BREEDERS

FAYE KNIGHTLY

Acknowledgements

The truth is most books wouldn't make it into the world without the support of a team of people and Breeders is no exception.

To my phenomenal editor, Rachel Mitchell, THANK YOU for all of your help in elevating Breeders to the piece it is today. I could not have done this without you. My books and my writing are stronger because of you.

To my early readers, you guys are superstars. Thank you for looking past the roughness of my first drafts and seeing the beautiful book Breeders would become. Your insight and encouragement helped shape this book into what it is today.

A special thanks to Alysha Stafford, who, in addition to being an early reader on Breeders, has shown an incredible amount of support for this book as a proofreader and promoter. Alysha, your love and patience with me and my stories has been boundless, and I'm eternally grateful for it. I'm also pretty sure I don't deserve it, but thank you anyways.

To my husband. This is the longest love letter I've ever written. Thank you for being you. Also, can you make me a quesadilla?

BREEDERS

To all the people who dreamed of meeting the love of their life while strapped to a hospital bed being railed..........you're sick.

I got you.

BREEDERS

Trigger Warning

This story includes a pregnancy loss and an attempted sexual assault. Please protect yourself and either skip these pages or PUT DOWN THE BOOK. Your mental health is important.

Chapter 1

"It's no big deal really. You just breathe this in and lay back on the bed." The breeding program coordinator sounded almost bored, his voice droning on tonelessly as he informed me about the safety protocols. His thick glasses gave him a bug-eyed appearance further emphasized by the lack of hair on his barren head. He wore a long lab coat that went to his ankles. I guess that made sense—he'd be fully protected from any fluid mishaps.

My fluids.

With a gulp, my eyes drifted to the central feature in the small room—a cramped twin bed with a black waterproof mattress and uncomfortable-looking black straps hanging off the sides. Soon, I'd be strapped to the thing waiting for man after man to come and fuck me for the glory of the pack.

The rest of the small room was surprisingly homey and designed to help the breeder relax, with two nightstands on either side of the bed and a painting of rolling country hills on the wall. But the cozy flower-patterned lamps barely gave off enough light to call the room dim, and I knew it was intentional. Wouldn't want me to see any details of the would-be-fathers of my children. Or smell them. Wrinkling my nose with disgust, I looked around the room for whatever was pumping out the obnoxious floral scent invading my nostrils and found a white plastic cylinder secured to the ceiling. A pile of water bottles in the corner had me rubbing my bare arms against the chill of the room. Right, that was in case any of the men became thirsty after exerting themselves.

They weren't for me though. It was said when you went into heat you didn't get hungry. Or thirsty. Or want anything other than sex, sex, sex. I swallowed hard, trying to imagine being that far gone. Those black straps hanging haphazardly from the bed would be locked onto my ankles soon, helping to keep me from thrashing my way off when the heat madness took hold. Shiny metal rails were slid under the bed right now, but I knew they'd be pulled up and secured in place once we began. Yet another safety measure for poor sex-crazed Cassie.

Sex-crazed Cassie. It was hard to believe I'd soon be reduced to an animal needing to be strapped to a bed lest she harm herself. Coughing nervously, I frowned down at the freckles peppering my fair arms. At five foot four with hardly any breasts to speak of, green eyes, and straight dirty blonde hair with a tendency to frizz— would I measure up to their expectations? And if I did, would I be able to perform my pack duty and go through with this?

Say the heat madness took hold, and I became the lust-filled creature the pack wanted me to be, what of the men? I hadn't seen a boy my age since they separated girls and boys at puberty. The boys I'd played soccer with and who had helped me jar fireflies at dusk were completely different creatures who watched us from a distance with a predatory gleam in their eyes, their round boyish features replaced with hard angles and gangly limbs teeming with thick muscle. They were enigmas with deep, rumbly voices and broad shoulders.

A new fear emerged. Would they find me attractive enough, or would they see me lying on the bed, and turn to leave—water bottles left without use, my entrance slick, my body desperate?

I wanted to call the whole thing off, to say that the signs of my heat coming must be false. The feverish chills and dry mouth, the restlessness all a part of my imagination, but I couldn't back out.

Not when this was the only way I would ever be a mother.

I'd always wanted that, always, and my heart had swelled with pride when the scholars had looked into my genealogy and assigned me the role of a breeder instead of a worker. I would be a pack mother, like I'd always dreamed. Younglings had always trailed after me, begging me to tell them more of my stories or to play some of my made-up games, and I wanted to have my own little ones someday to do those things with.

It was in the weeks leading up to my heat when the reality had started to sink in, and all those good feelings had turned into fears and nerves so powerful I could scarcely eat or sleep. I wanted this. I was meant to be a mother, but as much as I told myself it would all be okay, I was a mess by the time my heat started showing signs of starting.

To fulfill my dream of motherhood, I'd have to go through at least one heat cycle with a lineup of men visiting me in this strangely homey room, fucking me senseless in the hopes their seed would take root. Supposedly, I would enjoy it, but maybe I'd be terrible at sex.

I fiddled with the white cotton shift I wore, trying to stretch it over my exposed thighs. Even the coordinator was making me nervous. Was there hint of lust swirling in his hazel eyes? Maybe he was in the breeding program. Shit, shit, shit. For all I knew, he would don a mask and take a turn.

Maybe he was here to get me warmed up. Tension churned in my stomach as I assessed him. He was older, around fifty, but that didn't mean he couldn't be used as a breeder—not if the record keepers found him to be a good match for the woman. But he was wearing glasses, and the record keepers did hate to tarnish their perfect breeding program with hereditary issues that could impact a wolf's ability to defend the pack.

They could look past it though, for the right genetic combination.

The air became thin, and I wheezed, nearly jumping when the coordinator reached out a calloused hand to pat my shoulder fondly. I managed to meet his eyes and saw only kindness there.

"You're going to do fine. You've practiced, right?"

Practiced? Oh yeah, I'd practiced. I nodded, lowering my head and fixing my eyes on the hideous black ankle strap. All the breeding females were permitted to take a first when they first started showing signs of their heats starting. We were instructed to choose a man to have protected sex with so we would be prepared for our breeding days. We were supposed to practice with them as much as we wanted. They wanted us as comfortable as possible, but the whole experience had been so sweaty and unsatisfying that I'd only been able to do it twice.

At least the man had been eager enough. I hadn't dared to ask anyone outright, but my mother had found a gentle older man named Reg who had asked about me when I'd turned twenty-two and started showing signs of my heat. Wildly overweight, sex with Reg had been sticky and loud. I could still feel the slap of his belly against my back when he'd taken me from behind, and the throaty grunts by which he'd made his pleasure known. It hadn't hurt but it was unappealing, and now I was going to have to put up with that for however long it took for my heat to die down enough to regain my sanity.

"Just climb on up here and get comfy. You'll need to remove your nightgown. We don't want to risk you getting tangled up in it." He smiled, gesturing invitingly at the mattress. Get comfy? Was he serious? His hand remained extended expectantly, and the silence stretched between us until I couldn't stand it anymore.

With a shaky nod, I climbed up on the bed. The mattress crinkled noisily as I did, and I stripped off my cotton nightgown, dropping it on the nightstand just within reach. A button with a long cord sat on the table just in case I needed to tap out. I stared at the shiny red button longingly then turned my attention to the simple white door where my breeding males would enter once my heat started.

It took me a moment to realize I was trembling. I ran my hands up the gooseflesh of my arms, startling when the coordinator clicked something into place. A handrail. Right. They'd used these beds in hospitals, and the shiny metal grips were integrated into the bed. The coordinator gave me an apologetic look before moving to the next one and securing it.

Almost ready.

Gently, he took my bare foot and lifted it onto the bed, taking the strap and wrapping it around the ankle to secure it with a buckle. He did the same to my other leg, and I felt a stab of panic when I realized I didn't have enough leeway to close my legs. The cool air of the well-ventilated room tickled and teased at my exposed entrance—*no*—pussy. If I was going to do this, I needed to get comfortable with the big girl words all the women who went through the breeding program used.

I sat up straight, facing the door. My eyes fixed on the entrance. When the coordinator laughed, I startled. It was all I could do to glare at him where he stood, fully dressed and standing awkwardly beside the bed. *So superior.*

"We're not starting just yet. Relax."

Relax. Yeah, okay, like he could relax if his body was about to be ravished by a group of complete strangers. The coordinator reached into his lab coat and pulled out a small clear vial stoppered with a black plug. Curious, I squinted and was sure I saw a hint of a deep purple bloom within.

"Your heat is on the cusp of starting, but you're not there yet. One whiff of this, and it'll start."

One whiff of the flower in that tiny vial—practically crushed in the coordinator's meaty hand—and I'd be a mindless sex-obsessed doll for the breeding males to come and fuck. *Oh, no. This was really happening.*

My breaths came in short gulps that choked more than provided air, and I hugged myself. Stomach clenching, I began rocking back and forth, trying to find some comfort in the familiar motion.

"Hey, now." There was a pause and a rustle of papers as he checked his clipboard for my name. *Oh. My. God.* The coordinator didn't even know my name. My breathing became more erratic. "Cassie, this is all going to go fine. Hell, you're young and healthy. I bet you get pregnant on your first heat and we don't see you for a good couple of years, if at all."

Right, once I was pregnant, I could raise my babies in peace until I decided I was ready to have more children.

I breathed through the panic, fighting to take in air through my nose instead of my mouth.

A mother.

My children.

I was going to be a pack mother—the most sacred, honoured role in the pack. I just had to get through this night. Well, *nights* depending on when my heat let up. I'd heard about one breeder who had continued in her heat for two straight days and had to be coaxed into drinking water lest she pass out.

The thought of entering a state where I was so mad with lust that I could die of thirst when water was readily available, but too consumed with the heat to save my own life, did not help and my body shook uncontrollably.

Huffing, I caught some motion from the corner of my eye as the coordinator shifted from foot to foot.

"Just sniff the flower, please. I have three other girls to get set up."

Just sniff the flower.

He was right. I could do this. I had to do this. With a steadiness I didn't feel, I nodded and stretched out my quaking legs, sitting up and looking over at him.

"I'm ready now."

Stepping towards me cautiously, he held out the vial for me to see, moving slowly as though I was some cornered animal likely to take flight at the wrong move.

"This will induce you. I want you to empty your lungs of air and take a deep breath of this the second I unstopper it. Fill your lungs and hold it for ten seconds. Your heat will start about five minutes after that. When you're ready, press the call button twice, and we'll send in the first breeding male. Ideally, you get through all of them, but if not, we'll use them next cycle."

The coordinator shrugged like the potential father of my children wasn't a big deal, but it was and this was really happening. Once my heat was completed, I'd move in with my breeding males for the rest of my cycle in the hopes of encouraging fornication outside my heat window—a situation I was none too keen on, but two weeks I could do. It was what would happen if I didn't get pregnant that worried me.

I'd have to repeat my breeding party next cycle and do this whole thing over again. As much as I told myself this was a one-time thing, I'd heard of women taking up to four cycles before a pregnancy was achieved, and the thought made my head spin. I just wanted to get this over with so I could go home.

The coordinator must have seen my growing alarm because he held up one hand. "Don't worry, lots of women get pregnant in their first cycle, but it's good to have a plan if you do need to come back. Okay?"

I could do this. I would do this. It was just something I had to bear.

I nodded and the coordinator unstoppered the vial, holding it out for me to take. I thought I could smell it from a distance—a wild tangy scent that tingled on my tongue, like eating raw lemons with sugar caked on them in the summer sun. Tangy but sweet all the same.

"Remember, breathe out first."

Right. I pushed out the air from my lungs and snatched it from him, bringing the vial under my nose, almost close enough to touch.

I. Could. Do. This.

I breathed it in until my lungs screamed for air and counted out the ten seconds. My lungs burned with the need for release by the time I was done. The sooner I started my heat, the sooner I could get through this terrible ordeal. Only a few seconds after I'd released the breath, there was a burst across my senses, like everything was too bright and too loud, too fuzzy, and too sharp. All at once, the cozy room seemed wonderfully inviting and not as frightening. I felt the knots of muscles that had been squeezing my neck like a vise these past few days loosening.

What had I been so worried about? The coordinator daintily took the vial back and put in the stopper, muttering something about his timeline and beelining for the door. Well, I certainly hadn't made his job an easy one, fretting as I had.

Fretting. The idea seemed ludicrous. There was no need to worry. I was safe here in the heart of my pack and about to be worshipped. Warmth flooded me from head to toe. I was groggy, so tired and relaxed I could sleep, but also burning with a mad energy that demanded release.

Release. I'd found it myself beneath the covers a few times—not an easy feat when you share the room with your mother—but those had been stolen moments, filled with fear and worry, convinced my mother would hear me and demand I tell her what I was doing.

Now? I was exactly where I needed to be, doing what I needed to do. I leaned back, stretching my arms out luxuriously over my head. I didn't know how many breeding males were assigned to me, but I hoped a few of them liked freckles.

The burning started in my core and spread upwards until I felt consumed by it. My skin was on fire, and my nipples ached to be touched. Helplessly, I arched into the bed, using my own hands as best I could, but my touch did nothing—not really. I needed—*oh, shit*—I needed someone else's hands on me.

I grabbed the remote on the nightstand. What had the coordinator said? Press it twice? I hammered the button, tossed it back on the table and leaned back into the noisy bed, hoping that someone, anyone, had received the message I was ready. Beyond ready.

Burning and panting, it was all I could do to run my hands up and down my feverish skin, squeezing my nipples and trying to find some relief until—at last—I ventured lower, finding my pussy soaked. The last thing I wanted was for a man to walk in and find me spread and fingering myself, but I was quickly realizing what I wanted didn't matter. My body had other ideas. The physical need tore through me, a deep almost painful sensation that promised heights of pleasure yet unleashed if only I would give in to its call.

No wonder they called it a heat.

There was no resisting. Dipping a finger into the slick, I sought my clit, gasping at the intensity of the sensation. Everything was so much more sensitive right now. More gently than my initial attempt, I found the swollen bud and gave it a tentative touch.

Fireworks spread from the site, and I arched back as a wave of pleasure coursed through my body. All those times I'd touched myself, it had taken time to reach these heights, but now my body was in overdrive, ready to give me pleasure as soon as I relented to its devilish desires.

Just when I was about to dip my fingers into the slick and chase the sensation, I heard the squeak of the door. Startled, my hand darted away, and I sat partway up, pulling the offending hand to my chest and hoping whoever it was hadn't seen. Some part of me expected it to be the coordinator again, but the balding man in his lab coat didn't appear.

Instead, a naked man wearing a rubber hawk mask that covered his face and hair all the way to the base of his thick neck stood in the doorway. The cocking of his head matched the bird mask he wore, and I fought the urge to giggle.

Fuck. Number one. Of how many, I had no clue. Did he like what he saw? I nervously covered a freckled arm with my hand. But all thoughts of freckles and shyness were gone when he stepped closer to the bed, and I felt the warmth of his body close to mine. I was instantly consumed by an arousal so intense it pulled a needy moan from my lips.

How long would I be like this before the heat was satisfied? He moved slowly, and I drank in his body. Muscles rippled across his tanned abdomen, seemingly etched in stone, and—*shit, shit, shit*—his cock was already fully erect. He was ready for me and damned if I wasn't ready for him. Just the thought of him plunging into my wet heat had a phantom wave of pleasure sending me back to the bed, my eyes rolling as my head pressed into the mattress, and I arched towards him in a silent plea.

Hands grabbed my hips and steadied me, pulling me gently to the edge of the strap's reach, positioning me at the end of the bed. I gasped at the friction of the mattress on my oversensitive skin. I looked up to find him watching me, but I couldn't see his eyes through the deep, recessed sockets of his mask.

He gripped me more firmly and pressed in, groaning his pleasure. It was too much, and I threw myself against the bed, thrashing as I writhed on his cock, rolling my hips into him and trying to drive him deeper, though I could feel he was sunk to the hilt. I wanted more. I gripped the side rails to brace myself.

The friction of him pulling out and slamming back in nearly killed me with pleasure. He hadn't even touched my clit, and I was already near my release. Stars danced in my vision. Each thrust was a tiny orgasm. But it was all building to something even more. I desperately tried to meet his thrusts. The angle gave him more control over our rhythm, but I still slammed my hips down into his. He gripped my hips as he worked towards his own needs.

Faster, harder. I wanted it more than I'd ever wanted anything. I was spiraling, getting closer to something bigger than the tendrils of pleasure already tearing their way through my body. The Hawk came with a throaty groan that echoed in the room, massaging my thighs as his warm seed spilled inside of me. But I wasn't there yet, and my body craved more friction. With a final grunt, he pulled himself loose and moved one of the two bedside tables to retrieve a tissue.

Eyeing his limp cock with wide-eyed horror, I watched as he wiped himself clean.

I needed more. I wasn't there yet. I could cry with the cruelty of it, and that's just what I did. Embarrassing tears streamed down my face, and I couldn't stop them. Without looking back at me, the man paused before grabbing a water bottle and exited the room, giving me a perfect view of his tight ass. Frustrated, I moaned my misery as I lay on the bed. The burning, while partially sated by The Hawk, increased again, leaving me even more miserable. But I didn't have to wait long before the door cracked once again and a man wearing a plague doctor's mask walked in.

Like the man before, his mask covered his face and hair, leaving me no clue as to his identity. This man was heavyset, with thick shoulders and a belly that jutted out nearly to the length of his hard cock. Normally, I don't think I would like that kind of body, but right now? He looked fantastic. I was pretty sure I would fuck anything with a cock in this state, and the man didn't leave me waiting.

He went straight to the bed, grabbing my hips with a roughness I was surprised to find I enjoyed. The Hawk had taken me deeply, but I'd been craving a little more force, and The Plague Doctor didn't disappoint. His fingers made indents on my skin as he thrust hard into my pussy, grunting each time, the sound of his flesh striking me like music to my ears.

Teeth clanging together with each jarring thrust, I held onto the side rails for dear life. I sank deep into the ripples of pleasure, feeling each explosion building. The man came with a roar, and I got a taste of heaven, crying out and grasping his hands on my hips, desperate to hold him in place as the orgasm settled deep into my bones. On and on it went until he at last pulled away from my hands and left me on the bed. Craving more. I wanted to stay in that high, but it was impossible now that he had left. I was sticky and wet, but not satisfied. Never satisfied.

Damn, the other girls were right. I couldn't imagine caring about food or drink—not when all I wanted was release after release, until the beast inside of me was satisfied and would allow me a moment's rest. Everything else I'd wanted in my life—to be loyal to the pack, to serve the alpha, to be a mother—paled in comparison to this.

I imagined what I must look like—my heated cheeks a splotchy red, my long dirty blonde hair a mess from all the thrashing around. I groaned as another wave of need overwhelmed me, but all I could do was arch back into the bed, the waterproof mattress cover pinching at my skin. My pussy felt like a gaping, empty void without a man there.

This was pure, utter torture.

I barely noticed the next man entering the room and pulling me gently to the edge of the bed, not until he sank home, and the terrible emptiness was filled again. I moaned my approval, feeling my pleasure building anew as his hips found the right rhythm.

He didn't last long, coming far too soon and moving to the table to wipe himself. I found myself crying again. Was it always like this? None of the women I'd talked to had mentioned crying, but it had felt so good and now he was moving away, closing the door behind him.

I was lost in the haze of sex, constantly somewhere between torture and ecstasy. More men came, to touch me, to fill me, and it felt incredible each time. A rolling orgasm that was easily triggered and left my body begging for more. But then they would leave, and I would be alone in my bed—half mad with need and consumed by an emptiness begging to be filled.

Sex was all I wanted. Every other dream and thought I'd had in my life paled compared to the feeling of touching heaven and practically living there. How many men had been inside me? I didn't know, but I knew the moment I was exhausted because I simply could not thrash around as I had. My body was still desperately on fire. Begging for touch. Primed for it. The need to be filled and penetrated and stuffed with warm sticky seed overwhelmed all other thoughts and needs, but my energy was waning.

At last, the haze began to lift, and I looked up to find a man wearing a Ram's mask with one hand still on the knob, staring down at me. Silently, he closed the door and came to where I lay on the bed. Now, *his* body was beautiful, and even without the heat pumping through my veins as it was, I knew I would think so.

He was all compact muscle with thick forearms and beautiful hands I could appreciate even with the heat still clouding my vision. I couldn't see his eyes properly with the mask on, but I could tell he was looking down at me by the way his chin angled downward.

I wanted him. My heat surged, and my nipples tightened excruciatingly, desperately. I gripped at the side rails, pleased once again they were there for me to use as a brace for myself. Moaning, I arched my back, already imagining the sweet kiss of pleasure his cock would give me, but he just stood there.

He didn't touch me for an eternity—just hovered over my body, close enough I could feel his heat. I wiggled my hips, trying to encourage him closer, but he stayed put. I managed a strangled "please." My voice pitched so low and husky I barely recognized it, but still he remained motionless. Begging—shit, that was a new low—but I couldn't care less.

Frustrated, I slammed my head back, moaning as another wave of heat skittered across my skin, a rolling taste of the release I needed leaving me filled with an agony that promised the most exquisite bliss. Then his hands were on me, running up and down my legs, and it felt amazing. My body was in overdrive again and when he began to softly palm my thighs, tendrils of pleasure shot straight to my core.

His nimble fingers crept up towards my swollen nub, but I cried out when he grazed it. I was too sensitive for that right now, the feeling bringing more pain than pleasure. He moved away from my clit—thank god—lightly running his hands up my torso to play with my tight nipples. But they were just as sensitive, and the gentle pinch of his fingers sent a bolt of pain through my system. I would have launched off the bed if not for the railings holding me in place. Squirming beneath his touch, I moved further down the bed and closer to the cock I so badly needed.

"Shhhhh." The soft shushing was strangely soothing, and I felt my muscles relax in response. His hands returned to my thighs, massaging them more firmly now, and I felt another small orgasm tear through my body. Crying out, I gripped the side rails, and with my face turned sideways, I began to cry again. Big, wet tears dribbled down my face to soak the slippery material beneath me.

"Please." I was like an animal before him, but I no longer cared what this man or any other thought of me. I just needed so badly to be filled again. He stopped massaging my thighs for a moment to stare down at me again.

Finally, I felt him positioning his tip at my entrance. I gasped, trying to wiggle lower and press myself down on it, but the straps hindered my movement. He shushed me again, his hands moving in slow firm circles across my inner thighs as he carefully pressed into my soaking heat.

I cried out, bucking my hips to create friction. He was large, but between all the cum and my own juices, he slid into place until our bodies were flush with each other.

The rhythm was slow and steady—not what I'd wanted—but his hands on my inner thighs held me firmly as he pressed in to take me deeper. He spread my legs wider, stretching me around him and the extra sensation of his ministrations drove me towards the edge of something new.

I spiraled, coming undone beneath him. Wanting it harder and faster but settling for the pace he set. I couldn't stop it. My orgasm tore through me and continued. Screaming, my body clenched helplessly around him, craving the roughness he was unwilling to give.

Slowly, I came back down, spasming until the waves of my release lightened and I could breathe again. But he was still hard and still moving at that slow, maddening pace.

Gripping the cold metal of the side rails as tightly as I could, I whipped my head from side to side, seeking an escape from the pain and pleasure my heat brought. I felt it building again, coiling tighter and tighter, and I was a helpless passenger along for the ride.

The hands on my thighs moved to my hips, still gentle but more insistent and filled with need. He gripped me hard, and I got the punishing pace I'd wanted from him as he pulled away and slammed back in. If not for his hands holding me firmly in place, he would have shoved me up the bed with the force of his thrusts.

He was like a man possessed, the sounds of his throaty groans mingling with my own as tremors of pleasure took me higher. Then he was on the bed with me, pushing me farther up the mattress to make space for himself. His hands bracketed my face. The warmth of his body pressed closer to mine felt so damned good.

Faster now, he took me like he was experiencing his own heat. Like he was as caught up in me as I was with him, and it was intoxicating to watch him come undone with me. I cried out as another orgasm tore through me, just as violent as the last. It was all I could do to hold on to the rails and breathe through it. My core was tight around him for so long that I was sure I would die.

This was exactly what I'd needed, my own passion, my own need reflected in a man, like some part of me had been waiting for him. His guttural groan echoed through the room as his warm seed spilled inside of me, and my head dropped back as the exquisite feeling drove me higher. The push and pull around my clenching pussy was heaven, and it took me forever to come back down, pleasure continuing to consume me as he slowly went limp. He stayed inside of me until the rolling waves of my ecstasy finally eased, and I was a boneless mess beneath him.

He hovered over me, looking down for a moment longer before carefully pulling away. The Ram's body was covered in a sheen of sweat, and I wondered what it tasted like.

Stupid. I found my voice but didn't know what to say as he moved to the table and wiped himself down.

What did you say to someone who you had shared something so profound with? More than any of the others, I had felt like he had come to take care of me. To ease my suffering and focus on my pleasure, not his own, and with him, I'd climbed to a height previously unreached. The way he'd touched me, gripped me, stayed with me—there'd been a passion to it that went far beyond anything I'd ever expected from the breeding program. I wanted to say thank you, but the words refused to come. *Thank you, how stupid.* Saying thank you to a breeding male who derived their own pleasure from the act.

But I *could* talk if I chose to. I felt it. The only thing I'd been able to say this whole time had been the occasional pleading words, but now? I felt more like myself, and my skin didn't prickle with the heat and hypersensitivity that had so consumed my every thought.

The Ram paused at the door to look back. He breathed heavily, and I got the impression he wanted to say something, the urgency apparent in the tension of his hand on the doorframe. I waited, sure that his differentness meant something. But then he did turn, closing the door and moving away, off to clean up like all the others.

Sighing, I leaned back onto the bed—the first night of my heat had finally ended. Had it been a night or had it gone on for longer? I was hungry and parched enough that it may as well have been a week. I felt around the side of the bed for the call button to let them know my heat was finished. I'd been dreading this, wanting somehow to get a baby without engaging in the act of sex, but now? A part of me wished I didn't get pregnant this cycle so I could go again.

The heat faded, and a mousy young woman wearing a freshly pressed lab coat and rubber gloves so at odds with her messy brown hair came in. The coordinator's assistant. With an apologetic smile, she stepped between my legs and dipped a gloved finger into my pussy. I looked away as her finger squelched into place.

"Great job, Cassie, was it? I see plenty of opportunity for a successful pregnancy."

CHAPTER 2

Cassie.

Of course, it had to be her. The girl I'd had a crush on since I saw her making a flower necklace out of dandelions by the swings in the schoolyard. With her golden hair and bubbly smile, she was popular, but it hadn't made her cruel the way it did with some girls. No, not Cassie. She was nice to everyone. Even me. The outcast. The one always on the outside looking in.

I'd been the kid the others liked to tease and beat up, but Cassie had never been that way. She'd just grin and invite me to play, her cheeks dimpling as though it were the simplest thing in the world. Not that I ever said anything back, but she was my personal sunshine, and I'd always tried to stay near her, to bask in her seemingly boundless joy.

I'd seen her a few times since they had separated us from the family compound and taken me and the other boys to the barracks to trial us as guards, an all-important position only the most elite would claim, but I hadn't realized how beautiful she'd become. Not really. Sure, I'd seen the womanly curve of her hips and her pert breasts from a distance, but last night...

Fuck. I sent the wire wastebasket sailing across the smooth ceramic tiles, where it clattered into the wall, before falling over and spilling used tissues on the floor. Sebastian, one of my new roommates, had some kind of allergy and he'd stuffed nearly every wastebasket full of the snot-soaked rags.

Let him clean it up.

I should've seen who was in that room and backed the fuck off, told them I was sick or something. That would have been the smart thing to do, and I'd considered it, but the way she'd begged for my cock. Well, all the smarts went clean out of my head.

Had I really fucked Cassie? The memory of her creamy thighs and her desperate mewling noises sent the blood rushing straight to my cock.

Shit, shit, shit. Was she still there in the throes of her heat, in physical pain, without someone pounding into her? I gripped the counter hard enough to make the tendons in my arms stand out. If she was still there, I could go back. I could have her again—pound into her relentlessly until we were both roaring with pleasure. Maybe this time I would undo one of those fucking straps and hitch her leg up on my shoulder so I could go deeper. It was a mercy to go there and plunge myself into her wet heat.

A mercy. Yeah, right, as if I could pretend this wasn't my selfish desire to touch the untouchable girl, and be important to her, even if it was only physical. I could do it, too. I could go again. I was rock hard already, my cock straining against the grey joggers I'd thrown on after exiting her breeding room.

But then, that's what the heat did—it sent males into a frenzy and kept them so high on their girl they could get hard again and again, as much as she needed until her heat was through.

We didn't do that here, of course. The baby's father had to be anonymous. For the pack.

For the pack. The idea of maybe fathering children on a breeding female had never bothered me before, but then, there'd never been a girl in my life like Cassie. If only I'd looked at the file hung outside her door. Could I have known who was inside and avoided all of this?

But would I really have walked away if I'd read her name? Even I didn't know the answer. I liked to think I would have, that I would have known it would mean something to me to have her and put the pack first by walking away. With a sigh, I braced the back of my head with twined fingers and leaned back into it.

The pack's laws around mates had never bothered me before. It made sense after the pack wars pitted pack-loyalty against family-loyalty and chaos ensued. The twelve main packs had agreed to remove families from the equation. We were all brothers and sisters, aunties, and uncles, a unified pack. No family above Pack Family.

It just worked, but now? The thought of someone else walking in there and taking Cassie, satisfying her, and maybe even fathering pups by her made my blood boil. The very thing the alpha and our council of elders had wanted to squash by outlawing romantic entanglements and requiring children to be fathered anonymously.

The rage pumping through my veins was physically painful, filling me with tension until I didn't know what to do with myself. I let loose a feral scream and stood, slamming my fists into the wall hard enough to crack into the drywall. Fuck, we'd have to get someone in here to fix that, but in an environment where alcohol use was encouraged and wild parties were the norm, at least no one would ask what had happened.

I flooded my system with heaving breaths to calm myself, but I could already feel the need to change, making my skin feel too tight and itchy. Like it wasn't even mine, and I needed to rip it off and embrace my real skin. Find a way to run off all this anger and arousal. Not wanting any of my roommates to see me, I unlocked the bathroom door and slid out the bathroom window. It was plenty big enough to fit through and a short jump down to the ground. Nothing on our property was built higher—maybe because sometimes lycans really did need to get outside and breathe in the piney scent of the woods to calm down.

I let the peace of the woods and the distant birdsong soothe me. A calm change was a better change—a safer change—and one less likely to result in sprains or strains. It was a good thing I could get out to shift and run because at some point soon Cassie would be finished with her heat. Then she'd move into Pack Breeders 103C where her beautiful body would drive me mad with desire. Until her next cycle when I could once again don The Ram's mask and fuck her to my heart's content.

CASSIE

After a shower hot enough to melt my skin, and a quick change into the knit turtleneck and jeans, I felt more like myself, my long blonde hair tied up into my usual tight ponytail. I sat on the squashy chair, shaky, but working on processing everything that had just happened. Was that really me laying myself out on the bed, eagerly awaiting a slew of strangers to take me and fulfill the needs burning through my body?

Now I understood why anyone not assigned to be a breeder took drugs to suppress their heat. I couldn't imagine being able to work or focus on anything but sex when I was in that state. The heat had been all-consuming, stealing my identity and dignity in one fell swoop, and leaving me a helpless, crying animal splayed out on a waterproof bed.

And I'd liked it—welcoming each new man with the same zeal as the last. Even now, with my hips bruised and aching and every muscle strained from clenching and squirming for what turned out to be eighteen hours, the thought of my heat coming on again was exhilarating. Never had I thought of experiencing such pleasure or hitting such highs, but when I thought of the night and the parade of men who had claimed my body as theirs, The Ram stood out. His hands on me had been the perfect combination of feral need and gentleness with a focus on my pleasure that had taken me to a height beyond anything I had imagined.

The others had come in and done their duty to the pack, of course, depositing their seed into my vessel of a body with eagerness, but lacking an interest in helping me find my pleasure.

The Ram had been different, and the more I thought about it, the more I was convinced it was true. It was him I was most looking forward to seeing at my next cycle, his hands on me, his grunts in my ear.

With a shudder, I blew out a breath, standing up and brushing some invisible dirt off my jeans. I'd really lost it. My role here was simple—achieve a pregnancy and bring pups into the pack with the right genetic combination determined by the record keepers. Sure, I could enjoy it, but fixating on one man was forbidden.

The freshen-up room was cozy with comfortable brown chairs, but this wasn't a place where the coordinators wanted women to linger. A white plastic egg timer had been set after the coordinator had helped me to my room on wobbly legs. There were only a few freshen-up rooms, and while we were all expected to come out of our heats at different times, there was no telling when the next woman might need this space.

I made full use of the massive bathroom. I couldn't make myself rush as I took soap from the dispenser on the wall and grabbed a fresh washcloth from a metal hanging rack. I was stalling, and I knew it, running out my timer until it was almost at zero.

I was to be housed with the men and women in the breeding program until my next heat took hold, and I simply didn't know how to face all the men who had seen my face and would recognize me from my breeding party while I had no idea who had been behind the rubber masks they'd worn. It seemed a ridiculous arrangement, but the council and the alpha wanted us having as much sex as possible and housing us together encouraged fornication. Pregnancies happened outside of the heat even if they were less common, and the council was nothing if not efficient. The sooner I was pregnant, the sooner my pups would join the pack, and the breeding males could be cycled out and put back onto their posts.

Most of the males were members of the guard, having made the cut and been honed for service as fine physical specimens. The occasional worker was included, but it was less common. The record keepers favoured physical strength in the breeding program, and those selected as guards were the best of them.

All right, I couldn't put it off any longer. I slowly opened the door and squinted into the bright hallway. I'd still been a bit out of it when Ms. Lab Coat had helped me to the freshen-up room, and I hadn't realized how dim and soothing the lighting had been. My senses were still messed up from the heat, and the bright light from the hallway felt like it was burning straight through my skull. I shielded my eyes and shambled out, my gait off as I tried to walk through the lingering soreness in my hips.

Breeder housing was connected to this area, and I followed a few neon orange arrows directing me around the corner, past some more white doors, and to a plain-looking brown door at the end of the hallway. With a deep breath, I wiped sweaty palms on my jeans and swung the door open with a confidence I didn't feel.

A familiar scent slammed into me, and I looked up to find the same kind of air fresheners from my breeding room secured to the ceiling in a grid around the room.

I wrinkled my nose. I'd hoped it was just a breeding room thing, but apparently, they wanted to mask our scents here as well.

My eyes scanned the circular room and fell on a massive brown sectional dominating the space. The lush pleather looked ridiculously comfortable, and in front of it, a mounted large-screen TV was hooked up to at least three different gaming systems. My mouth dropped.

We had a few systems in 7C, but they were shared among at least fifty of us gamers, and it was always a struggle to get a turn. That, and there was always so much work to do in the family compound between tending the kids, cleaning, and preparing the meals—I almost never got a chance to game. Okay, maybe this wouldn't be too bad. I'd just get lost in a game and try to forget all the amped-up men who wanted to get into my pants. Well, back into my pants. I shuddered at the familiarity so many of the men I was about to live with would have with my body.

But my heat felt less like a real event and more like a dream the longer I was away from the room with its low light, bed rails, and black straps. Now that the arousal had drained from my system, I barely recognized the wanton creature who had begged man after man for more, more, more. But I was her, and the memories—hazy though they might be—were pleasant. I wrapped my arms around myself, feeling a sudden chill.

Where was everybody? I'd been told I would be housed with a few other breeding females and the same group of men who had been assigned to me with a few less desirable candidates assigned to the others. They considered it an acceptable risk to get pregnant from one of those not-genetically-incompatible, but not ideal.

This common room should be teeming with people, but it was empty. An expansive kitchen looked out onto the living room area, barstools neatly tucked under the counter, and I slowly made my way over to it, marvelling at the gorgeous drop lights illuminating an oversized white marble kitchen island. My fingertips grazed over the smooth counter, and I admired the swirling white marble. But my purpose here tainted my thinking, and I couldn't help but wonder if they'd made it so big to allow the occupants to use their surroundings for more variety—vegetables and meat shoved aside in favour of the new angle a countertop height would provide.

Different types of alcohol lined one of the kitchen walls, and while I barely recognized the various shades of amber, I knew the wooden barrel with white tubing coming out of the top must be beer. We'd had one of those to celebrate the harvest last year. I opened the double fridge to find the whole side door filled with beers. All right, message received, we were supposed to drink and fuck during this rare time where men and women mingled freely, but that wasn't me. Swallowing, I moved around the island to find a handwritten note in front of the coffeemaker. I frowned down at my name in the scrawling black ink.

Cassie,

Welcome to our little hideaway. We wanted to give you a chance to explore without everyone crowding you. Please do whatever it is you want to make this space feel more like home. We've got the absolute best video games, and the fridge is STOCKED, and I do mean stocked. Just let the staff know if there's anything you're craving, and they'll get it for you. Your room has a marker with your name on it, so you'll know where to go. We're out for a group run and will be back after 5.

Welcome to the family!

–Pack Breeders 103C

Pack Breeders 103C? I guess that was us, or at least, the name I'd seen on the sign outside the front door. A small smile crept up my face as I stared down at the note. Maybe I'd been freaking out for nothing. After all, if they were kind enough to give me my space, they couldn't be half bad. If I could pretend I'd never met them before—certainly never been fucked by any of them—and we could just hang out and eat delicious food while gaming. I just had to forget what *his* hands had felt like on my body, and maybe this could actually work.

THE RAM

Even the run wasn't helping, and it was usually the only thing that could ease my tension. Or maybe it wasn't the run, but the company. A bunch of frisky wolves out for a simulated game of cat and mouse in the woods that always ended in a hyped-up fuck.

But she was all I could think about. *Cassie.* Cassie coming into the apartment and checking it out, touching my things. *Cassie, Cassie, Cassie.*

Fuck. I stopped running, foregoing fur and fangs for skin and teeth as I leaned heavily against a tree trunk and took a few shuddering breaths to recover. My muscles twitched from the change as my spine fell into place.

Would Cassie like what she saw back at the apartment? Was she going through our things right now, running a delicate finger along the pleather couches? I wondered if she would check out any of the bedrooms. Hers was clearly marked with her name, but I'd purposefully left my door unlocked—an invitation she only needed to turn the knob to discover. The thought of her looking around my room made me rock hard.

A rustle in the bushes on the other side of the tree caught my attention, and I peered around curiously to see a large grey wolf playfully nipping at the heels of a light brown wolf as they raced through the bush. The brown wolf came up short in the small clearing beside where I hid and began circling behind the grey wolf.

Shit, she'd been caught. Well, not really, but she was admitting defeat, which meant—I swallowed back a groan when they shifted into their human forms. The scent of their arousal drifted over to me, gliding along my already frayed nerves and leaving me even harder.

The she-wolf—Rebecca—was gorgeous. Stunning really. She'd been with us for three heats and found she enjoyed sex—a lot. We were encouraged to sleep with one another, and I'd had Becca more than a few times myself. She was quite the exuberant partner, and my stiff cock twitched in reaction to her hardened nipples and smooth tanned flesh. She eyed Bentley like he was a plate of food, and she was starved.

Poor, sweet, shy Bentley. He'd found that he liked to fuck too, but he'd never gotten over his nerves with the girls. I wasn't surprised when Becca was the one to close the distance between them and grasp his cock in her hand. Fuck, why was this such a good vantage point? Fucking torture.

I could join them. Step away from the tree and offer myself. I imagined Becca's luscious lips curling up in delight when she saw me. Damn, those lips had always felt so good wrapped around my cock, but Cassie refused to leave my head. The image of her writhing in pleasure, her tight pussy clenching around my cock as the near constant orgasms of the heat took her, kept me rooted to the spot.

But I didn't want Becca, damn it. Not even when Bentley finally gathered his courage and walked her over to a neighbouring pine, and she hiked her leg over his hip obligingly. He took her, hard, and without warning. Her gasp of surprise carried over to where I stood, still hiding like a coward behind the tree. Shit, no foreplay. Bentley really wasn't great with the ladies, but Becca didn't seem to mind. Her hands reached around to grasp his butt and massage the cheeks in encouragement.

He groaned, and I grasped my own painfully hard cock at the sight of him slamming into her. Fuck, I imagined it was Cassie and that it was me shoving her into the ground, spreading her hips wide, and pressing her into the dirt and twigs of the forest floor. Shit, that must've stung, but Becca was lost in the act, her heavy breasts bouncing in time to Bentley's grunts and thrusts. Her throaty moans blended into one long note of pleasure.

With a roar, Bentley hoisted Becca up into his arms and lifted her up and down on his cock. *Wow, okay, Bentley wasn't so hopeless after all.* Becca clung to his shoulders, her mouth open in an 'o' as he relentlessly impaled her on the full length of his cock. But it wasn't Becca. In my mind, I was watching Cassie, and I grabbed my painfully hard cock and pulled on it, hard. Pumping it with a ferocity that matched the rutting couple I spied on. I tilted my head back against the rough bark and got lost in my memories of Cassie and me, how good she'd felt—how right—how perfect. The girl I'd always wanted, but had never spoken a word to, clenching around my cock like she'd been born to do it.

We all came together, and I could only hope my own involuntary grunt was lost in the sound of Becca's dove-like cry and Bentley's thunderous roar. I continued pumping as my cum trickled out, staining the surrounding patch of twigs and rocks. Becca and Bentley would only have to wander past this way to know they'd been watched, and that the watcher had enjoyed himself. Would they care? I'd been considering joining them not long ago, but the thought of them knowing I'd chosen to watch rather than participate made me balk, and I gently tugged some weeds loose and placed them over my spill to hide it from prying eyes.

CHAPTER 3

It had been so long since I'd had time for gaming, and I'd forgotten how fun it was. Of course, they would have first-person shooters and the bright red pop I loved to sip on while getting lost in a mission. This place was practically made for me.

Maybe that's why, despite being exhausted and eager to explore the apartment to learn more about the people I would spend the next month with, I grabbed some cheese puffs, my precious drink, and planted myself on the smooth, supple pleather cushions.

By the time I checked the clock, it was already four. If I'd been back in the family compound, I'd be helping with food or starting to corral the cows in from the field. Instead, I found a fuzzy blanket hidden between two thick couch cushions and settled in.

I'd never been in a fight and certainly never seen a gun before. Ever since the fall of the human world and the rise of the lycans, they'd been outlawed. Not that they did much good against us anyway, but humans didn't heal as quickly as we did. They'd damned near wiped each other out, scorching the land with their bombs and guns—an event we were hardy enough to survive, but they weren't. They'd practically handed this world to us, and I took a moment to be thankful the only thing left of those days were video games. My character hunched down in camouflage clothes. Because that's what humans did—I reminded myself—they couldn't shift into a wolf and blend in seamlessly with the forest. They had to wear clothes that allowed them to hide. So weird to think about.

Lost in thought and the mechanics of the game, I drifted off, awaking to the game over screen flashing an angry red. It was dark. Shit, someone must've returned by now. Had they found me sleeping like Goldilocks on their couch? Ugh. Sighing, I rubbed at the pillow creases on my cheek from the ribbing on the armrest and stood up.

But the apartment was quiet. Even if they'd come in and gone to their rooms, I was sure their entrance would have woken me. What I'd done to deserve this much time to process things, I didn't know, but I refused to waste it. With a squeal, I raced into the kitchen, grabbing some fried chicken from the back of the fridge and cramming it into a flower-rimmed bowl. I crammed the food into the microwave and hit start, dancing on my toes as I anxiously awaited the bing, letting me know it was done. I couldn't wait to satisfy my rumbling stomach and retreat to the safety of my room. With any luck, I'd make it out of here before the others got back, figure out which room was mine, and hide out for the rest of the night. *Just the night*, I promised myself. *In the morning, I'd be ready to face them. I had to be.*

The microwave had just beeped when the sound of a key jingling in the lock made me jump. I slammed the button, popping the irritated microwave open with a squeal, and grabbed the hot bowl in my bare hands. Hissing in pain, my fingers went slack, and the bowl clattered to the ground. Luckily it didn't break, but the sound drew attention to my location. Somewhere behind me, a light switched on, illuminating the room and nearly stopping my heart.

Oh, shit, shit, shit. I looked up in alarm as guys began entering the room, laughing and ribbing each other. Where were the other women? Surely there were other women in this housing arrangement. There were supposed to be. The ratio was something like one woman to every three men, but there were definitely more women here other than me, right?

The laughter stopped when the guys saw me watching them with wide eyes. A handsome man with a chiselled face and a swagger smiled at me, showing a set of too straight pearly whites. He sauntered over, his head of shaggy blonde hair swaying at every step. He wore khakis and a soft-collared grey shirt with green stripes across his chest—a clean-cut look at odds with his unkempt hair.

Although, on further examination, his hair wasn't shaggy, it was intentionally cut to *appear shaggy*. The man's green eyes twinkled merrily as he looked me up and down. His gaze lingered on my breasts, like someone had left him a present and he couldn't wait to unwrap it, and I shifted uncomfortably. He looked like the sort with a speck of alpha blood—a leader.

"Welcome, welcome. You're Cassie, right?"

I couldn't answer. More and more people began trailing in behind him until they crowded the door, and every one of them seemed to stare into my soul. My eyes grazed the sea of well-dressed men, but I couldn't focus on any of them, not with my flight or fight kicking into high gear.

Nodding quickly, I ducked down, scooping the chicken back into its flowered bowl. Mr. Green Eyes came around the counter and offered me his hand to stand up.

My gaze dropped to his hand. It was large, the fingernails dirty—no doubt from roaming the forest floor. Had I seen this hand before? Had it held me in place while he pounded into my lust-crazed body? Not knowing was maddening.

I shook my head quickly, securing the fried chicken in its flower prison with two well-placed thumbs.

"I have to go to bed now," I squeaked, avoiding his inquisitive gaze and fixing my eyes on his impractical brown loafers. Who even wore those out for a run?

Hurrying away, I dashed down the hall, ignoring the calls of my name from the others. Luckily, my room was easy to find. A sign dangled from twine wrapped around a single nail, with my name written in stark white chalk.

At least they'd spelled it right. With a free hand, I slammed the heavy door behind me, heaving as I leaned back into it. I worked to control my breathing, counting down from ten before pressing my ear to listen at the door. I could barely hear a thing.

They must've installed soundproofing in the rooms, probably to give privacy to those who wanted it. Were all the rooms like that, or did they know the thought of communal sharing terrified me?

Hell, the idea of taking a lover here, outside of my heat, terrified me. Only, I was kidding myself if I thought those twinkling green eyes and those large hands hadn't awoken something in me. That my core didn't pulse even now, knowing the kind of pleasure those men could give me. It was as though something inside of me had been sleeping, and my heat had awakened it. A carnal desire I hadn't known I was capable of—one that threatened to consume everything I thought I'd wanted before coming to this place.

While the main room had the latest gaming system and a huge wall-mounted TV, my room was bare, with only a nightstand, tall dresser, and double bed. The message was clear: they expected us to socialize. And if we wanted to bring someone—or some-ones—back to our room, there was enough space in the bed for everyone to fit. I sighed, standing while I dug into the now cooled chicken, not quite ready to test out the bed.

The chicken was pretty good. Even reheated, it was decently crispy and had a spice to it, but I'd foolishly forgotten to grab a bottle of water to bring back to my room. My mouth was on fire, but my belly was full by the time I'd eaten every delicious piece in the bowl, chewing off the precious gristle around the bones.

Stomach sated, my attention turned to the others, and I took up my vigil by the door, pressing an ear against it. Whatever soundproofing they'd used in here was surprisingly effective—the sound of voices barely audible. The tightness in my chest eased when a woman's laugh rang out. So, there were at least some other women here. Thank god.

Hopefully, they'd go to bed soon, and I could sneak out for a drink of water. Moving back to my bed, I stretched out, staring up at the popcorn ceiling to pass the time, and trying to make the swirling patterns make sense like I'd done as a kid. But after my heat, I'd downed four bottles of water, and I was starting to feel it. Of course, they wouldn't include a bathroom off the bedrooms, not if the goal was putting us together at every opportunity. *Oh, damn, damn, damn.*

Wrapping my arms around myself as if it would help, I danced from foot-to-foot until I couldn't stand it anymore. My mouth was on fire, and my bladder uncomfortably tight by the time the voices died down. There would just be a few people out in the main area, or maybe they were all just busy doing other things with their mouths. Ugh, my bladder spasmed, and I squeezed my legs tighter. There was no choice.

I flung the door open, banging it into the wall, and dashed out like a shot. Looking up and down the hallway—yes, there! At the end of the hallway was a bathroom. I could make it, maybe without saying a word to anyone.

Just a few quick paces and I was almost past the hall of bedrooms—nearly embraced by the brightly lit white tiles that meant my salvation—when a door to my left opened, revealing an entirely too cut naked man with sleep-ruffled blonde hair half covering his eyes. I stopped short, my bladder forgotten as I gaped at him.

Damn, it was the guy from earlier. The one who seemed like he must have alpha blood. He smiled with recognition as he took me in, rubbing his stubble thoughtfully.

Don't look at his dick, don't look at his dick, don't look at his dick. But it was too late. It was on display, and I couldn't help myself.

My eyes drifted down, and shit, was he ever well endowed. The guy clearly manscaped, his cock standing out proudly among the trimmed hairs. Had I seen that cock before? Who the hell knows. Those men could've been fucking me with a metal rod, and I probably wouldn't have noticed.

"Hey, Cassie," he said with a smirk, his green eyes twinkling playfully as he leaned one arm over his head on the doorframe. "How you doin'?"

Did he just forget he was naked? The way he spoke to me certainly seemed so. Only the smirk gave him away.

"Good," I squeaked out. He wasn't exactly blocking me from the bathroom, but I would have to walk past him to get there. And going back to my room to pee in the flower bowl was starting to seem like a much better idea.

"Okay then, have a good night." *Oh, thank whatever deity looked after shy women.* He headed back inside, stopping to look back at me briefly. "I'm Jace, by the way."

Jace, okay, that was actually a really nice name. I nodded, giving him a watery smile. His entirely too sexy lips curled up, and he shut the door behind him.

Before any more gorgeous, naked men could appear in my path, I hurried the last few steps into the white-washed bathroom and closed the door quickly behind me with a loud *shlock* sound that made me cringe.

With a sigh, I leaned back against the door, wishing I had a friend to talk to. I thought of my mother, and her brief explanation of what I could expect. She hadn't been able to express how alive I would feel in this place, how it would change me and make everything so much scarier and exciting.

She'd had me and settled down in the family unit. Done her duty. Talking with her about how she'd never chosen to go back, her voice had been filled with a longing I didn't understand, only now I did.

Now, I understood the appeal only too well.

I pushed away from the wall and took the time to really look around at the bathroom. Everything was crisp white, from the long double vanity to the oversized shower. There was only one reason you would need a shower big enough to fit five people, and I noted there was only one knob to operate three showerheads. You'd have to shower with a few other people or waste a ton of water—something the higher ups could be rather strict about.

Apparently, we were supposed to eat, sleep, bathe, and do basically everything together while we were here.

I took a few deep breaths through my nose, counting to ten. Jace came unbidden to my mind. He was hot and nice, even if boys did still seem like a foreign species, but the worst part was not knowing who had visited me in my heat state. Had Jace? He'd certainly make some beautiful babies. I took a moment to imagine what they might look like with his unruly mess of blonde hair and my freckles. They'd be so damned cute.

Now that the adrenaline was fading, I remembered my too-full bladder and my burning throat. I took a moment to appreciate the fact that there were individual stalls before making a break for it.

Between my agitation and the heat, it had been well over forty-eight hours since I'd slept. The bed here had some kind of thick foam with a gel pad on top that supported every inch of my body and made me feel like I was resting on a cloud. It was so much better than the old spring-filled ones we had at the family compound, and my aching body sank into it gratefully.

I'd never slept so long or so well in my life, and when I woke up, the light slanting through the blinds was strong enough that it could only be midday.

Midday. My mother would think I was sick if I ever slept this late. I rubbed the sleep out of my eyes and yawned, stretching my arms over my head and flexing my sore muscles. Everything hurt like I'd been pushing myself too hard during a harvest, but it was nothing some food and rest couldn't cure.

That would mean leaving the safety of my room and finally meeting my new roommates. Something I was not prepared to do.

A peek outside my door revealed someone had dropped off my large black duffel. Busying myself, I emptied it and put my things away in the set of brown wooden drawers provided for me. My drawers back in 7C stuck, making every opening and closing a stuttering fight, but this one glided as smooth as butter. Everything here was so much nicer than my stuff back home.

Drifting over to the window, I got my first real look at the field outside the building. It was well maintained; the grass cut uniformly short, with the wildness of a forest brushing up against its edges. This place really was a dream, or it would be if I could find a way to relax.

I blew out a breath, selecting a set of blue jeans and a long-sleeved, grey knit turtleneck. The thought of exposing my skin to these people made me uncomfortable. Never mind it was warm in the apartment and I'd be sweating bullets in no time.

Reaching into the side pocket of my duffel, I pulled out a hair tie and secured my hair into a high and tight ponytail. On my days off back home, I liked to wear my long blonde hair down, letting it curl just past my shoulders and enjoying the heavy weight of it on my back. Here, I had no idea what I was about to walk into. Tying it up seemed the right choice, like I would be better prepared for whatever I would find when I left my room and joined the others.

My stomach growled, the sound echoing in my empty room. I felt refreshed after sleeping in, but my stomach still played catch-up, and the spicy chicken was long gone.

Okay, okay. I can do this. With a steeling breath, I stalked over to the door and pulled hard on the knob, intending to swing it quickly open. Only, I lost my courage partway through the pull and it ended up creaking rather slowly when it gave way. Damn it, I really needed to develop a backbone if I was going to live here for the next however-many-months it took to conceive.

I crept down the hallway toward the light coming from the main room. A deep pounding music played, the kind where somebody had jacked up the bass and you could feel the music rattling your bones. As soon as I rounded the corner, I understood why.

Oh. My. Right on the couch where I'd played video games earlier—that easily wipeable pleather couch—a tall brunette was taking two cocks in her pussy, her hole stretched to the extreme as one man lay beneath her and another on top. Her mouth was put to use too, and somehow, I knew the guy making her gag on him while he held her hair to keep her in place was Jace well before he turned and smiled at me.

He stood there, fucking her mouth and smiling at me. But I couldn't move, couldn't say anything. I was frozen until a sound from the kitchen drew my attention.

I'd been right about the counters here. A trim blonde sat atop the counter with a red-headed man standing between her legs. Her body jiggled with the force of the man's violent thrusts while two others stood around her, touching her breasts and whispering to her. She moaned her pleasure while I stared, unable to look away.

Only now they noticed me, just as Jace had, like they had some kind of sixth sense for fresh meat. *Shit, shit, shit.* All three of them were gorgeous, but I tried not to look. I wasn't prepared to take in any more naked flesh today—I'd seen my fill. My mouth gaping open, I was still frozen when the sound of someone coming up behind me made me nearly jump out of my skin and shift into my wolf form right there in the common room.

"Hey, are you okay?" The words followed me as I spun and raced back to the safety of my room. Third on the right, but I checked the nameplate to be sure. If that was what they did in the common room, something told me a whole new kind of fuckery was going on behind closed doors. I'd never been so happy to see my name in my life, and I yanked the door open like my life depended on it, rushing in and closing it behind me. With my back to it, I sank to the floor, hugging my knees.

I was never going out there again. I'd still do my duty to the pack and emerge during my next heat, but I refused to take part in the debauchery going on in the common room.

CHAPTER 4

It was difficult to fall asleep with a grumbling stomach, but somehow the soft mattress lulled me into a fitful rest. When I awoke, it was to the sound of a polite knock on my door. Just the lightest of taps, but it sent me into a panic. Flinging myself off the bed, I hid behind it on the far side of the room. There I waited, eyes wide and unable to do anything but stare at the damned thing like it was going to swing open to reveal a whole gang of naked men at any moment.

Only the door remained firmly shut, and the knock didn't come again. Hesitantly, I crawled around the bed, wincing at the pain of the hardwood on my aching knees. Staying near the ground felt safer.

When I reached the door, I pressed my ear against it and listened carefully. No sounds reached me. The music from last night was absent and there were no voices I could hear. I stayed in that position, ears straining, certain I would hear the person outside my door shuffling about. After a few more minutes of absolute silence, I turned the little nub lock on my door handle and pulled it open a crack.

The scent hit me before I saw the plate of food, and I gasped. Resting on a dark cedar tray was a plate piled high with eggs, taters, and thick slabs of glistening bacon. My empty stomach growled hungrily at the divine aroma tickling my taste buds. Before I knew what I was doing, I pulled the door wide and grabbed the tray, bringing it inside with a furtive look in either direction.

They'd even given me a glass of orange juice, and I smiled at the sight of clinking ice cubes floating in the pulpy liquid. Whoever it was, they had gone through some trouble to prepare this for me, and the gesture was kind. I thought of Jace whistling away while he prepared my food in the kitchen and carefully placing it outside of my door. No, it just didn't seem like him. Something about the predatory way he'd watched me while getting his dick sucked last night made me think he wasn't one to woo his women. Chase them, yes. Woo them? No.

The bacon was so damned good, and I moaned as the greasy salt hit my tongue. I made quick work of it. Before long, I'd eaten the whole plate of food. Rubbing a finger through the grease stains, I eked out every last trace of my gift from some mysterious stranger.

I'd still need to go out there at some point, but for now, I could stay in here longer, blissfully alone with my thoughts as I worked through what to do next.

THE RAM

"Why the fuck did you bring her breakfast?" Jace gaped at me, clearly confused by my actions, and of course he would be. Even though he was my squad alpha and half-brother, Jace had been in the breeding program a few times over the past couple of years. He was a favourite of the women here, participating in every bit of play—no matter how deviant—and always trying to convince me to do the same. To relax and have fun. Yeah right, as if there was any chance of relaxing here of all places.

I enjoyed the sex, sure, but I wasn't ravenous the way Jace was. And I definitely didn't have his easy confidence or charming smile. Mostly, I settled for his leftovers—the girls who couldn't get enough of Jace but who had been forced to move on when something sparkly caught his eye.

I wouldn't let that happen to Cassie. Couldn't let her become another one of his puppies, following him around the apartment and banging on his door while he ignored them. There were more men than women here, but it was always him they fell for.

But Cassie had been scared last night when she'd finally emerged from her room and walked into one of our nightly fuck parties. Her face had gone such a sickening shade of white that her freckles had stood out against her pale skin, and I'd been worried she was going to faint. It was all I could do to stand there, gaping, and once again, not talking to her but wanting to. Fuck, did I want to.

The very least I could do was to make her a nice breakfast. She had her door firmly shut since coming out to the common room, and I can't say I blamed her. We must've been a sight to someone not used to it. Hell, I still hung around the sidelines, and I'd been here for a few months. I could still remember my first time arriving, and understanding what life here was going to be like.

Of course, I'd had Jace to urge me along.

Cassie had no one.

"Dude, hey? Are you even listening to me? Why would you make her breakfast? Don't you want her to come out of her room so you can tap that sweet pussy?" Jace rolled his eyes—clearly done with me—sinking further into the couch and selecting his character from the menu.

The guy he chose had a tall green mohawk I secretly envied. We weren't allowed to do much with our hair—nothing that would make us stand out in the pack—but I found it fascinating humans had gone to such extremes to make themselves appear different from one another. I smiled quietly to myself. Yeah, right, like I'd have the courage to do something like that with my hair when I mostly felt I had too much attention as it was.

Naw, I'd probably have just kept my hair nice and neat, and unremarkable like the way I wore it now. Trying my best to fit in and not draw attention, but the idea of standing out and attracting Cassie's attention was an exciting one to entertain.

"The key to getting into Cassie's pants isn't breakfast." Jace frowned when a sniper took out his character with a headshot. Maybe not the best plan to sneak into enemy territory with brightly coloured hair. "You have to actually talk to her, dude."

I nodded my agreement.

Why Jace had ever adopted me as his best friend was beyond my understanding. We were related, but it wasn't something we talked about, and he attracted friends in a way I could only imagine. I was lucky if the people in our social circles, Jace's circles really, even remembered my name.

He was outgoing. I was introverted and much happier to spend an evening gaming on my own than with other people. He was athletic. I was okay at sports but my lack of interest had resulted in a sincere lack of effort, and it showed. I treated my body like a temple, but sports had never interested me. I had no need to pit my skills against others in a mad bid to see who was better.

The one thing we had in common was our commitment to guard training, pushing our bodies as far as they could go until we were the strongest and fastest pairing in the pack. We worked seamlessly together out in the field when we were defending the border. Even I had to admit that.

Jace and I were just so different it was hard to get into his head. Unless we were tracking an intruder or hunting together, then it was simple. I cleared my throat when I found him staring at me with raised eyebrows. He clearly wanted me to say something.

"Yeah, man, I'll do more than make her breakfast, I promise."

"Fucking good. I'm sick of your mopey ass." He threw a piece of popcorn at me, and with a huff, he turned back to his game, leaving me to my thoughts.

He wasn't wrong. I did need to find a way to talk to Cassie. It felt like fate that we were both here in this breeding program, in this pod at the same time, and I couldn't waste the opportunity to get to know her better. Then there was the cyclic nature of the heat. It was rare for a she-wolf to get pregnant on her first cycle, but it did happen. If she didn't, we had a few more weeks before Cassie would be splayed out in front of me once more, begging me to fuck her. No clever words required.

CASSIE

Whoever was supplying me with food was committed, bringing me fully plated meals for breakfast, lunch, dinner, and even the occasional snack. I laughed the first time a little bag of cheese puffs and a glass of milk appeared on my tray at midnight. I guess he figured I had the munchies.

The idea of someone carefully curating my snack tray was ludicrous, but I couldn't help myself from getting a little overexcited every time I heard the light knocking from my mystery man. Even though there were women in the apartment too, something told me it was a man. I kept picturing Jace standing on the other side of my door, rapping lightly with large hands matching The Ram's.

While I still couldn't picture Jace cooking and preparing my meals, his confidence aligned with the way The Ram had played my body like a musical instrument, finding every button and stroking it until I was a whimpering mess beneath him.

I sighed, staring down at my chicken piccata and pushing a few capers around with my fork. There was no reason to believe The Ram and my mystery benefactor were one and the same. But he was out there. One of the men here was the one who had taken me to heaven and kept me there for so long that time had lost all meaning.

In my room, I was safe from any unwanted social interactions with my roommates, but I was also bored as hell. Luckily, I'd brought my precious pile of forbidden books from home. They were old romance novels, written by humans years ago. Romantic fantasies were forbidden for their emphasis on partnering, and they'd been my favourite for as long as I could remember. My family had been hiding them for years, and all the girls took their turn. The books spoke of love and connection with men, and while mating was forbidden, they evoked in me the kind of excitement usually associated with reading about a mythical creature that existed long ago.

Pride and Prejudice was my favourite—a story filled with misunderstandings and passion. Though the last chapter was worn beyond readability, the ink faded to practically nothing by eager fingers, I liked to imagine an ending where all the couples were happily wed.

Whoever had set this apartment up as a breeding ground had planned for the breeders to pass the time by socializing, partying, and fucking, but they hadn't accounted for residents bringing their own source of entertainment

With my books for company, I lasted four days of nighttime trips to the bathroom before the burning curiosity and need to do something—anything—drove me to listen quietly at my door.

It was early afternoon, and I'd seen a whole troop of people heading out to the woods through my window. Now was the best possible time to explore the apartment. I only hoped everyone had left this time.

I turned the knob quietly, the crazy sex party at the forefront of my mind. If they were at it again, I wanted to be able to slip back into my room, but there was no thumping music drifting down towards me from the common room.

There was *a* sound though, and I carefully padded closer to listen better, my bare feet making almost no sound on the dark hardwood.

Someone was gaming. I could hear them smashing buttons on a controller and the accompanying gunfire from the TV. My fingers twitched to pick up a controller, or at least to round the corner and see what game they were playing.

Before I could think about it further, I burst into the room. Just as I'd surmised, there was no sex party going on. The high-end black and white kitchen was pristinely clean, the hanging lights practically shone, and the large comfy sectional was empty, save for one very startled guy with spiky black hair. He sat up, his body rigid with tension at the sight of me. His dark eyes quickly scanned my face, before he looked away and forced himself back into a slouched position on the couch. His eyes were strange. What colour were they? It was hard to tell. Dark enough to almost be black but surely that was the trick of a light, and they were truly brown.

He didn't even say hello, and I found myself smiling at the thought of him being afraid of me. Something about that idea put me at ease, and I looked the stranger over more thoroughly. He wore blue jeans and a baggy black windbreaker with red stripes down the side. For running. I'd heard of those before. The colour made whoever wore one more visible in the woods. Guards were required to train in their human form as well as their wolf form, and these kinds of clothes were what they used during their conditioning.

Carefully, I moved closer. The guy wasn't as big as Jace, but he looked solid with broad shoulders and a strong jawline. Maybe he had alpha blood somewhere in his history. It was hard to tell, but then the way he'd startled when I came into the room made me think he must be harmless. Somebody's beta, a lowly foot soldier.

That was fine with me. Whoever he was, he didn't appear to be a threat. Instead of engaging with me, he kept his focus on the game. Relieved, I blew out a breath, coming closer so I could see what was on the screen.

Yessss, he was playing *Marine Corp X2*—one of my favourite multiplayer games, and he was fucking good at it. Only, he was being creamed, and I frowned at the way the crappy Ais on his team failed to cover him when he advanced. Without a word, I fished out a brilliant lime green controller from its charging cradle and sunk into the plush cushions beside the stranger. A few feet away, but beside him none-the-less.

I should've been more freaked out by being around a man, but somehow, I wasn't. After quietly setting up a profile and joining his round, I soon fell into the rhythm of the game.

The stranger didn't say a word to me, but we worked well together, taking down the enemies one by one and advancing on their base.

We were just about to pass the threshold and force a surrender when the lock on the front door clicked behind me, and I scrambled off the couch. I made a mad dash for my room, dropping my controller with a sickening thud in my haste. Fuck, I hoped it hadn't broken. It was such a beautiful colour. I didn't look back to see if the stranger had finished the round or if he'd been taken out during my absence, but I couldn't imagine him losing.

Sneaking out to meet and play video games with the stranger became my routine. Meals and the occasional snack were dropped off to me, and I'd found the perfect time to use the washroom. A little while after midnight, but not too late for anyone's bladder to wake them.

I lived for the early afternoons when the muffled sounds from the other side of my thick bedroom door quieted and my roommates left. I'd hear them getting ready in the front, talking to one another and laughing, and then I would peek out the window and watch them disappear into the forest to be absolutely sure they were gone. Well, everyone but him.

Without fail, I would enter the common room, and there he'd be. His long legs splayed out with our game already on, and my favourite controller laid out on the seat next to him in silent invitation. How he'd sussed out I preferred the lime green one was beyond me, but I appreciated the gesture.

The first few days, neither of us said a word. We played and when the others came back, I exited the space as quickly as the consuming cushions of the plush couch would allow.

Nothing changed, and five days went by like that. No words between us, just a cozy video game camaraderie only broken when the others returned. Until one day I became hungry while we were playing and my rumbling stomach broke the silence. He'd looked at me sharply, his dark eyes scanning my face, his brows furrowed, and that had been it.

Or so I'd thought. The next day, I came out to find he had left a bowl of cheese puffs on the couch between us. I stared in surprise at the bowl of snacks, and my stomach grumbled in betrayal. He could have just as easily put it on the arm of the seat next to him, but no, he'd put it directly between us knowing exactly where I would sit. My controller was laid out just to drive the point home.

He didn't look up at me as I sat down. Fine, he could leave a bowl of snacks there, but it didn't mean I needed to share them. No way was I going to fall for his trap. But the game dragged on, and the sound of him crunching the occasional cheese puff finally became too much for me. I reached out to grab three at once, stuffing them quickly in my mouth.

They were all salty, cheesy goodness, and I moaned despite myself. My gaming buddy looked over, meeting my eyes briefly before looking quickly back at the screen and shuffling himself further into the armrest beside him.

He was like a frightened little rabbit, and I couldn't help but laugh.

His eyes met mine once again, and I muttered a sorry around the cheese puffs in my mouth.

Slowly, he relaxed beside me, and we fell back into the rhythm of the game. Now that the silence had been broken between us, I was feeling more comfortable around my gaming partner, and that made me curious.

"You don't like going out into the woods with the others?" The question practically leapt from my lips, and I realized how long it had been since I'd spoken to anyone—at least six days. My voice was hoarse from lack of use, and I cleared my throat to get the gravelly sound out of it, feeling the sting of embarrassment.

He frowned, guiding his character around a building with an expertise I couldn't help but admire. "I do. It just gets boring after you've been here for a while." The man's voice was deep, and it did something to me when he spoke—like a little shiver at the base of my spine. Who the hell was this guy?

"You've been here for a while then?"

"Yeah, about three breeding cycles." Shit, so he'd definitely been here for mine then. I hazarded a glance over at him, taking in his lean compactly muscled form just barely outlined by the light windbreaker and jeans that he wore like a uniform every day. Did I know that body?

Careful not to attract his attention, I sniffed the air, trying to focus on his scent. It was hard with the ceiling air freshener that had been present in my breeding chamber, and the ones I'd seen carefully positioned around the communal room, but the fresh clean scent of my mystery guy's soap did seem familiar.

Then again, we had communal showers here. It was very possible everyone used the same soap. Fuck.

"Did you," I paused, trying to build my courage. My hands had gone sweaty on the controller, and I clumsily mashed buttons. I fucked up and my character took a shot to the arm as I worked to get the slippery buttons to do what I wanted. "Participate in the last one?"

Maybe they didn't, maybe they rested the guys, and I could maintain the illusion that there was no way this guy had fucked me senseless.

"Yes." Something about the way he said it made me shiver, and not with fear. I wasn't afraid of him—he'd let me make every move so far, and even the way he admitted he'd participated in the last breeding cycle seemed cautious. He wasn't gloating, he'd only answered because I'd asked him directly. No, my shiver had nothing to do with fear. There was something exciting about this conversation with him, like we were at the beginning of something—standing on a cliff waiting to jump.

He wouldn't lie to me. The thought took me off guard, and I studied the man at my side again. There was zero tension in his muscles, and his attention seemed completely fixated on the screen. His calm energy soothed my nerves, and I decided not to pursue the conversation further.

Maybe he'd fucked me, maybe he hadn't, but I desperately needed a friend, and there was no reason we couldn't hang out and chat. Especially if video games and cheese puffs were involved.

CHAPTER 5

"Whoa, buddy, slow it down, man! We don't have enough ammo yet!" Ugh, of course, he was headed straight there, skirting around the debris, just expecting to find ammo along the way instead of securing it beforehand. "And you forgot the fucking MedPac again, didn't you?" I glanced over at him and saw his lips were quirked up in a smirk that had become increasingly annoying over the past few days. "Come on, they are going to smoke us! Hold up!" I turned towards him, my trusty lime green controller still in hand, raising my arms at him and trying to get his attention, but he just kept looking at the screen, marching into certain death.

What was a girl to do?

"All right, fine. But next mission, we do things *my* way, you got that?" He didn't answer, but my mouth hung open when his guy knocked over a trash can and found four full clips of ammo. "What, no way. You knew that was there!" I punched his arm in annoyance, nearly breaking my fist on his muscles, and wishing I could knock the smirk right off his face. His answering chuckle was almost enough to push me off the edge.

Almost. The ache in my hand I was trying to subtly shake off with a few finger flexes prevented me from taking my revenge.

"Maybe I did, and maybe I just had faith I'd find a way."

"What is this bullshit about faith? You've played this level before, admit it!" He didn't answer, just loaded up and continued towards the enemy base. They were positioned on a mountain and would not go down easy, but I had a strategy for that. "So, now that we actually *have* ammo, let's flank them. I can set up one of my bird decoys and activate it once I'm close enough to their position, draw their fire while we sneak around."

"Solid."

That was his answer? Solid? As stellar a player as my new friend was, he wasn't big on talking. Too bad for him, I was an expert at it.

"Ho, yeah!" I held up a hand in victory before snagging another cheese puff and sitting back on the couch with my feet up on the coffee table. He eyed my feet like he wanted to say something, so, naturally, I settled them in a bit more.

"That's unsanitary." He speaks!

"Oh, sorry about that. Do you often eat at the coffee table?" It was meant to be a tease, what with a dining table and all those beautiful stools he could just pull up to the counter. But I saw a flash of hurt in his eyes before he looked away. Shit. I took my feet down and sat up a bit on the couch.

"You have something against sitting with the others?" I sat forward awaiting his response.

He shrugged, but I could see the tension in his shoulders, and I cringed at my stupidity. This wasn't what I'd meant to happen. The last thing I'd wanted to do was make him uncomfortable. *You're an idiot, Cassie.* I never knew when to shut my mouth.

"I don't have many friends."

What? I looked over at him in shock, noticing his jaw was set tight enough the tendon stood out against his skin. Without thinking, I put my hand on his bicep.

"Well, you've got me. I'm your friend." He looked at my hand in surprise, then up at me with wide eyes. He really did have beautiful eyes—the deepest brown so close to black, I could only tell the true colour when I was sitting right next to him. Nice lips, too. There was an electricity between us I couldn't explain, but I let it guide me closer until my lips pressed against his. I closed my eyes, and I lost myself in him, my tongue darting out for a quick taste. A moan escaped me at the sweetness I found, but it was then I noticed he hadn't moved to reciprocate. His lips were stiff and unyielding against mine.

I pulled away, dropping my hand and moving over to plant myself firmly in my seat. I could feel his eyes on me, and I blushed as I tried to reposition myself to get back into game mode—and pretend like I'd never kissed him.

Had I even done it right? I'd never kissed anyone before. Not Reg and certainly not during my breeding party. That had been about sex. This was...I didn't know. The blush crept up my neck, and I pulled the cowl of my turtleneck tight.

I liked my new friend. I couldn't deny it. He was hot and nice, and really the only one I'd said more than a word to since coming here. I craved the social connection he provided, and well, it didn't hurt that he was easy on the eyes. I'd be lying if I said I didn't wonder what those nimble fingers of his could do to my body, but there was one truth I couldn't ignore— he hadn't kissed me back.

I may not know much about men, but I knew that wasn't a good sign.

"What's your name?" My new friend frowned down at his controller. Unlike me, he liked to pick a different one every day. Today's was a garishly bright red.

"What?"

"Oh, come on, you heard me. I assume you have a name."

He gave a long-suffering sigh like I was asking him to take my shift mucking out the barn and not giving him an opportunity to introduce himself.

"Listen, I can't keep calling you *'Dude'* and *'Buddy.'* It's getting old, and I'm not creative enough to come up with a new nickname each time. If we're going to keep doing this—" I gestured at the spread of delectable snacks he'd set out for us on the coffee table: chips, my favourite cheese puffs, pretzels, and a huge jug of lemonade with a dash of pop to give it the perfect fizz. We had our own bowls of each type, but my friend had also set out a bowl of nuts and dried fruit on his side of the table.

"I'd like to know what to call you." I didn't think he was going to answer. He reached out to take a potato chip and slowly crunched it between his teeth while staring off into space. We were taking a silently agreed upon snack break when I'd decided to try initiating conversation.

"Damian. Well, Dame. Everyone calls me Dame, or well. My one friend calls me D." He shuddered, before giving a small barking laugh at himself and looking over at me with a twinkle in his eyes. "Take your pick, I guess."

"Um, but that's not very helpful. What do you like to be called?" Another chip and Damian—Dame, D, whatever—sank back into the couch cushions until he was so far reclined, he was almost lying down.

I took a moment to admire his lanky form at rest. Even in a reclined position, he looked poised and ready to jump at a moment's notice. My friend was not someone who relaxed easily, and his compact muscles told the story. Being a guard was a prestigious position within the pack, and they were picky about who they recruited.

"Whatever you want to call me is fine."

"Well, Damian is a bit too formal, and you clearly don't like being called D, so, I think I'll go with option number two. Dame. It suits you."

He nodded, thoughtfully, before pulling himself out of the couch long enough to snag a few more chips. He sank back in with a sigh. Pleased my questioning was over and done with, but I had no intention of letting him off so easily.

"Hey, Dame?" I asked. His only reply was a noncommittal grunt with a hint of annoyance that made me all the more eager to push. "You wouldn't know anything about the food outside my door, would you?"

He frowned, eyeing the greasy chip he held between his forefinger and thumb. "Food? What food?" I stared hard at him, watching him take a cautious lick of the chip before putting the whole thing in his mouth and finishing it off with a crunch. His face was completely relaxed, and I didn't think he would lie to me. If he wasn't the one leaving me food, then who was?

Ugh, I'd been hoping it was Dame, so I could thank him and be done with it. The last thing I needed was to live with not knowing who my secret benefactor was, but also knowing how much I owed someone in this house. I guess the only way to find out was to get to know the other guys in the house. Something I was entirely unprepared to do.

Instead, I grabbed a few chips and settled in next to Dame on the couch. I could only hope I was pregnant and going home soon, then all of this would be a nonissue. I let the idea of home—my mother's warm embrace and the kids I took turns teaching at school—comfort me.

Staring down at the rivulets of blood coating the white porcelain, I was a mess of emotions. The dream I'd had of staying hidden in my room until they confirmed I was pregnant and sent me back home was dashed. I hadn't conceived. The breeding frenzy hadn't worked. *Shit, shit, shit.*

No way could I hide out for another two weeks. I was already bored of the books I'd brought, and while Dame had proved good company, my curiosity about the others had only grown.

Blowing out a breath, I tucked a strand of long blonde hair behind my ear and tried to find some composure. I'd need to go through it all again. The heat, the breeding frenzy, and then this terrible waiting period where I was trapped in the apartment with the others until my cycle started anew. An endless repeat until I got pregnant, or they deemed me infertile and removed me from the breeding program. That couldn't happen. I refused to lose the only chance I had of becoming a mother. If I failed, they might try again in a few years if my genes were strong enough to warrant another attempt.

If not, well, my grades had never been good enough to work in the offices. They'd be more likely to send me out to work the fields the way they had with my mother's sister.

When the humans launched their nukes and poisoned the lands, lycans had been hardy enough to survive the fallout, but even we struggled to coax the dead earth to produce food. Working the fields was a hard life filled with manual labour while suffering with the ill effects of working so closely with the poisoned earth. No family, no children, and nothing to look forward to except the knowledge you were helping pave the way for future generations. Shuddering, I rubbed my arms to comfort myself. I wouldn't allow myself to consider failing. They'd selected me as a pack mother. I wouldn't allow myself to consider failing. I would be a pack mother like I'd always dreamed.

I just had to be.

Having sex outside the breeding frenzy was supposed to be helpful, but I hadn't been able to stomach the idea. I'd hoped my heat and the breeding frenzy would be enough, but it hadn't, and now I was staring down another cycle.

"All right. This is okay, Cass. You can do this." Speaking out loud helped to steady my nerves and reduce the tremble in my hands. I grabbed one of the tampons from the top shelf of the tall wire rack tucked behind the door and turned to one of the mirror-sink combos lining the wall. The girl in the mirror—no, woman—looked worried. Setting the tampon on the sink, I pulled a hair tie from my pocket and swept my thick hair up into a tight ponytail, staring myself down.

"No more hiding."

I dared the woman in the mirror to disagree.

CHAPTER 6

No more hiding, no more hiding. I repeated to myself as I stood in front of the door, holding the cold brass knob in my hand. Laughter drifted to me from the common room. Laughter and music, just like the last time I'd gone out there and found everybody tangled up with each other.

How the hell was I supposed to do this? I only hoped Dame would be there so I would at least see a friendly face. But what would that friendly face be doing, or rather, whom? My stomach grumbled loud enough that anyone walking past my room might have heard it. My mystery meal provider would bring me a plate soon. If I went out there right now, I might even catch him still cooking it and know who it is. I wanted so badly to give him my thanks and clear the debt weighing on my heart.

Cooking. Right. If my mystery man was cooking me dinner right now, maybe they weren't all in the kitchen fucking like last time. They couldn't always be going at it. Surely, they must break for food.

Okay, Cassie, just go. I turned the knob with a mostly steady hand and swung the door open to reveal an empty hallway. At least my first encounter wouldn't be right outside my room. Holding onto the doorframe, I leaned my head out of the room and looked towards the common area, quickly darting back inside when a body passed in front of the mouth of the hallway.

A clothed body. Definitely a clothed body. I'd caught a glimpse of blue jeans and a deep maroon sweatshirt. Not Dame then. I'd never seen him outside of that striped, black windbreaker of his, but it didn't mean others weren't fucking. There was only one way to find out. Self-consciously, I smoothed the fabric of the floor-length powder blue dress I wore. The scooped cut accentuated my delicate neck without putting my tits on display. I was going for pretty and approachable, not ready to fuck.

Okay. With a steadying breath, I walked out into the hallway and strolled down it as though it was perfectly normal that I would join the others in the common room, and not at all like a recluse who'd had to be fed like a pet in a cage.

The first thing I noticed was the eyes. It felt like there were a thousand eyes on me all at once, like every single one of the men and women stopped whatever they were doing to stare at me. My gaze sought Dame, and I was relieved to spot him in the far corner lost in a game of foosball with some leggy blonde. The woman wore shorts easily mistaken for underwear, and a top see through enough I could count her freckles. She had a lot of those, particularly around her very obviously erect nipples. She laughed, bending over the table, with her eyes on Dame and not on the game in front of her. Dame, on the other hand, displayed a laser-sharp focus I had seen many times. His eyes tracked the tiny ball delivering swift wrist flicks without mercy.

I cleared my throat and tore my gaze away from the foosball table, my face colouring at having intruded on a private moment. I guess maybe they had plans to all get naked later. The woman playing foosball with Dame already looked halfway there.

Some of the girls were dressed like Miss Practically Topless, but others were more conservative like me. I saw a girl sitting on the couch with short brown hair wearing a similar dress to mine, but with a navy blue flower pattern that complemented her bright blue eyes. I didn't recognize her, and it annoyed me. If any of the girls from 7C were here, I'd feel so much more comfortable, but the secretary had told me they avoided mixing houses, and preferred the breeders to focus on members of the opposite sex until pregnancy was achieved.

Not that any of us were likely to see each other after conception. The idea made me melancholy. Any friendships or acquaintances I made while here would mean nothing. The secretaries were careful not to repeat the same breeding pairs for future pregnancies. It helped produce variety and variety strengthened the pack. It was all part of their process.

The feel of a warm hand encompassing my shoulder startled me out of my thoughts, and I nearly jumped. My face flushed as I fought to hide my embarrassing reaction. The boy who had approached me was someone I'd never met before. Taller than me by a whole head, he watched me cautiously with light brown eyes nearly the same shade as his skin. He wore his hair short and had on a plain grey t-shirt with some kind of old-school graphic of a movie I'd never seen. It looked cool, though. Some kind of monster flick with a fanger positioned above a haunted house, his hands stretched out like claws as though preying on those inside.

The shirt made me want to give him a chance. If nothing else, it seemed like a good conversation starter.

"Hey, I'm Cassie. I'm new here. Well, not new exactly, but new to here, to this room, er, to all of you." I was rambling now, and I allowed myself to trail off, plastering what I hoped was a friendly grin on my face.

"Yeah, I know who you are. You're the chick who's been hiding out. I thought maybe you could use a beer and some conversation after being cooped up so long. The name's Tristan."

He was nice, and the curl of his delightfully thick lips was adorable. He held up a beer with a yellow label towards me like a peace offering, and I quickly snatched it out of his hands. But once I had it, I had no idea how to open the thing. So, I just smiled and nodded my thanks, holding the cold bottle by the neck.

"What's with the shirt?"

"Oh, this?" He gestured down excitedly at his jersey like he was waiting for someone to ask him. "Only the best movie humans ever made. There's a secret werewolf in it too, the kind that can't control their shift. Picture this: everyone's scared of this Dracula-looking motherfucker when one of the guys from their group shifts and starts tearing them apart. Oh man, humans really had some ideas about the supernatural."

I nodded, giving a more genuine smile back. I hadn't seen too many movies. Every free moment I had was spent playing games in the common room with the other kids. Luckily, most of us were into gaming and not so much into movies or there would have been some serious conflict. But the way he described it made me want to watch one.

I was just about to tell him so when the same woman who had been flirting with Dame slung a perfectly tanned arm across Tristan's broad shoulders. He was taller than her and her nipples rubbed against his arm as she reached.

"Hey, Trist! What's up?" In Tristan's defense, he didn't seem thrilled that the blonde bombshell interrupted our conversation. I liked him all the more for it.

"Just talking to my new friend here. Cassie, this is Becca."

Becca gave a start, as if noticing me for the first time—although I swear, I'd seen her size me up—and smiled in greeting.

"Oh hi, yes, The Girl Who Hides in Her Room." She laughed, the sound thick with mockery. It brought a flush to my cheeks and made me want to run back to the safety of my bed. I longed to throw myself on the thick coverlet and cry and read and never even contemplate coming back out here and dealing with these people, the plan be damned.

"Not anymore, Becca. She clearly came out of her room. She's just Cassie now." The words were spoken in a growl, and I turned with relief to find Dame walking up, and his lips pressed into a thin line. He looked damned good tonight, his midnight-black hair spiked up contrasting against his pale skin. The sharp cut of his jawline was tense, his eyes unforgiving. I'd never been happier to see another person in my life. I fought the urge to run to Dame and throw my arms around him in thanks. Instead, I turned to Becca with renewed confidence.

"Yes, you see, my room got a bit *boring*. I don't think I'll be going back there anytime soon."

Becca's mouth fell open in an 'o.' I thought for a moment she was going to say something nasty, but she released Tristan and raised the beer in her hand.

"Hey, everybody, listen up. Cassie here is joining us for real. She's not going back to her room," she finished her announcement with a rowdy whoop that was quickly echoed by those present.

Everyone raised a beer to me, and I raised the one I held in solidarity, not sure I liked where this was going. I still hadn't worked out how to open the fucking thing, but I guessed if holding a beer helped me fit in, it was worth it.

THE RAM

Tristan's arm snaked across Cassie's shoulders, and I didn't like it. Not. One. Bit. Jaw sore from how hard my teeth were clenched, I worked to cool the rage building in my chest. It wasn't like Cassie was mine to begin with. No, she never would be mine. That beautiful ray of sunshine was well outside of my reach, but she was out of Tristan's too, and seeing him sidling up to her all chummy made my blood boil.

There had to be a way to get used to this. Cassie had the right to go to bed with any man here. In fact, she was encouraged to do so. As sweet and shy as she was, it would happen. I could tell by the look of resolve she'd worn when I'd watched her casually stroll into the main room like she hadn't been a hot topic of conversation for the past few weeks of her self-imposed confinement.

So, why couldn't that man be me? Why couldn't I be the one to take her to bed? My mouth went dry at the thought of approaching her. It was so much simpler during her heat. There she lay begging for my cock, no words, no embarrassment. Even my identity had been hidden from her. It was so simple. I'd wanted her, and she'd wanted me.

No, that wasn't true. She hadn't wanted me—as much as I wanted to believe she did. I'd been nothing but another hard cock to impale her needy pussy on, and I'd been only too happy to oblige, to bury myself in the sweetest, prettiest pussy I'd ever seen and give her every last drop of my seed.

Fuck. Cassie. Her pink tongue darted out to lick chapped lips, and I realized for the first time the beer she held still had the cap on. I couldn't suppress my groan at her innocence. We were the same age, but she'd never left the family compound, never drank or partied.

"Hey, Bash." The slim nerdy guy running past paused and turned to me with a question in his eye. "Grab the bottle opener and go help Cassie with her beer. The cap's stuck."

Bash gave me a drunken salute and changed course, heading back to the kitchen to find the bottle opener.

I'd be damned if I was going to go searching for it and leave Cassie unattended and surrounded by a bunch of horny wolves. She was the new girl, and everyone wanted a piece of the new girl.

As hard as it had been to rise through the ranks of the guard, being a superior had its perks.

Cassie's tinkling laughter made me cringe. *Would she laugh like that with me?* I had barely managed a few words to my personal ray of sunshine, and here she was surrounded by a growing group of guys just as social and chatty as she was.

Fuck. I was screwed, but I could never give up on Cassie. Not now that I knew how good it felt to be inside of her. That tight pussy clenching hard around me, her eyes rolled back, and lips parted in a perfect 'o' as orgasm after orgasm crashed into her. But it was more than that. She touched my heart like no other. Her natural warmth and care for others was something special. Something to be treasured.

Tristan whispered in her ear, pulling her in so close that his lips brushed against her skin when he spoke. Damn, he was smooth. All I could do was look on, staying at the outskirts of the group, but not so far I couldn't hear the melody of her voice. Just like when we were fucking kids.

Bash came over a few seconds later with the bottle opener and took Cassie's beer, but the moment he snapped the lid, frothy white foam poured out, splashing all over her light blue dress, leaving navy splotches. She hunched forward, the cold liquid dripping off her soaked chest. Her nipples quickly became erect and visible through the thin material of her shirt.

Shit, I looked at Tristan, but he wore a look of shocked confusion himself. Becca, on the other hand, looked about as satisfied as a dog with a fresh butcher's bone.

Poor Cassie's mouth worked, and I moved quickly to take off my shirt and offer it to her, only to be beaten to it by a few of her more admirers. Tristan had his horror movie shirt off in a heartbeat. His was the first to go on followed by a ridiculous striped polo with a chewed-up collar. A moment later, Cassie found herself wrapped in a variety of shirts and surrounded by a group of half-naked men watching her eagerly.

Freezing, I waited to see what she would do. This was too much. *Fucking Becca.* What a bitch. She must've shaken up the bottle and given it to Tristan. That idiot never thought past the next move.

Thank fuck Cassie tucked a loose strand of her long blonde hair carefully behind an ear and reached out to take the now mostly empty bottle from Bash. With a small brave smile, my girl held up the bottle.

"Cheers." The resulting whoop was nearly deafening as everyone around her raised their beers together in a loud clink.

I held mine back, not much wanting to participate. It was tiring always being the loner, but whatever. At least I was here if Cassie needed me.

She took a sip. The way her little mouth wrapped neatly around the bottleneck made me half-hard. *Great, now I was jealous of a bottle.* I had to get it together.

"It's bubbly." She giggled, and I couldn't stop myself from smiling. I wasn't prone to emotional displays, but something about Cassie always got to me.

Shit. I was in so much trouble.

CASSIE

Everyone was so nice. I couldn't remember what I'd been afraid of, but to be fair, I couldn't remember much of anything. The world tipped and turned like a top on its point, never settling on one spot. Everything was a blur of handsome faces and hard muscles, all of them staring at me, wanting me. Never would I have imagined anybody would want me, and now there was a room full of men looking at me with hunger in their eyes.

Laughing at the absurdity of my situation, I stumbled, catching myself from falling at the last minute and felt a steadying hand on my shoulder.

"Whoa, Cass, maybe take a break there, Babe." *Was that Jace's voice?* I struggled to focus on the man still holding my arm. Yes, Jace. Hot Jace with that cocky little smile of his.

"Babe? I'm Babe now?"

His smile widened. "Only if you want to be. I'd also consider, Sexy, Baby, or Bae."

I laughed violently enough that I needed to cover my mouth to keep from spitting all over him.

"Baby, Bae, Babe? Aren't those all kind of the same? Why don't you just call me Ba like a sheep—*ba, ba*." I snorted, nearly falling over when the force of it made the world spin like crazy.

"This is your first time drinking alcohol, isn't it?"

I peered up to see his brow crinkled, his green eyes soft. "Nooooo, I've had lots before, and I've been to lots of parties, and had lots of sex." I gave him a toothy smile, hoping he bought my bundle of lies. The hard set of his jaw told me he didn't.

"Come on, Ba, I think maybe we should set you up a nice little spot next to Mr. Toilet."

I laughed at that, Mr. Toilet. How silly.

But he was right. After stumbling down the hallway towards the bathroom, I realized just how affected I was. The damned world just couldn't keep still. The porcelain toilet beckoned me, and I fell in a heap beside it, pulling myself up to the edge as my stomach heaved and I threw up.

A little more clear-headed after losing half my body weight in fluids, I looked up to find Jace holding a neatly folded piece of toilet paper out to me. I took it from him, delicately patting my dirty mouth. *How embarrassing.* Really embarrassing. The more my mind sobered up, the more I wanted to somehow retract my promise to be done hiding and go back to my room forever.

But Jace still looked at me with a heat in his eyes that made me blush. That intensity. Could Jace be The Ram? Then he came up behind me, looped his arms under mine, and hoisted me to my feet.

I turned to see he still wore that self-confident smirk, his lips curling seductively. He reached out to stroke my cheek, and I knew. There was no way Jace was The Ram. Something about his touch didn't feel right, and I pulled away from his fingertips.

"Come on, Ba, I've got some space in my bed for you tonight."

What? Like I should be honoured to fuck him? What a pig.

"No, thank you." My voice was weak, and he moved in closer, looming over me.

"Are you sure about that?" He didn't seem at all put off by rejection. If anything, the heat in his gaze had only grown. My mouth opened and closed as I fought through the remaining bits of drunken haze for something to say. Something more clear than no?

The bathroom door swung open, and I looked up to find Dame in the entryway, his normally handsome face contorted into a feral scowl.

"Back off her, Jace." The words came out in a low growl, and it was impossible to ignore the threat in his blazing eyes. With his dark hair spiked up and rage pouring off of him, he'd never looked hotter. I thought back sadly to my failed attempt to kiss him. He was definitely not interested.

"Whoa, whoa, D. What are you talking about? She wants me, don't you, Ba?"

Horror-stricken, I drank in the casual way he leaned against the sink. Could he convince Dame to go? My throat worked, but no words came. I was working up the nerve to tell Jace to go to hell and fuck a demon if he was so horny when Dame stepped between us, getting in Jace's face. I took one tottering step to the side and watched the conflict nervously, unsure of what I could do to help diffuse the situation. Dame was a few inches shorter than Jace, and he had to look up to meet his eyes, but I admired the stony glare he gave Jace as though the size difference between them didn't matter. Dame had always been so shy and unsure, but seeing him now, I could see the wolf deep within.

Both men appeared completely relaxed the longer they faced off, but I could see hints of tightly controlled muscles ready to spring into action. Their arms and shoulders might be loose, but it was there in the stiffness of their necks and the fists at their sides.

"I didn't know you cared so much about what I did, D."

"Well, I do."

Jace held Dame's gaze for an extra moment before taking a step back and holding up his hands in apology.

"Well, okay then. I hope you know what you're doing, buddy." The last word was practically spit at Dame, and then Jace was leaving, turning to smile and wink at me once before the door shut behind him.

Adrenaline fled my body, leaving me woozy and dizzy once more. I tried to take a step towards Dame, but somehow my wobbly legs got tangled up, and I started to fall. Strong arms caught me and pulled me into a rock-hard chest. I looked up to find Dame's midnight eyes.

"Cassie, Cassie, Cassie, what do we do with you now?"

CHAPTER 7

THE RAM

Watching Cassie sleep was the most wonderful thing I could imagine, and also, the most exquisite torture. Could you die from a hard on? Because it felt like you could die from it. I sat at my desk, only too aware of the stunning creature passed out on my bed. I'd needed to carefully remove her vomit-soaked clothes, and while she was tucked neatly beneath the blankets, I'd seen enough to know my memories from her breeding party were not mistaken.

Cassie was easily the most gorgeous woman I'd ever seen, with creamy soft skin, delicate limbs, and pouty lips more often twisted up into the sweetest smile. Breeding parties be damned, I wanted to see those lips wrapped around my dick, her beautiful smile replaced with one of lust. I wanted to touch her and make her come outside of the shackles and desperation brought on by her heat.

A breathy sigh from the bundle of blankets she was buried in caught my attention, and I turned to see she'd pulled down the blankets, exposing the top of one perfectly round breast. I couldn't touch her, wouldn't touch her. She was passed out, but the need to do so was hard to ignore, and I pressed a hand onto my painfully stiff cock.

We'd have her again. *Later.*

Pregnancy had failed to take, and Cassie reeked of the telltale blood. She'd be here for at least one more breeding party, and then maybe she'd go. My heart clenched in my chest at the thought. One more time with her, and then she could be pregnant, she could leave, off to have children that could be mine, and raise them far away from me. I wouldn't see her with the children and would almost certainly never see her again. The administrators preferred to choose new sets of breeding pairs for each pregnancy to encourage diversity.

Frizzy blonde hair covered her face, disturbed from her tossing and turning, and the strands came to life with each of her sweet breaths. Tenderness—not lust—pulled me to her bedside, and I carefully disentangled her from the hair, tucking it behind an ear. Fuck, even her ears were pretty. I wanted to suck on the lobe and find out if she was sensitive to it outside of her heat. Everything was heightened in that state. I was pretty sure she would've been turned on if I'd touched her elbow, but she had liked it when I'd focused on her earlobe and maybe she still did.

The memory haunted me, and my cock twitched painfully in protest, not understanding why we couldn't take her right now. The fucking thing had found its home, and it was eager to get back.

Not today. Even if Cassie was awake and asking for it, I didn't know if I had the strength to take her to my bed outside of the breeding party, to have her look at my face, and know me. The thought was terrifying. What if she didn't like what she saw? The vulnerability wasn't something I could face, and I found myself pulling the blankets up to cover her exposed breast.

She wasn't mine, not physically or emotionally, and never would be. My issues aside, starting something real with her was forbidden, and would only end in heartbreak. If for some reason she did like me and we were caught, I would be dismissed from the guard. My life's purpose as a protector would be lost, and I'd be sent to the fields to work. I wouldn't have my respected role within the pack, and I certainly wouldn't have Cassie. That lonely future meant Cassie could never know how I felt about her.

With a sigh, I returned to my desk, pulling out a fantasy book from some old human author. Life would be so much simpler if we were elves or orcs, hell, even humans. There wasn't any romance in this particular story—reading romance novels was forbidden—but

I could imagine it. They had married couples within the story, though they never showed their beginnings.

Marriage was a human concept, but with Cassie asleep a few feet away from me, her beautiful face smooth and peaceful in sleep, one I could well understand. To have someone for the rest of your life, to have them be only for you and you be only for them, my heart ached at the unfairness of never knowing what that felt like.

Pain stabbed from behind my eyes, and my head ached as I fought for consciousness. With a groan, I flung an arm over my eyes to filter out the light coming from the window next to me. That helped, but only just. My head still felt like someone was inside trying to bust their way out.

The window next to me... wait, what? My window was on the other side of the room. With a start, I sat bolt up, ignoring the flare of pain as the sunlight continued its assault on my retinas, and looked around.

This was not my room. *Oh, shit, shit, shit, where did my dress go?* I pulled the thick coverlet across my naked chest and scanned the floor. No dress, but there was a cream towel neatly folded over the only chair in the room, and it looked like salvation. Some part of my brain processed how incredibly sterile the room felt, with no personal identifiers and everything cleaned with military precision, but that was as far as I got before the panic took hold. I needed to get the hell out of here before the owner of the room came back. I struggled to pull myself from the bed, snatched up the towel, and wrapped it tightly around myself, pleased it was large enough to reach almost to my knees.

Moving with urgent caution to the door, I listened for a moment to ensure no one was there, before whipping it open and dashing out into the hall. But I was disoriented. Where was my room? I stumbled down the hallway, searching each name tag for my name until

I found it halfway down on the opposite side. I couldn't breathe until I was back inside the familiar white walls pressing my back to the thick wood of my door.

My heart pounded almost as hard as my head, and I dropped the towel to the floor as I fought for air. I was in someone's bed? In only my underpants? What happened to my dress? The last thing I remembered was Dame showing up to rescue me like one of the heroes in my books. Was it his room I'd ended up in, or Jace's?

With a shudder at the memory of Jace's insistence, I took stock of my body. No, no one had done anything to me. I wasn't sore, and nothing stained my thighs. A quick check confirmed that my tampon was still in place. I sighed, the stress draining from my body and leaving me to feel the full aftermath of drinking.

Head spinning, I kept a hand on the wall and made my way over to my dresser, pulling out my favourite cotton nightdress with its familiar pink rosebuds and fitting it over my aching head. I never wanted to drink again. Never. Or eat, or well, anything really. The neatly made bed I'd left when I'd foolishly gone out to attend the party called my name, and I slipped beneath the soft blankets, nearly asleep the moment my head hit the pillow.

Thoughts of Dame filled my mind. How fiercely protective he'd been confronting Jace. If he could react that strongly, maybe there was something there, or maybe, he'd just been being my friend. A genuinely good guy.

Of one thing I was certain, after my encounter with Jace last night, I knew there was no way he was The Ram. I had a few weeks left before I'd go into heat again and see *him* in the breeding chamber—the one who played my body effortlessly, like it was an instrument he'd spent his life practicing on. Memories of the way he had run his hands over my skin teased at the edges of my mind, and I felt myself react, my skin growing oversensitive in anticipation of The Ram's touch. I traced the soft cool fabric of my silk pillowcase—brought from home to keep my hair smooth—and imagined I was pillowed on The Ram's hard chest.

My body jolted awake, and I sat up in alarm before remembering I was back in my room now. My pillow had a wet spot on it I could just make out in the waning light. A swipe at my cheek revealed drool, and I rubbed it away, hoping I hadn't been drooling in whoever's room I'd slept in before.

It was past seven o'clock when I looked at the unforgiving numbers on the clock, meaning I'd missed my chance to talk to Dame and find out what had happened after I'd blacked out.

I sighed. My mouth felt like it was stuffed with cotton balls, and my stomach was rolling painfully, at once demanding and rejecting the idea of food. But I'd gone all day without, and I knew I needed to eat so I padded my way to the door on bare feet hoping against hope.

Yes. A tray of buttery croissants and sausages sat alongside two tall glasses of water. Thank god my mysterious benefactor had decided to visit me once more, and based on the food, he knew just what kind of a state I'd be in. Not surprising since I'd made a fool of myself in front of everyone who lived here. Peering out into the hallway to make sure no one was there first and finding it empty, I crouched down and pulled the tray towards me, all the way into the room before shutting the door. I didn't want to see anyone now, or worse, talk to them.

I ate until I was stuffed, feeling an intense amount of gratitude to whoever had left it for me. The flaky croissant had a satisfying crunch to its exterior, and the grease of the sausages soothed my roiling stomach. I finished eating, wiping my face with the cloth napkin, and drank down both glasses of water. Expecting my stomach to revolt at the sudden influx of liquid, but it sat well now that I'd had some food. I breathed a sigh of relief, sitting back against the headboard. I'd eaten in rapidly dimming light in tribute to my poor abused eyes, but if I wanted to read, I'd need some light.

The lamp turned on with a click of the wall switch next to me, but I flinched away, disturbing the plates on my tray and nearly upending it. Arm shielding my eyes, I switched it back off. Carefully moving the tray to my bedside table, I lay back down. I'd slept all day, but I was still exhausted and not quite recovered. With a full belly and a dark room, it wasn't long before I drifted off to sleep once more.

CHAPTER 8

"Cassie, reports of your behaviour are troubling." Tapping his pencil, the man leaned forward in his desk chair and tried to catch my eye. Administrator Samson must've been sixty, with a pair of glasses so thick his eyes appeared huge and a kind face. He'd long ago lost his hair, with only a few remaining white wisps clinging to his scalp. Why he didn't choose to trim them and neaten it up was an oddity, but then, his tiny office was filled with old books and DVDs. Perhaps he was clinging to the past.

He squinted down at the paper. With eyesight like his, no wonder he'd been cast into the role of an administrator. I bet he'd never been chosen as a breeder—never known what it was like to live in a group setting like mine. My throat turned dry, and I fought to clear it as I searched for the right words to put him at ease. *This couldn't be it.* I had to stay on as a breeder or miss my chance at being a mother. But if they did decide to reject me, I could go home. Back to my mother and friends. I'd be free of Pack Breeders 103C forever. No more heats, no more tiptoeing around the apartment terrified of running into anyone. No more Dame.

No more Dame.

The words hung in my mind. The quiet comfort of his presence was something I'd grown used to, and I was shocked to find my heart ached at the thought of leaving and never seeing him again. Okay, wow. I did not expect that, and I didn't know what it meant other than I needed to find out, to talk to him more, to be around him more until I understood it better. There was something about Dame that made me feel safe in an environment where I felt constantly on edge. He'd been a comfort to me, and if I lost him now...

"Please don't send me away." The words sprang from my mouth in a nervous jumble that had Administrator Samson chuckling and putting down his neatly sharpened pencil without writing a thing. There was a knowing look in the twinkle of his brown eyes.

"Cassie, I know you want to be a mother. I interviewed you when you were first selected, after all. It's just that..."

I waited with bated breath while he paused to frown down at a piece of lint on his blue and white striped shirt. He brushed it away before continuing. "You don't seem very committed to the process. Hiding in your room? Getting blackout drunk? These don't seem to me to be the signs of someone committed to the breeding program."

Palms flat on the table, I stood up and stared him in the eye.

"I swear to you, I am committed, it's just been a bit of a transition. But I will fulfill my duty to this pack, to the Alpha."

Administrator Samson gave a slow nod, studying the rigid tension warping my posture. "Okay then, I can see you feel strongly about your role. May I offer you some advice?"

I gave a shaky nod in response.

"Shift."

"Shift?" My mouth hung open in surprise.

"Yes, embrace your wolf and let yourself race through the woods. It's not natural to deny yourself the shift, and by all accounts, you've been doing just that. How long has it been since you shifted and went for a run?"

"Oh, um." My mind went blank, and I slumped back into my chair, defeated. How long had it been? I hadn't shifted since coming to the apartment. Before that? I'd been too nervous to go out with my mom when she'd asked.

Administrator Sampson gave a nod as if I had already answered him. He took his pencil to paper, scribbling something I couldn't quite make out no matter how hard I tried. His handwriting was atrocious. Bad eyesight and bad handwriting, what a bummer. Maybe he was a good singer. I could just picture him as a crooner, his hand on his heart as he belted out some slow old tune in an amazing tenor.

"You'll start going on a daily run just like the others, whether you copulate with them or not, I don't care. Sex outside of your heat is encouraged, but not required. Just try to let yourself go a little bit, relax. Have some alcohol."

Suppressing a shudder and the creeping nausea threatening my stomach, I gave him the best smile I could manage.

"Go on now, Cassie. If you hurry, you can make it back in time for today's scheduled run. I wish you the best going forward."

So, the runs were scheduled, were they? That was interesting.

I hurried out of Administrator Samson's office, trying to peek again at what he'd written. There was a question mark at the end of the statement, and I could make out the word wolf.

Okay, so his advice was to lighten up, relax, embrace the freedom of a shift, and run through the forest. It didn't even need to be with the others, not according to him, or at least, he hadn't said so explicitly.

No, I wouldn't be joining the pack run today, but I would try what he was suggesting—by the light of the moon, I would shift and let myself go, work my muscles until all these petty insecurities faded. I would let pounding blood renew my spirit and sweat cleanse my body until the troubling attachment I had to Dame became clearer. Whatever had me desperately unhappy at the thought of never seeing him again, I would face it head-on, and find myself under the moon's glow.

Fuck, it felt so good to be outdoors breathing the fresh spring air tinged with pine. I wished I could share it with Cassie. Hell, I wished I was inside with Cassie right now. Or just inside Cassie.

No, bad thoughts. I had to focus here, forget about her, and recommit myself to the pack. She could never be my mate.

Mate. The word stayed stuck in my mind like a drop of oil polluting pristine waters, spreading across the surface until it consumed everything in its path.

Only, I wouldn't let it, wouldn't let her. There was no way for us to be together, so I should just stop thinking about it. Focus on the sights right in front of me, like the small busty brunette shimmying out of her skin-tight jeans in anticipation of the change. Of course, she wouldn't be wearing underwear. She caught me watching and winked, but I was already looking away, not willing to engage.

But I *needed* to engage, to lose myself in another woman's body so I could forget hers. Everything felt so tainted since I'd sunk into her heat and felt her tight pussy clench around my eager cock. Nothing was good enough. Every time I thought I was starting to get better, to recover from this illness she'd inflicted upon me, I'd see something that reminded me of her. The brightness of her eyes. The warmth of her smile. The way she sighed with her whole body, her slender shoulders settling back into the couch when she was truly relaxed.

Fuck, I should go back. Maybe she'd come out of her room today and I could catch a glimpse of my personal ray of sunshine.

It'd been three days since she'd passed out in my bed, two days without even a whisper of her in my life, and I was damned near ready to crash through her door and demand an audience. Only, if I did that, what the fuck would I even say?

Hey Cassie, how are you doing? Can I get you some more food?

Stupid, I'd say something stupid, and she'd laugh at me. The sexy brunette in front of me stepped back in line beside where I stood, naked and waiting for the signal. I kept my gaze straight ahead, but I could feel her eyes on my half-hardened cock.

I wasn't getting hard for her, but by the smirk on her pretty face, she thought I was.

Fuck, I couldn't even distance myself right. When had Cassie started bleeding? It'd been at least ten days now, which meant only another two weeks before she'd be induced into her heat again and strapped into a bed, awaiting my pleasure.

With a growl, I embraced the animal part of myself and dropped to all fours, stretching my changing spine and feeling the power in my powerful hind legs as the transformation completed. A power waiting to burst forward. I glanced at Jace, who was still half-dressed and flirting with some women at the end of the line. He wasn't nearly ready to signal our start, and I was done waiting.

I howled into the day, wishing our daily runs could be scheduled when the moonlight could fall on my fur, and dashed off for the line of thick spruce across the clearing. But I wasn't alone. The thundering sound of paws hitting the grass echoed around me, and I looked over my shoulder to see that *my howl*—not Jace's—had started the run. Fuck, he was going to be pissed. We'd both always known my wolf was the more dominant between us, but I'd never asserted myself, and hadn't wanted all the leadership and social obligation that came with being the most dominant in a group. I'd always been happy to follow.

Not today. No, today, I howled into the welcoming thicket, tearing through the underbrush. If I couldn't have Cassie, I would at least have this.

I returned to the apartment at a near run to find it empty, the squashy couch missing Dame's lithe form. No dark head with spiky black hair, no sounds of games being played. He must've gone out on the run with the others, which meant I was Dame-less. With a sigh, I rounded the couch to find the table full of neat little snack bowls next to the spot where I always sat.

Warmth spread through my chest at the sight. He might not be here today, but he'd still thought of me. I wasn't surprised to find extra cheese puffs in the bowl. While Dame always appeared aloof and cold, he paid attention.

I flopped down on the couch, not in my spot but his. From his position, I looked over at the space I usually occupied and wondered what he saw when he looked at me. He must like me just a little bit. He'd stood up for me, after all, and set out snacks.

But that kiss, I leaned back, letting the couch nearly consume my slight frame. He hadn't responded at all. It'd been like kissing a statue. I stared up at the air freshener on the ceiling. Yeah, wouldn't want us to be able to smell each other. I picked up a cheese puff and chucked it at the lavender-scented monstrosity above my head. Of course, the cheese puff didn't have the weight to go anywhere. What did Dame really smell like? Would it be familiar? The breeding rooms were kept just as nauseatingly scented to help maintain the masked male's anonymity, but I felt I would still know. I'd been close to each breeding male, and maybe I'd be able to recognize a familiar scent.

Air fresheners were plugged in everywhere, but this seemed to be the only one right over this part of the couch and the ceiling wasn't that high. There was a basketball net on the back of the front door, and always a few balls rolling around. It would be believable for an air freshener on the ceiling to be hit without anyone realizing it.

With a grin, I ran to my room and grabbed a thick white plastic hanger from my closet. The couch was sturdy, and I didn't weigh so much that it would tip. I jumped up on the cushion and then stepped up onto the back of the couch to gain the extra height I needed, carefully balancing on my socked feet. Good thing these had grips. It took a few swings before I connected, but when I did, the lavender scent intensified. Holding my nose with one hand, I hit it again and gave a little whoop when it hit the floor.

I climbed down to stand over the little piece of plastic with clear liquid spilling onto the dark wood. Carefully, I picked it up and rushed to the sink, washing it out with water until no more of the atrocious smelling scent remained. Then I sopped up the wet spot from the hardwood and tucked the empty piece under the couch, as if it had been mistakenly knocked down and rolled under.

The self-satisfied smile spreading across my face as I sat down would've put the all mighty alpha to shame. I yawned and pulled my favourite bright green controller from its cradle. Hopeful that being able to smell Dame properly would help me to better understand the intense emotions that had overtaken me when I'd thought of never seeing him again.

Dame would be back. He might be mad at me for getting drunk, or just giving me space, or who knew what went on in that spiky head of his. But he'd made sure my controller was charged and waiting, and he'd left out my preferred gaming foods.

He hadn't given up on me yet, and if all went as planned, I'd get a good whiff of him at our next meeting. A whiff I might be able to place from my drug-induced heat state. For now, I was perfectly content to stuff my face with cheese puffs and hone my skills so I could be more effective when next we teamed up. Dame was one helluva shot, but I wasn't far behind. I'd just have to use this Dame-less time as a bit of extra practice, so I could see the shock on his usually emotionless face when I took the lead on our next advance.

Game on.

CHAPTER 9

The full moon's light welcomed me home even as the cool fall air pebbled my skin. I quickly stripped off my tank top and cargo pants, knowing I'd feel warm again once I settled into the form of a wolf.

Deep breath Cassie, you've got this. It had been a while since I'd shifted, and while I loved the feeling of running through the woods on all fours, shifting had never been my favourite activity. Letting go and allowing the change to happen always made me feel uneasy and vulnerable. Everyone else talked about how freeing it was, but it just wasn't that way for me. My dislike of the act was a carefully guarded secret of mine and something I hadn't even shared with my mom.

I let go of my human self and embraced the animal part of my soul, my stomach dropping in a sensation that was at once both hungry and nauseous. Fur sprouted across my bare skin, and I fell forward as my spine twisted into place. A few quick shakes helped to settle me into my new shape, that of a russet wolf with a white patch on her chest.

The world before me became alive as the scents of the forest hit my nose, and I couldn't stop myself from yipping with excitement before racing off into the trees. Shifting might have been just as awful as ever, but this? I could do this forever. My powerful legs pumped, propelling me faster through the trees at a reckless pace as I dodged tree after tree on nimble feet. I ran until I no longer recognized where I was, and I started to worry I was approaching the border where the pack guards patrolled.

Panting, I pulled up to a stop next to a small stream and lapped up the water. Fresh and ice cold from the fall chill air, the water tasted like heaven on my parched throat.

Thirst slaked, I looked up at the moon visible through the thick canopy provided by ancient oak trees stretching high overhead. So beautiful. The moon goddess called to me, and I threw my head back to howl into the night, letting loose my voice in her honour.

A twig snapped behind me, and I spun around, splashing in the shallow water.

An enormous pitch-black wolf watched me from the shadows, studying me with glowing yellow eyes. My body reacted instantly, leaving me cold and too warm all at once. The male stepped forward, sniffing. There was something feral in his eyes—feral and familiar.

The Ram. If I'd have had my human mouth, I would have gasped. As it was, I took another step back into the icy stream. It was him. I knew it in an instant, and my pulse quickened with something much stronger than fear.

He was here. It was him, really him.

The wolf lowered his head and gave a low growl that I felt low in my belly. I'd wanted him in the breeding chamber, but of course, I'd been induced into my heat. This? This was completely different and somehow exactly the same.

Trembling, I backed further away until I was walking up the hill on the other side of the stream. The black wolf stopped advancing and watched, his lip raising to reveal sharp fangs. I wanted him, but I didn't just want him, I wanted him to take me. The thought sent a shiver of desire straight to my core.

Before I knew it, I spun around and took off through the trees. My heart sang when I heard the sound of him following close behind. His grunts and sounds sent me careening through the trees, pushing myself faster and faster until I was just barely dodging trees and at real risk of injury. He kept pace, dodging just as well as I did, but his larger size was a hindrance in the thick brush.

I broke through to a clearing of tall grass and raced across it, no longer impeded by trees and the underbrush of the forest. But neither was he.

His heavy form knocked me to the ground, and I felt his teeth grip my scruff gently but firmly. He growled, his hot mouth soaking the fur at the back of my neck even as the sound rattled through my bones and left me wriggling with need beneath him.

There was a commotion at my back, and I felt the teeth in my scruff replaced by a hand.

"Shift." His voice was somewhere between a man and an animal, his hand in my scruff holding me down so I couldn't turn around and see him.

I obeyed without thought, taking my human form and trying to twist around to see the man I'd thought of every day since my heat. His grip on my neck was punishing, pushing me further into the ground until I tasted dirt. A feral growl and hot breath at my ear sent a new shiver of desire skating across my skin, and I shivered in the cool night air.

"Stay down."

As if I had a choice. As if I'd want to get up when all I could think about was feeling him inside me again. I ceased struggling against his hand on my neck and moaned, pushing myself up against him.

A hand moved down my back with a tenderness so at odds with the way he kept me pressed into the ground. His hand moved lower to find me soaking and ready for him. Without warning, he sank two fingers into my wet heat like he owned it, and I cried out.

"You're so wet for me already." His voice was distorted, still mingling with the animal, and somehow it turned me on even more. I groaned in acknowledgment of his claim, as if the need dripping down his fingers wasn't answer enough.

He removed his fingers and slammed them home again, pumping in and out of me, his thumb circling my clit. I screamed, tasting earth as he relentlessly hammered his fingers into my needy pussy.

Tendrils of pleasure curled low in my belly as the tension wound tighter. I was so close I could taste it. But I cried out in disappointment when he pulled away, leaving me empty. All thought left my mind when his cock slammed home a moment later, and I gasped at the feeling of fullness and the stretch. But he didn't give me any time to process the sensation before pulling out and slamming in again, reaching around to pinch my nipple before circling my swollen clit.

He pounded me hard into the forest floor, shoving me forward. My arms splayed out fighting for purchase I couldn't find. The sound of his balls slapping against my soaking pussy filled the night air. His grunts and growls wound me tighter and tighter.

I wanted to sit up. To be an active participant. To take some kind of control, but he had it all. His hand moved to my head, twisting painfully into my hair and arching my neck up towards him. He was relentless as he chased his release, driving me closer to a heaven I didn't know existed.

During my heat, I'd always been on the edge of an orgasm, but this? A wave of pleasure tore through me, leaving my core trembling in its wake singular and powerful, unlike the waves I had ridden in my breeding room. A guttural cry tore from my throat as I shook with the force of it.

But he didn't stop. His thumb on my clit only increased, until I moaned at the intensity of sensation building toward another release.

He came with a roar, his warmth spilling inside of me leaving me full of him. Consumed by him. Desperate to find a way to be even closer. I was finished with my orgasm, but not at all finished with him. I struggled in his grip, eager to turn around and see him, but he leaned over me and growled into my ear.

"No."

The word cut through the haze of pleasure shaking its way through my system, and I stilled. Hot tears sprung to my eyes as he pulled out, his hand firmly gripping my hair and holding me down while he did so.

Then it was gone, and I turned to find a black wolf where the man had been, watching me with steady yellow eyes. Sad eyes. He blinked and it was gone. The sadness was there for a moment and gone the next. He turned away, and the wolf took off at a quick clip through the woods and back toward the compound.

I couldn't get her out of my head.

Why did she have to be out in the woods last night? The one damned night I stay out after dark to try and clear my head of the cobwebs *she* put in there, and don't I hear the most beautiful howl. I follow it, and I find her, even more stunning in her wolf form with a white patch on her chest that I swear looks just like a fucking heart.

Cassie. I'd been helplessly drawn to the scent of her arousal, and the way she'd moaned beneath me when I'd caught her.

Smoke blew into my face, and I cursed. Digging out the quesadilla from the pan where it was burning and quickly flipping it, I cursed again when I saw how blackened it was. I mean, I'd still eat it, but no way was I going to serve burnt shit to Cassie.

I sighed, dragging over the butter dish and fetching another tortilla and some shredded cheese. They only took a few minutes to make, and I was careful to seal the edges with an extra bit of butter. Cassie had lost a bit of weight these past few weeks, and I didn't want her getting sick.

Cassie. Slamming into her tight pussy had been just as good as I'd remembered it, like coming home after being gone for far too long. I'd told myself it couldn't have felt that good to be with her, a pussy's a pussy, but Cassie. Those sweet breathy sounds she made and the way her hands scrabbled at the grass when she came. Everything about her turned me on. Sex with her was both incredible—and addictive. I'd wanted another hit of her ever since her breeding party, and I'd been completely unable to resist when she presented herself to me.

It had been wrong for me to indulge myself in her again, and outside of the breeding room where she could catch a glimpse of my face. That wasn't allowed. No woman was supposed to know who their breeding males were, and I could tell she recognized me. But why would she recognize my wolf form and not me as a man?

Grumpily, I flipped the quesadilla and moved to take out the sour cream from the fridge. I'd add a sprig of chives from the herb in my window box to finish it.

"Hey, what's cooking, man? Didn't we just pound back some wings like an hour ago?" Jace came up beside me, leaning back into the counter, not quite in my way, but close enough to be imposing.

Yes, we had, and I'd more than had my fill but Cassie didn't like wings, at least, the ones I'd included on her tray in the early days when I was still learning her tastes had come back untouched. I frowned at the quesadilla.

"Yeah, we did eat."

Jace wore a tight black shirt that clung to his considerable muscles, with even tighter pants showing off his package. He must be having a harder time with the ladies than I'd realized if he was putting his assets so front and center.

News of how Cassie had turned him down had spread.

At least he hadn't thrown a fit about my leading the run the other day. He'd acted like it had never happened. Like I hadn't just taken his authority in front of all the others. I was happy to hand the reins over and never talk about it again if he was. It was much more comfortable in his shadow. Safe.

"You're making it for her, aren't you?"

I shrugged casually. "Yeah, maybe."

"But, dude, why?"

I shrugged again, trying to keep my cool. He was just concerned, I reminded myself. I would be too if I was in his position. "She needs to eat."

"Yeah, she does, but you don't need to be the one to feed her. She could just come out here and grab something from the kitchen whenever she wants."

I fished a square white plate from the bottom of the stack in the cupboard and plated Cassie's quesadilla, cutting it into wedges with a pizza cutter. The roundness of the quesadilla looked great on the square dish just as I'd planned. A dollop of sour cream in the center, some salt and freshly ground pepper on top, and it was almost ready.

"Are you even listening to me? This shit is dangerous."

He was right, it was very dangerous. In more ways than one. If Cassie had seen my face, and known I was Dame—the man who could barely utter a word in her presence, who handicapped himself in games so she wouldn't feel less than, and spent his days planning out more and more elaborate meals to try to impress her—she'd laugh at me.

I clenched my jaw and caught his eye. "It's fine."

"You aren't getting attached? D, look at me and tell me right now that you aren't interested in Cassie."

"Of course, I'm interested. She's hot, all right. I'm looking for a good fuck is all."

Jace clapped an arm across my shoulders, leaning into me and knocking me dangerously off balance and close to the lit burner.

"Pack above all, brother."

"Pack above all." I nodded.

How does one get over getting held down and railed on the forest floor, and loving every minute of it? Of sharing something so special with someone and not even knowing who they were or what they looked like?

I had the weirdest feeling when I did, it'd make sense. I'd see The Ram's face, and all the pieces would fall into place. No more worry, no more fear or distrust, just...

What, love? I barely knew him. Sure, we'd slept together a few times now and no one had ever made me feel as good as he did. He had a way of anticipating what my body needed that left me dying for more. That sad look in the black wolf's eyes haunted me.

No, he wouldn't be out there again tonight. I wouldn't see him again until my next breeding party in just under two weeks, or whenever the powers that be decided I was close enough to my natural heat that they could induce me.

What would it be like to be with The Ram in a proper bed? To talk to him and fall asleep next to him? *Pah, talk to him about what?* Oh, yes, I could just picture it.

Mr. Ram, the weather out here is simply splendid.

Why, yes, Cassie, now please be quiet while I fuck you into oblivion.

I didn't know him, so I couldn't love him. But I wanted to know more, and the only way to do that was to find my courage and leave this room to mingle with the others.

I needed to spend more time with the guys and try and figure out who he was. At least I knew I'd be able to get a proper whiff of Dame the next time he showed up for some gaming. I didn't for a second think the meek man who quietly played games beside me on the regular could have the same fiery passion as The Ram, but I'd have a chance of knowing if we'd fucked before.

Sighing, I revisited the mirror. This time, I'd chosen a pair of tight jeans and a white belly-revealing tank top with spaghetti straps. I'd go out there in the day this time, and there'd be no more drinking. My stomach turned just thinking about it.

Chapter 10

Tristan had the most adorable dimple in his left cheek that only appeared when he smiled, which was pretty well all the time. The man was a breath of fresh air after dealing with Dame's moodiness for so long. Not to mention damned fine.

"Can I get you another drink? Non-alcoholic, right?" His eyes twinkled with mischief.

I glanced down at the dwindling glass of orange juice I was holding.

"Sure, that'd be great! Definitely non-alcoholic." I laughed nervously, hoping I hadn't earned the title of lightweight for the foreseeable future.

Being out in the main room wasn't so bad, and Tristan had been excellent company. There was an energy to the way he gestured wildly with his hands while telling me about his horror movie collection. Somehow he'd managed to have a TV set up in his room, and he kept his precious DVD collection squirreled away in there for his use only. He'd been regaling me with swamp creatures and killer dolls for over an hour now, and I didn't mind a bit.

The large room only had a few occupants, and I was much more comfortable not having to deal with a crowd. Both Jace and Dame were curiously absent, and I wondered if they were off doing something together.

I didn't have to wait long for Tristan to return, bounding over to me on long legs looking every bit like a bouncy puppy. This man was seriously adorable, and I'd been trying to lure him over to the couch so I could give him a sniff, but that would require its current occupants to move their butts. Something that didn't seem likely as I side eyed the two guys sitting on the edge of their seats and playing an arena battle game. They seemed pretty well prepared to stay there all day, with a mix of almost meals arrayed in front of them—pepperettes, chips, guacamole. No way I was getting Tristan into the smell zone. *Damn it.*

But could he be I Ram? There was a liveliness in him that did align with The Ram—I couldn't deny it. And the room had been dark. I'd thIt The Ram had light skin, but I could be wrong.

"So, do you want to come check out a few flicks? Chill in my room?"

So, this was what he was building toward.

Tristan gave an exaggerated pout, and his beautiful brown eyes went wide. "Please."

Did I trust him? After Jace had been so pushy, I hadn't had a lot of faith in male kind.

"Only if we can leave the door open, and if you have *chairs not* just a bed for us to sit on."

He grinned so wide I thought his face might split, showing gleaming white teeth and making his dimple stand out even more.

"Deal."

Well, at least he wasn't offended. That was a good sign. I nervously followed him back to his room. All the rooms had air freshener plug-ins too, but maybe the smaller space would be helpful.

I trailed behind Tristan's large form, admiring the peaks of his broad shoulders through the baggy shirt he wore, and the curve of his ass just visible through loose grey sweats. He didn't exactly dress to impress, but impress he did. I hummed my approval too low for him to hear, quickly bringing my eyes up to his face when he opened the door to his room. He reached in to grab a green plastic t-rex to prop the door and turned to gesture me inside.

What I saw had me laughing out loud. I'd known Tristan was a horror junkie and a bit of a nerd, but this place was to the extreme. Horror figures lined a tall bookcase filled with DVDs, and three big monster movie posters adorned the opposite wall. Two comfy-looking bean bag chairs in navy blue sat across from a wall-mounted flat screen.

Stepping closer to the bookshelf, I admired the figurines. They must have been difficult to collect—relics of another time—but most of them were in pretty good condition. Except for an old vampire-looking dude with chipped paint across his lapel and a faded cape.

"Ah, yes, you've noticed Drac. He's a limited edition but obviously wasn't taken care of. I found him in the wreck of an old house. I've been trying to get a hold of the right paints to clean him up, but they're difficult to find, and not exactly something that's made anymore."

I nodded thoughtfully, looking sadly at the chipped miniature figure and its story.

The wreckage of a human house, no doubt the result of one of the deadly bombs that had all but decimated the human population. I wondered what else could be found in that wreckage. Had a child once owned this figure, or maybe another collector like Tristan?

"You okay?" Tristan's arm rested across my shoulder, and I looked up to find his eyes filled with concern.

A delicate sniff I hoped was subtle enough to escape notice revealed only the same soap all the guys used. Damn, I'd have to get really close to Dame to smell him properly. The thought of cuddling up to my stoic friend made me blush, but I coughed to cover up my reaction, hoping he'd interpret my flushed cheeks as a result of the violent hacking.

"Yeah, fine. I hope you find the paints you need soon."

He studied my face, his eyes drifting down to my lips and then lower to my breasts, just visible through my V-neck due to his higher vantage point. I flushed, pulling away. He let me go, holding up his hands in a consoling gesture.

"Sorry." I grabbed my V-neck to hold it closed. It'd seemed a perfectly reasonable top when I'd put it on, but I hadn't planned on standing next to any tall guys with their superior height. I cleared my throat.

"Do you like to cook?" The words filled the awkward silence between us, and there was that dimple again.

"Well, I mean, I can microwave a mean burrito?"

I laughed. Okay, so, Tristan was more of a microwave chef, which meant he wasn't the one whipping me up four course meals and leaving them in front of my door. At least I could solve one mystery.

"All right, let's see what we have here." Tristan peered past me and started running a finger along the spines of his DVD collection. "You want vampires? In memory of the little Drac guy you like so much?"

"Sure, I don't think I've ever seen a vampire movie." The way his mouth dropped open was almost too much, and I burst out laughing. "I've watched lots of monster mashups, though! I promise, I'm not totally new to all this." I gestured at the bookcase full of horror memorabilia.

With a grin, he grabbed a DVD from the shelf, then another and another until he had a stack of five in his eager hands.

"Sit down, Cassie, and get comfortable. We've got work to do."

The first movie was good, if a bit corny. A man went on a mission and became a vampire to impress his girlfriend, only to return and find her in bed with someone else. The ensuing bloodbath was cringeworthy, but the setup was well done, and Tristan? Tristan was in heaven, half sunk into his beanbag chair, long legs bent at an uncomfortable-looking angle. He wore a smile the whole time, reaching over to grab my arm excitedly as the man left a bloody trail on the way back to his beloved.

His enthusiasm was contagious, and I surprised myself by chuckling along with him at the bad special effects—blood that was as red as ketchup, and wounds on obviously fake limbs. By the end of the film, the muscle tension had drained from my body, and I was genuinely enjoying myself.

But as it ended, my thoughts turned to Dame. Tristan was a joy to be around, but I found myself wishing to share this experience with Dame. To see if any of the gore broke his usual composure. To make him laugh the deep throaty laugh I'd only heard once before when I'd missed my shot, and my avatar had tumbled off a cliff. It had been magic, the sound, so rare and yet made even more precious for it.

The film ended in a blood spatter across the camera, and Tristan moved to start the next one. Thoughts of Dame had soured my mood, and I didn't think I could maintain my cheerful facade through another one of Tristan's films. I just wanted to be alone.

"Hey, sorry, but I think I'm going to call it a night, if that's okay?"

Hand paused on the button, Tristan looked back at me with a heartrending look of disappointment etched into his features.

"Aw, Cass, I thought we were having fun! I have about four more films for you until I can deem your vampire history lesson complete."

I shook my head.

"Please?"

"No, I'm sorry, Tristan. I just—I'd like to go back to my room."

With a defeated sigh, he ejected the disc and reinserted it into its case, fitting it snuggly back on the shelf in an empty slot that I was sure must be categorized in some way. It sure wasn't alphabetical—maybe by director?

I felt bad for wanting to leave. How often did people come in here for movie marathons? It seemed a unique interest, and one I could understand. No one in my family was nearly as interested in reading as I was.

"But, listen, I'll come back again, okay? We'll watch the next one?"

Tristan's face lit up. "Yeah, okay, that sounds good. Really good. I'll leave these out so we know which ones we're going to watch, and in what order. The order is very important to your vampire education." He grinned, exaggerating his top row of teeth and giving a vampire-like hiss I couldn't help but laugh at.

"Okay, goodnight, Tristan." I extracted myself with great difficulty from the beanbag chair and sidled past him on the way out. So close I could feel his warmth. He flattened himself against the wall as I slipped past.

"Night Cassie, don't let the hidden vampire in your closet *get ya.*"

Laughing, I left the room, walking backwards, and right into someone.

"Oof, sorry, are you okay?" I turned in a hurry, another apology on my lips when I realized it was Dame I'd run into. My mouth hung open in surprise, but he didn't look surprised at all.

He looked pissed.

"Fine." The tense line of his jaw muscle twitched, and his dark eyes blazed.

"Hey, um, HEY." I struggled to form words; my tongue glued to the roof of my mouth.

"Sorry, I didn't mean to disturb you and Tristan." He turned to go, and I grabbed his arm, wrapping my hand around his bicep.

"Dame, hey. Dame, wait." His arm was hard as a rock, and I couldn't help but wonder what he looked like in something more form-fitting, or nothing at all. Heat rose to my cheeks, and I snatched my hand back. "Where have you been?"

"Around."

"Around? Come on, we always play when the others go out for their run, and you've been a no-show. I think you owe me a little more than 'around.'"

He opened his mouth to say something but closed it without uttering a word. His posture eased, and he stood more casually, the fire in his gaze dying.

"Yeah, nothing to worry about. I'd be down for some gaming tomorrow if you'd like." Dame's tentative smile was everything, and I couldn't help but grin back.

"You're on."

He moved to shuffle around me awkwardly. "Oh, and Cassie?"

"Hmm?"

"I've got way better taste in movies than Tristan and his weak collection of B-horror movies. If you're ever interested."

I laughed at the mischievous twinkle in his eye.

"I'm down for whatever." Ugh, why did that sound so sexual? "L-like games or movies or—"

Not much better, but Dame just gave a smirk and continued on his way to the common room. I wanted to join him, and my hands itched to take hold of my controller and play a round with him, but not now. There were too many others in the main area, and it wouldn't be the same. Maybe I was a selfish fool, but I wanted my time with Dame to be just the two of us. Whatever that was.

One thing was for sure, the way he'd hinted at watching movies with me, and the look on his face when I'd bumped into him, he was jealous of my spending time with Tristan. Maybe there was hope yet.

Fucking Tristan. I'd been minding my own business coming back from the bathroom when I'd passed his open door and heard the all-too-familiar sound of Cassie's tinkling laugh. She was damned near to laughing hard enough to snort, an adorable discovery I'd made during a mini game with dancing rubber ducks. It was so sweet and so Cassie that I'd wanted to make happen again and again.

Only Tristan was the one making it happen, and all I could do was stand outside the door with clenched fists and so much jealousy pounding through my veins that I was frozen to the spot. Thankfully, they had been almost done. When she'd emerged only to bump into me, and I'd had to suffer through the pure joy of her closeness, it was almost too much.

But Cassie didn't deserve my anger. She was right. I had been avoiding her. It was only natural for her to seek some other form of companionship. I'd have felt a lot better if it'd been with a girl though, or Jerry, otherwise known as the guy with the oversized nose and a unibrow.

The problem was that having a taste of her out in the woods wasn't enough, and it had only made my obsession with her all the worse. But by the look on her face when she'd confronted me about my absence, she wanted me there with her, and I wasn't about to say no. Not when I could spend just a little more time with my personal ray of sunshine.

There wasn't so long to wait until her next breeding party, when she'd be strapped down and zoned out on lust, dripping wet and waiting for me. But I couldn't deny it'd felt so damned good to make her squirm and come without her heat being involved, to think she wanted me and wasn't trapped in an induced state of lust she was helpless against.

No, in the forest, she'd wanted me, and I'd smelled it on her. Her arousal was thick in the air from the moment our eyes connected by the stream. In my agitated state, I'd been helpless, and then she'd run. I hadn't been able to resist a chase, especially not knowing where it would lead.

I couldn't do that again—wouldn't. My feelings and desires for her were too strong—dangerously strong. Besides, she might get pregnant at this next breeding party. Whether by me or someone else, I wouldn't even know, and then she'd be gone. Back home to 7C, never to be seen by me again. They were strict about not using the same breeding males for subsequent pregnancies, and males weren't allowed in the family area. Fuck, that'd be torture, knowing where she was and not being able to see her. I had to stay strong, to keep myself at a distance or I wouldn't survive her absence.

So, we'd play some games, enjoy each other's company, and then go back to our lives. That had to be the end of it because there could be nothing else. I just needed stronger walls with her, to build my defenses up a bit better, and we'd be fine. I could do this. Just a few more weeks.

Chapter II

I stretched out luxuriously on the pleather couch, settling into my spot beside Dame with a huge grin on my face. A glance at him revealed the same emotionless mask he always wore. But his quiet presence was a comfort I had sorely missed.

Dame had set out our snacks, and even secured some ice cubes for our pop, something in short supply with limited freezer space and a large group of mostly twenty-somethings. Despite Dame's usual grumpiness, I was content. The only bummer was someone had reported the missing air freshener, and a new one was now installed and pumping its obnoxious scent down around us. I'd have to figure out a better plan and try again, but for now, I wouldn't let it spoil my good mood.

"What do you think? Should we hit Bathas Rock today? Are we ready for it?"

Dame's answering grunt was noncommittal. Shit.

"You know, there's nothing going on with Tristan and me." Why had I said that? Putting it out in the open was probably a terrible idea, but I couldn't stand the way he was acting like a stranger.

Dame looked at me, really looked at me, and the cautious way he considered me told me I'd hit on what was bothering him.

"You do what you want, Cassie. You and I both know sex is encouraged outside of breeding parties, and I've certainly had my share of women. It doesn't bother me if you fuck around with Tristan or whoever you want."

My mouth hung open at his candor, but the jealousy he'd displayed when I'd bumped into him in the hallway had been real. I was sure of it.

I didn't know what to say to him. In one brief statement, he'd denied any hope I'd harboured of us becoming a couple and pushed me towards another man. Swallowing, I tried to breathe through the hurt in my chest.

"Well, I don't want to 'fuck around' with anybody outside of my breeding parties. I'm here with a purpose, and in the meantime, I'd much rather play video games with your grumpy ass."

He snorted, and I looked over to see his dark eyes alight with laughter. He shook his head, giving another snort and looking back over at me. Damn, he was beautiful. His face all chiseled lines, and while his smile was rare, it never failed to take my breath away.

An answering smile spread across my face.

"Me, too. Well, okay then. Glad we got that cleared up. You said something about Bathas Rock?"

I sighed, the tension draining from my shoulders. *Cleared up.* Yeah, it was cleared up. We both enjoyed our time together a helluva lot more than screwing random strangers, and if that was all I got for now, okay. I could work with that.

"Only if you think you're ready for it," I joked winking at him playfully.

"Oh, I'm ready for it. I don't know about you though. The last time we played, your shooting game was weak."

With a guffaw, I punched him in his stupidly hard arm. "My shooting game is *not* weak, besides." I grinned over at him, "While you've been off doing whatever the hell you were doing, I've been practicing."

Dame quirked an eyebrow at me, and I saw a touch of mirth in his eyes that almost made me want to punch him again, but then he turned back to the screen.

"Bathas Rock it is."

"Yes!" With a squeal, I sat up to grab a few cheese puffs from my bowl, stuff them in my mouth, and take a sip of fizzy, icy pop. Best to be ready.

I kept glancing over as we played, eager to see if my new mad skills were impressing him, but Dame's face was as untouched by emotion as ever. The advance went well, but the AI had planted guys in the shadowy rocks off to our side and flanked us before we could reach the top. They took us out and I sat back defeated, staring at the screen in shock.

"We were so close, so close."

"Yeah." He sounded just as disappointed as I was, and I peeked over to find him staring at the screen with his mouth twisted down into a frown. It was true Dame wasn't the most expressive guy, but each time he dropped his mask was delightful.

"So, Jace is the guy who calls you D?"

"Yeah, I'm his beta in our squad."

"Are you guys..." I hesitated, trying to think how to word it. "Close?"

"Yeah, sort of. He takes the lead, I follow. It's always been that way." Dame frowned down at his controller. I got the impression there was more to the story, but I didn't want to pry if he wasn't willing to share. The last thing I wanted was for him to close himself off again.

"But you don't want to be his beta, do you?"

Dame's eyes flashed to mine, and I knew I was right, but he only held my gaze for a moment before looking away. He sat up and snagged a pretzel from one of his bowls. "I don't mind having someone else organizing people and leading." He frowned at the pretzel he held between his index finger and thumb. "I'm not so good with people."

"See, I don't think that's true. I think you don't try to be good with people."

"Hm," he hummed, shrugging and sitting back on the couch. "Maybe. People are difficult for me to be around, I'm always sure I'm going to say or do the wrong thing."

"Am I difficult to be around?" I leaned forward to catch his eye and failed. He continued examining his pretzel, like he was considering each grain of salt. I was sure he wasn't going to answer when he broke the silence.

"No," he said the single word quiet enough that I had to strain to hear it. A warmth spread through my chest, and I smiled to myself. I knew he cared just a little bit. But what he said next surprised me. "Did you want to join the breeding program?"

Leaning back into the couch, I thought about what he'd said. Of course, I'd been assigned to this role like anybody else, but...

"Yes, I did. I wanted the chance to be a mother." Sighing dreamily, I thought of all the sweet little babies dangling on their mother's hips back in the family compound. "I—just. Well, I love children and babies, and I want that for myself."

He turned to study my face, his dark eyes roaming over every inch as he sought the validity of my reply.

"You don't seem to like the process, hiding out in your room all the time."

"No, I don't, but I know that at the end of this, I'll have children to raise." The image of them in my head was so beautiful. Normally women had two babies, and I had no trouble imagining mine. They'd be a boy and a girl, and I'd hold them to my breast to feed them from my body. Carry one on the front and one on the back while I moved throughout my day. Cuddle them when they cried. And when they were older, I'd teach them about life, show them how to do things.

"Why is it you want to be a mother so badly?" Confusion swam in Dame's eyes like the idea of wanting children was unheard of, and I struggled to think of how to explain.

"Every night before bed, I tell the children of the compound my made-up stories."

"Okay, but you could do that with other people's children."

I frowned knowing I wasn't explaining myself very well, but for some reason, his question brought the bedtime routine at the family compound to mind.

"Well, yes, I do, and it's always a large group of little ones who come. They sit on their mothers' laps and their eyes go wide at just the right parts. They laugh when I tell a joke. It—it brings me so much joy."

"Yeah, so, why do you need your own kids? It sounds like you've got a pretty good setup."

"I do, but then." Sorrow settled into my chest. "The story ends, and the mothers bundle up their little ones, kiss them, and take them to bed. I can tell stories all I want, but I want to be the one to kiss them goodnight, too. I want that bond with them. I want to be someone's mother."

Dame nodded thoughtfully, and I caught a touch of sadness in his eye.

"That's...Well, that makes sense, I guess. Most breeders get pregnant after two or three cycles so you might get your wish sooner than you think. Then you can go back to your family." There was a note of bitterness in his tone that made me want to give him a hug, but his posture held me back. He was tense, stiff even, like he was ready for a fight.

"What about you? What do you want? Out of life, I mean."

Startled dark eyes met mine. Had he never really thought this through?

"To serve the alpha and the pack faithfully until my final breath." A textbook answer, but one that didn't ring true.

I studied his face, sure I'd touched on something real. But if Dame didn't want to tell me now, that was okay. I had time, a few more weeks at least, and this was the most he'd opened up to me since we'd first started gaming together.

I elbowed him playfully.

"Okay, you serve the pack until 'your final breath'." I grasped my chest dramatically. "And I'll have my babies. But for now, why don't we give Bathas Rock another try? I can set some timed bombs on our flanks to clear out those guys before we get to their trap."

He gave me a small smile in reply and sat up to push my bowl a bit closer to what had become my side of the table.

"Fuel up, Sunshine. It's going to be one helluva ride."

Sunshine, I liked that.

Chapter 12

The manacles around my ankles were tighter than I remembered—and metal. Weren't they straps? They weren't anymore. The metal bit painfully into my skin but moving against the restraints only made them dig in more.

A wave of flaming desire spread across my skin, and I gasped. My heat was starting. The horrible burn began in my core and spread out until every fiber of my being was consumed by it and only sex could cool me. I writhed around on the bed, soaked with sweat I knew from experience wouldn't be absorbed by the waterproof lining on my bed.

The door opened with a bang, revealing *him*—his silhouette even more imposing with a light shining from behind him, casting the curve of his horns into deep shadows. *The Ram. Yes.*

He approached the bed slowly, and I mewled with need, bucking upwards in invitation as the heat drove me to near insanity at the sight of him, and the knowledge of what would follow. Those hands—those talented hands—would know just where to touch, just how to work my body until the desperate need was at last sated.

The Ram was who I needed. I gave a breathy gasp as he stepped between my thighs and reached out with a firm hand to grip my trembling thigh just inches from my pussy. So close, but not close enough. I cried out in frustration when he kept his hand there, but then his other hand took hold of my opposite thigh and he started massaging on both sides, sending delightful shivers of sensation straight to my core.

"It's okay, shh." His voice was exactly as it had been out in that field, half-animal as though he weren't fully shifted back to his human form. Only he was. Hard muscles glistened in the low light of the room, and I wished I was free from the bed so I could run my hands along them and lick along the grooves of his perfect body. Make him squeal for once.

I was half sitting up just thinking about it, but he stepped forward to push me back down. I went willingly, watching him with trusting eyes as he positioned his tip at my soaking entrance.

It felt so good when he pushed inside. The fullness was everything I needed to soothe my heat back into submission. I wanted more, and I tried to scoot farther down, to push him deeper, but his grip on my thighs was unrelenting. We would go at his pace then.

His thumb moved to my clit and began circling it while he pushed in inch by satisfying inch until he was fully seated, and I felt the heat of his body flush with mine. My eyes rolled back, and I arched, needing the friction only he could provide.

The Ram didn't disappoint. He pulled out and then hammered back in at a pace that left me panting and inching closer to what I knew would be my first of many orgasms. His grip on my thighs moved to my hips, holding me bruisingly hard as he fucked me. I liked it, and I wanted more. I sat up to hold onto his arms and see him thrusting into me, but as I did, I realized something.

I could reach his mask. With a gasp, I reached out and pulled it off, revealing shaggy blonde hair and flashing green eyes.

Jace? The Ram was Jace? No, no, no, it wasn't supposed to be Jace. I cried out even as he brought me to ecstasy, a smirk on his face.

"Come for me, baby."

No.

I sat up straight in bed, gathering the duvet around me as I fought to reorient myself. Disentangling my legs, I kicked free of the covers and perched at the side of the bed, dropping my head into my hands.

The Ram was not Jace, there was no way. A shiver tore through me, and I hugged myself. Why had I dreamed of him? The mystery bothered me—that's why—and with my body showing signs of my approaching heat, I knew I'd meet The Ram again soon.

It wasn't Jace though, couldn't be. I repeated the words inside my head, hoping they'd sink into my subconscious and banish him from my mind.

I got dressed slowly, my limbs still shaky, and tried to read a bit of *Pride and Prejudice* to calm myself. Its yellow frayed edges failed to provide their usual comfort. What I wanted was to get back to sleep, but it was family day, and I found myself annoyingly awake long before the sun came up. Once per cycle, we were permitted to return home to our compound to see our families, and today was the day. The men could go back to their squads, and I would see my mother.

My mother...what would my mother think of me now? I felt so changed from the last time I'd seen her, and then there was the knowledge of her knowing what I'd done since coming here. Just the thought made my ears grow hot with embarrassment.

The kids, though, I did miss the kids. The mental image of their excited faces was enough to get me moving. I picked out some stretchy black yoga pants and a long-sleeved, blue shirt—all the things to allow me the movement necessary to roughhouse with my little friends.

Smiling at the thought of their sticky fingers and boisterous voices, I headed to the kitchen. Leaving my room was becoming less and less of a stressor as the days wore on. Aside from Jace, nobody had been pushy, and things with Dame just seemed to get better and better. He talked to me a lot more than he used to, and despite his insistence he was awful with people, he could be damned funny with a dry sense of humour that left me in stitches.

We never talked about anything deep, but that was okay. There was still time, at least another month's worth.

I dodged around a group of two guys chatting up a brunette with short spiky hair and shiny white teeth, to go to the kitchen and pour myself a bowl of cereal. There was quite a selection of sugary treats, but I looked past them for the bran flakes I knew my stomach could handle. They didn't taste like much, and they were a healthier sort, grainy and dry. I wasn't surprised to find the box almost full, but it was surprising to find it open at all.

With a chuckle, I imagined Dame was the other person who liked the crappy cereal. His body was in peak condition with very little body fat. Even the extra gaming snacks he set out for himself trended towards healthy— nuts, grapes, and protein bars. His only indulgence was a bowl of pretzels, although I'd seen him detour mid reach to help himself to a few of my cheese puffs and the occasional chip from time to time. I was pretty sure he just gave himself matching bowls of snacks for my benefit, a gesture that was both sweet and infuriating, and, well, Dame.

"What are you smiling about?" Tristan stood on the other side of the counter, his lips twisted in a smile and twinkling eyes that begged to be let in on the joke.

"Oh, Tristan, good morning."

Tristan wore yet another horror themed t-shirt and his signature baggy sweats. This one had a monster alien attacking a group of astronauts on what appeared to be their home planet. The creature looked like it was made of mud with the way its flesh drooped, and its arms were raised as the helpless humans scattered in front of it.

I approved.

"Good morning yourself. What's so funny?"

Embarrassed, I looked away. "I was just thinking that I'm pretty much the only one eating the bran flake cereal." I gave a nervous chuckle at my admission.

Tristan used his superior height to peer into my bowl, and when he saw dry brown flakes, he tsked and shook his head.

"Not even the flakes with sugar on them? Really, Cassie? I'm disappointed in you."

I snorted and chucked a flake at him. "Hey, it's a healthy choice. Besides, my stomach isn't feeling up to sugars right now."

"Family day?" His eyes softened.

"Family day." I nodded.

"Well, if it makes you feel any better, I haven't seen my mother in about four years now."

My mouth hung open. "What? I thought meetings were arranged between children and their mothers?"

Tristan gave a sheepish grin and looked around before making his way around the counter to stand beside me. "Yeah, but my mom's been pissed at me for joining the guard. She always wanted me to be a worker, and when I chose the guards, well, she *chose* not to see me anymore."

"But why? How could she do that?"

"Being a guard isn't always the safest choice, and I think maybe it was easier for her not to see me, to cut ties in case something happens. Kinda sad, but that's life."

I stared at him still not processing how his mother could be so cruel. Especially to a happy-go-lucky guy like Tristan. Denying herself of his company for fear he would be lost to her one day? It was madness.

"But, but you're her *son.*"

He shook his head sadly.

"Yeah, and she has four more just like me. She was a breeder a few times over, my mother."

"Oh." My heart broke for Tristan. So strange to think that such a cheerful guy like him had such a sad past.

Like a light switch turning on, Tristan's face lit up and his dimple came through. "But hey, it's not half bad. I actually love my squad, they're such an awesome group of guys, and Jace and Dame do such a great j—"

"You're in a squad with Dame?"

Tristan turned sheepish, scratching the back of his head. "Well, yeah. Sorry, I know you're not supposed to know these things about us, but, yes. It's just the three of us from our squad here. One of the lower ranks is taking control in the meantime. Why they thought it was a good idea for Dame and Jace to both be in the breeding program at the same time is beyond me."

"What's Dame like in the field?" Maybe I played my hand asking after Dame, but I couldn't help it. I wanted to know what Guardsman Dame was like.

"Incredible, actually. He hates to speak out and give his input, but he's methodological and one hell of a fighter. He's a smaller guy so you wouldn't think it, but he's deadly out there. Best I've ever seen, and I've met a lot of fighters."

"Oh?" The image of Dame kicking Tristan's ass just didn't compute.

Dame stepped into the common room and I startled, moving away from Tristan with a nervous smile. Why had I asked after Dame anyway? It wasn't like we were together. We couldn't be, and for all I knew, we hadn't slept together either.

Dame bristled when he saw me standing with Tristan, and I found myself worrying he'd overheard us talking about him. But he was across the room, and I didn't think he could make anything out from that far away. Shit, I hoped not. He walked past, shooting Tristan daggers as he went to the fridge and pulled out a carton of eggs. He wore his usual windbreaker with its red stripe paired with blue jeans. I was starting to wonder if he even had another wardrobe choice.

"Good morning, Dame."

"Morning," he muttered, giving me a grumpy look and turning to the fridge. Someone wasn't a morning person.

I hid a smile behind my hand and saw Tristan was also snickering.

"Wake up on the wrong side of the bed, *D*?"

Dame rolled his eyes and gave Tristan a look that couldn't mean anything other than shut the hell up. I struggled to think of some safe conversation.

"Are you going back to your squad today?" Dame brought out a carton of eggs, started up the fire, and poured some oil into a cast iron pan all without answering me.

"Yes." He grunted, running a hand through his rumpled hair. Sensing Dame's bad mood, Tristan held up his hands, and with wide eyes backed out of the area, winking at me before heading over to the window where a pretty brunette with long shiny hair was sipping a coffee.

"Are you looking forward to seeing your mother?" Dame's question surprised me, and I looked up to find him studying my face. It was a perfectly logical question, but...

"Yeah, I guess so. It's weird. I feel different after coming here." I sighed, and he nodded, turning back to the stove and cracking four eggs into the pan expertly without spilling a bit of the egg white. He flipped the eggs as he cooked, whipping them with the spatula and turning the pan with a practiced turn of his wrist.

"Yeah, well, that's understandable, but you're also still the same person." He finished his eggs and retrieved a plate, sliding them onto it in one movement. I sniffed at the aroma, now wanting something more than dry bran flakes for breakfast. The smell was mouth-watering, and I practically moaned when he shredded a bit of fresh parmesan on top. Delicious.

"You going to eat all that?" The words came out in a moan.

Dame smirked at me, and I caught a bit of playfulness in his eyes.

"I could spare an egg or two." He deftly retrieved a second plate and gave me half of his meal. I took the plate from his outstretched hand with a squeal of joy.

"Thank you!"

"You're welcome. Good luck today." Then he was gone, turning away and heading back down the hallway to his room like he hadn't just shown up, calmed my nerves, and fed me.

Chapter 13

The common room was crammed with nervous energy as we waited for our turn to head out. I sat at the kitchen counter, sipping water and tracing the swirls of marble, bored out of my skull, but too tense to do anything more engaging. My heart leaped into my throat as time and again, someone would knock and call a name, but never mine. The room cleared out until there were only a few of us left.

An older plump man in an all brown jumpsuit came for Jace, Dame, and Tristan. It was still hard to believe they were from the same squad, but seeing the way they headed out in formation—Dame falling into step behind Jace and Tristan bringing up the rear—it became more believable.

Late in the day, someone finally came to me. A woman wearing black pants and a button-up beige blouse. She had a stern face and short silvery hair she wore swept back off her prominent forehead. Her brown eyes sought me out.

"Cassie...Silverfish."

Yes, Silverfish! That was my part of the compound, and I jumped up on numb legs only to nearly fall flat on my face. Luckily, I caught myself on the counter. *Great first impression, Cassie.* I smiled apologetically at my guide and followed her out the door.

We stepped outside, and I was blinded by the sun, flinging an arm across my forehead as we made for the path home. The family compound wasn't that far from the breeding apartments, just a ten minute walk down a tree-lined path. The lower branches were kept trimmed to allow good visibility, and I saw the familiar red buildings come into view.

There were fourteen buildings divided into coded sections. Mine was building seven, quad C—or 7C—of the Silverfish section. Of course, we all got together regularly, but 7C was home. As we walked past the community gardens, I was overcome with homesickness. I'd helped to plant some cherry tomatoes in our garden but had missed their prime growing season. I wondered if my mother had dried any for me.

"I trust you know your way from here?" The stern-faced woman had stopped walking, and I'd just kept on going, lost in thought.

"Oh, yes, I can find my way."

"Good, you will return to the breeding compound by twenty-one-hundred hours. Someone will come to escort you back. You will meet them here." Her tone brooked no argument, but I was delighted I'd be able to stay so late.

"Yes, ma'am."

She gave a curt nod in reply and headed back the way she'd come, her brisk pace speaking of purpose.

Home sweet home. I took off at a quick jog, following the familiar winding paths through the paved courtyards connecting the buildings, seeking out number seven. The red building loomed before me, and I grinned at the sight. All on one floor, each building was huge but flat. I blew through the front door and went hunting down the aisles for mine.

"Cassie!" A shrill voice caught my ear but before I could turn, a small body crashed into my side and I nearly tumbled.

"Mabel! Hey, kiddo!" The little girl wrapped herself so tightly around my body that I couldn't turn to see her face. Mabel had always been one of my favourites.

"I missed you, Cassie! I'm so glad you're back." Twinkling dark eyes in a light brown face peered up at me.

"There you are. Wow, Mabel, I think you've gotten bigger. Let me look at you." I pulled her to arm's length and squatted down beside her, trying to take her measure. Yes, there was a little less girlish roundness to Mabel's cheeks. It wouldn't be long before she'd start to bleed.

I squeezed her tightly, pressing my cheek to hers, and sinking into her embrace. Her hair was tied up in braids and they tickled my face. I drank in the familiar smell of the peppermint she liked to chew.

"I missed you, too."

A brown-haired boy with tanned skin ran up beside Mabel and it took me a moment to realize I was looking at her brother, Lucas. What were they feeding these kids? Lucas and Mabel were from a double pregnancy, so I knew they were the same age, but still. Both of them having a growth spurt at the same time felt unusual, but maybe they hadn't. I'd been gone for over a month now. The thought made me sad. I'd missed so much.

"Hey Cassie, welcome home." He hesitated a moment, fiddling with the button on the collar of his shirt before launching himself into my arms and giving me a quick squeeze. Pulling away a moment later, Lucas rubbed his hands on his pants as if he were too cool for such things as affection and gave me a nervous grin that revealed a missing front tooth.

"Hey Lucas, I see you lost one of your front teeth. That's pretty cool."

"Yeah, Cassie, do you think you'll tell us a story again tonight? Maybe the one about the uh—uh, there was this big animal thing with leathery wings, and it stole a gemstone from the palace."

I smiled, letting him take a minute to work it out without interruption.

"The Dragon's Hoard."

Lucas' eyes lit up. "Yes, that's it! They go to retrieve the gem and they find a huge horde of treasure and a girl, too!"

My smile turned sad. In my head, the handsome prince, set on retrieving the gem meant to protect his kingdom, freed the girl and made her his mate, but I couldn't tell it that way to the kids. Instead, he frees her at the end, and they go their separate ways. Alone, but happy. As if being alone was something to celebrate. I cleared my throat to dispel the lump lodged within.

"Okay, I'll do The Dragon's Hoard tonight, but I really do need to go find my mother. See you guys later?" The kids gave me identical toothy grins. Well, nearly identical. Lucas had, of course, one less tooth than Mabel. They raced off back down the aisle where Mabel had come from. Lucas took the lead, and Mabel called him back to her in a shrill voice. I chuckled at their childish games, wishing I could have had a brother near my age so I would understand the opposite sex better.

Most Breeders chose to continue in the breeding program, having multiple pregnancies, and were supported by the others in the family compound to do so. Not my mother. She'd had exactly one pregnancy. Me, a rare single.

With a sigh, I stretched out the kink in my back and continued down the aisle, watching for the coloured dots at intersections though I hardly needed to look. There was the old lady, Aunt Mary, making her trinkets—figures made entirely of straw and bound with twine—and trying to pawn them off on whoever would pass. I declined with a raised hand and a polite nod. There was damn well near a shelf full of them at home. Mary insisted she had witch blood, and they were a protection she provided to the pack by giving them out, but no one believed her. All the older women in the family compound were called aunties, but I was happy to have no true familial relation with Mary.

Next a right at Aunt Sally's fix-it shop, and through to the very end of the row to find the familiar navy curtain pulled back as though she were waiting for me. And there she sat, my mother, occupying a recliner in her favourite aquamarine shawl and knitting something long and flowy that could have been a scarf. Since I'd joined the breeding program, my mother had been left alone. Her purpose reduced to helping with food distribution and supporting young mothers with their children.

She startled at my appearance, looking up at me with wide brown eyes so different from my own. Setting down her knitting on the table, she crossed to me slowly at first and then quickly, wrapping her plump, light brown arms around my neck in a bruising embrace.

"Hey, Mom." I hugged her back, marveling at the silky dress she wore—blue with white flowers throughout. The style of it was so out of date it was almost criminal. The material flowed straight down to her ankles with a ruffle along the scooped neckline. It could be worse. At least she wasn't making little straw men and giving them out at our front stoop.

"Hello, sweetheart. How are you? How's it going?" She pulled back to clasp my arms, and the warmth of her smile melted my heart. The embarrassment I was sure I'd feel was curiously absent. Better we get this out of the way straight off so we could have a proper visit.

"Oh, pretty good. First cycle down." I laughed, feeling a little bolder when she nodded along encouragingly. "It sucks that I didn't get pregnant on the first try, but it's not so bad having to stay longer."

"What do you mean, dear?" My mother's eyebrows pinched together in concern.

"Well, there are actually some pretty nice guys at the breeding compound." My thoughts drifted to Dame, and I wondered how returning to his guard squad was going.

My mother's sharp eyes missed nothing, and she gave me a disorienting shake.

"Cassie, 'some pretty nice guys'?" She tsked, shaking her head. "You're there for the pack, to do your duty, not to make friends, especially not male ones. Make sure to keep your wits about you." Her reprimand caught me off guard. At least I knew I couldn't talk to her about Tristan, Dame, or The Ram.

"I know, Mom. I'm just saying it's been okay."

"Good." She gave my arms a squeeze, and the warmth returned to her eyes. The conflict from a moment ago gone as quickly as it had come. "Pack above all, dear. No family, but pack family"

"Right, Of-of course." I tried to smile, to reassure her, but I knew it didn't reach my eyes.

"Are you hungry? I have some jam to send back with you."

Now, my mom's delicious homemade preserves, I could get behind. She left the strawberries whole and added some chopped up mint to bring out the flavour. The bit of tartness from lemon zest brought everything together, and I could practically taste it as I eyed the neatly stacked rows of jars on the shelf.

"Yes, please."

CHAPTER 14

I should've known better than to trust the squad's leadership to Warren, but with both Jace and I being selected for the breeding program, what choice did we have? He'd seemed a good enough kid—thorough with a head for formations. A bit young, maybe, but the responsible sort that made you want to give them a shot.

Responsible. Hah. I kicked an empty can of beer and watched as it skittered across the floor coming to rest beside four others. They hadn't been patrolling; they'd been having a fucking party. And it was past time for Jace and me to find the little delinquents and sort them out.

"Warren," Jace barked out his name, sounding every bit as angry as I felt.

Where the hell were those fuckers? We were at their campsite. The fire pit was still smoldering, but no one was to be found. Almost as if they were avoiding us. I gave a devilish grin. They were absolutely right to do so.

"Well, Jace, it looks like the hunt is on."

"You're damned right, brother." He was already taking off his jean jacket, his movements jerky with the rage I shared.

Those punks needed to be taught a lesson.

They were pathetically easy to find, making almost no effort to hide their trail. The woods stank of the alcohol mixed into their breath, and I had no trouble tracking them through the thick woods. I heard a yelp somewhere to my right and knew Jace had caught up with one of them. They'd all split up, scattering once they realized we were on their tail.

With a growl, I spotted one cowering behind a sparse pine. The russet wolf whined and took off at a run.

He should've known better.

I shot after him into the trees, overtaking him in no time at all and crashing into his side. With a cry, he fell over, and I planted a paw on his face, pushing it into the ground. Then I snarled, letting him see my deadly sharp teeth.

His answering whine and the fear in his eyes were satisfactory, and I released him, allowing him to rise before gesturing with my head back towards the camp.

Still at least five more little pups to hunt down.

We managed to find them all in a pathetically short period of time. Lined up and in their human forms, downcast eyes, I could still smell the alcohol on them. Nobody here was sober, and it pissed me off. Warren was the most messed up, his hair caked with mud and his lip bloodied. Jace had been the one to find him, and I was pleased to see he looked properly cowed.

"Do you realize what could have happened?" Jace's voice had an edge of rage I seldom heard. He was furious.

No one answered as feet shuffled and eyes looked anywhere but at the three of us. Even Tristan looked grumpy, his usual cheery personality completely dampened by what they'd done with the squad in our absence.

"Our job is to make sure we guard this section of the perimeter. Somebody could have gotten *in*," Jace hissed, stepping up to a gangly youth with red hair and a face full of pimples.

The poor kid looked like he was about to piss himself, and I could tell he was close to bowing down at Jace's feet and embarrassing himself in front of his peers. The sweat was starting to stand out on his forehead when Jace walked on, clasping his hands behind his back like he was on a stroll, sizing up each guard.

"We guard because we have something to protect. Maybe you *pups* don't realize how important your position is, but you're about to. There will be no more alcohol. Zero. You're cut off, and I want you all running double patrols until your fucking legs fall off. You get me?"

All seven of them stood at attention, clasping a fist over the center of their naked chests. "Yes, Sir."

"You start now. Each of you will do two laps of the perimeter, paired up, and then I want Dean and Samson to report back here for further instructions."

The two guards he had named stood a little straighter, their chests puffed out further.

Leaving the squad felt like abandoning my post, and I *hated* it. Jace and Tristan were both quiet on the long walk back from the perimeter, probably stewing like I was. Just when I thought we'd passed the time living inside our heads, Jace broke the silence.

"I don't trust them to do a good job." His statement didn't seem to need either of us to respond. We all knew we'd left a couple of kids in charge of pack security. "I think we need to talk to an administrator and be excused from the breeding program."

No. I nearly tripped over a weed poking out of the brush. Leave it? Leaving the program would mean leaving Cassie, and I wasn't ready for our time together to end. She wasn't even pregnant yet which would mean I'd have to live with knowing there was no possibility I was the father of her children. An image of Cassie strapped down and moaning in her heat state welcoming man after man while I relentlessly patrolled the pack's perimeter compelled me to speak out.

"Jace, I don't think the automatic solution should be for us to drop out. Maybe they can move some guys from 122 over. Swap around."

He grunted. "The guys from 122? They'd take over, D. It's my squad, yours and mine," he amended. "And I don't want anyone thinking they can steal it away from us."

The only stealing that worried me was someone else stealing Cassie's heart.

"When have you and I ever shied away from a challenge? Listen, this is our chance to be potential fathers, and all the sex is pretty great, too. I agree something needs to be done, but if the administrators will do a swap, you and I will get any new guys in line. We always do." I snarled so he'd know I meant business and hoped it was convincing enough to let him consider the alternative I'd presented.

Let us stay for at least a few more cycles. Once Cassie was pregnant and headed back home, I'd throw myself into being Jace's squad beta.

"Come on, man."

Jace nodded his shaggy head in acceptance.

"Yeah, those guys have got nothing on us." He gave me a wolfish grin that oozed confidence. "Plus, we've got Tris." He grabbed Tristan and pulled him down into a headlock. Tristan was a whole head taller than Jace, and he was walking basically folded in half, clearly torn between struggling his way free and allowing his alpha's manhandling.

"Aw, Jace. Man, let me go. My back's going to break."

That got us all laughing.

My chest was lighter for the rest of the walk.

Back to Pack Breeders 103C.

Back to Cassie.

The day back at the family compound was amazing—laughing with my girlfriends, hugging my mother, reading stories to the kids like old times. I felt so much more relaxed on my way back to the breeding compound, even if my guide was a crotchety old man who used a cane and grunted at each step, who turned to glare at me each time he did, as if I was personally responsible for his discomfort.

While I'd been afraid to join the others in the apartment, Pack Breeders 103C now felt like another home, and I marveled at the realization as we traveled the little dirt path leading back. I'd never thought I could feel that way about the breeding compound, but I was excited to be going back and it wasn't just spending time with the children had reaffirmed my desire to have my own. No, it had everything to do with my new friends—Dame and Tristan.

Dame and Tristan. Now there was a pair. It was hard to imagine them on the same squad, but the hero worship I'd seen in Tristan's eyes had made it clear they were. Dame, so shy when we'd first met, was someone who'd inspired loyalty in Tristan. I smiled to myself, passing a grove of pines all growing together. Like a family.

Family, the pack was my family—all our family. I chanted it to myself as we walked, earning another angry look from my surly guide.

At last, the familiar building came into view, and I gleefully waved the old man off. Taking the stone front steps two at a time, I headed down to the apartment door. Hardly anyone was in the main room, just the two guys who always seemed to dominate the TV to play games and shout excitedly at each other and a girl I didn't recognize having a snack of marbled cheese at the counter. No sign of Dame, Tristan, or Jace. Their absence made me wonder if everything was okay back at their squad.

My eyes drifted up to the new air freshener installed on the ceiling above the couch. I had a plan, but I'd have to make it work when the main room was empty, which meant this was not the time for it. With a sigh, I headed to my room for a night of reading my old, yellow-stained pages in secret.

At regular intervals, I opened my door a crack and listened carefully for sounds from the common room. The tension in my shoulders released when I heard the guys come in, their voices carrying to me. They were talking and laughing like they'd just come from a party. Even Dame sounded like he was in a decent mood, although I didn't hear a laugh from him. I smiled to myself. I knew those were hard-won.

Only when it was much later did silence greet me from the crack, and I snuck out to the main room, pleased to find it dark and empty. Only a few night lights left on for breeders leaving their rooms for a midnight snack. No one in this first cycle had gotten pregnant yet, but I could imagine the first sign being some kind of middle of the night craving for something really weird, like baked gouda on sardines.

The air freshener mocked me from its place in the ceiling, and I climbed onto the back of the couch, using a white plastic hanger from my room to knock it loose and send it crashing to the ground. It landed with a loud thud, and I held my breath. The extra soundproofing in our rooms proved to be my advantage. No one came out to check what the sound was, and I grinned in triumph as I hopped down to pick up the offending piece of junk.

This time, instead of rolling it under the couch, I brought it to the sink, opened its compartment, and dumped the clear, vile-smelling liquid down the drain. After a careful wash with extra soap, I secured the cap and grabbed a tall cup from the cupboard.

Using the cup, I lifted the air freshener back to its mount and screwed it carefully into place. It took an annoyingly long time, but once it was up there, it looked secure, and most importantly, untouched.

Yes. With my mission a success, I jumped back down off the couch as quietly as I could and headed back to my room.

The plan was set in motion.

CHAPTER 15

The next day, I made sure to come out for breakfast. I couldn't hide if this was going to work. Tristan stood at the counter pouring himself some sugary puff cereal that looked obnoxiously sweet even from across the room. He grinned and waved when he saw me.

"Hey, Tristan!"

"Hey there, Cassie! Did the visit go okay yesterday?"

I couldn't help but smile at the fond memories. "Yeah, I had a great time seeing everyone. How was the squad?"

Tristan's face darkened. He shook his head, frowning down at his cereal bowl and making waves in the milk with his spoon.

"Not so good. Jace is getting it sorted out, though. I know he's going to figure out something."

"Oh, okay, so it was bad, but not *that* bad."

"Yeah, you could say that." I frowned, hating to see his normally cheery face look so glum. Good thing I had a distraction in mind.

"Listen, I was going to ask if you and Dame wanted to stay back from the run today to watch one of Dame's movies. He said he has quite a few horror films he loves, and I thought you might be interested."

Tristan stuck his tongue out and scrunched up an eye. "Ew, no thanks. All of Dame's favourites are 'artistic' films that are boring as shit and depressing as fuck." His gaze turned thoughtful. "Classic Dame, really."

I couldn't help but laugh, and Tristan's eyes twinkled from his place across the counter. "But if you'll be there, I'm in. Just don't say I didn't warn you."

Tears were practically leaking from my eyes as I struggled to contain the giggles threatening to burst from my throat. "I won't."

All right, that went pretty okay. Tristan was in and Dame always stayed back to game with me, which meant the plan might just work after all.

I walked around the counter to find my plain bran flakes. While the sugary cereal Tristan had looked good, I was finding I enjoyed the ease of pure bran on my sensitive stomach. This place was always a whirlwind of emotions, and my stomach was never up for a sugar dump like what Tristan was eating.

"Where's Dame?" I popped a bran flake into my mouth, crunching it and savouring the grit on my tongue.

"Pfft, probably still sleeping. It was a pretty long night for all of us."

"Okay, so how come you're up?"

"Oh, well." Tristan snorted and heaved his broad shoulders. Then his eyes narrowed, and he held a hand up to cover the side of his face like he was telling me a secret. "I'm not much of a sleeper."

It was just a harmless comment, but the way Tristan's eyes lingered on mine made it seem like something more. I blushed furiously, gesturing a farewell with another bland flake and heading back to my room. As much as I was comfortable coming out of my room now, it still wasn't a place where I wanted to linger.

"Hey Dame, Cassie told me you wanted to chill and watch a movie today during the daily run time."

What? My hand paused on the bran flakes box mid-pour. I was in a bad mood. Somebody had been eating my cereal, and I was irritated to find it low. Everybody knew it was my cereal, and nobody else ever ate it. Until now.

The thought of Cassie thinking of me, though, helped.

"She told you that?" I smiled to myself, wondering what Cassie was up to. Or maybe it was because she had made a point of wanting to watch a movie with me after I'd stumbled upon her watching one with Tristan. Of course, I'd meant for it to be a private affair, not one that included a gore fanatic like Tristan. "Well, yes, I'm down if you are. I have the perfect film to watch."

It was one no one else had been willing to sit through, but I personally loved. Told from the perspective of a vampire tormented by his curse, the film followed him throughout a life spent trying to find a way to kill the monster within while preserving the man. It was a work of art with musical scores that had made me go all misty eyed, and I was dying to share it with Cassie.

I wished I'd run into her this morning instead of Tristan, but she'd just grabbed something to eat and scampered back to her room as usual. With a sigh, I finished pouring myself some cereal and went to fetch the milk. At least I didn't have to cook her meals and bring them to her anymore.

Only I wanted to. There was a feeling of pride in knowing I was the one to feed her, like I was her special person.

Now I was just like anyone else. Even Tristan was intruding on my video game time with Cassie, and I didn't like the way they'd been laughing together the other day. My hand tightened on the plastic handle of the pitcher, and I heard it crunch.

Fuck. I caught it just as it gave way, losing only a few drops of milk. I looked up to find Tristan watching me carefully.

"You okay, man?"

Where Cassie was concerned, I was never okay.

"Yeah. Just fine."

My collection of films was kept in my room, next to the science fiction books on my shelf. Truthfully, most of my movie favourites were sci-fi too, but a few were horror. *The Heart of the Vampire* was the best of them. Reverently, I slid the all-black case from the shelf. The DVD was old, and I was chronically worried it would break.

I brought it to Cassie, who snatched it from my hands and searched the cover for some kind of artwork. Fighting the urge to call her out for the way she manhandled the disc, I studied her reaction.

"Oh, there's no artwork or text on the cover. It's not one of Tristan's films."

"Hey!" Tristan gave me an offended look, sitting up on the couch.

"Please, you know your films all have monsters on their fronts." I smirked at Cassie.

Tristan rolled his eyes, settling back into the couch with his hands folded behind his head. The fucker had taken my usual gaming spot.

"Yeah, because they're *normal* movies, not whatever you have there."

"Well, if you'd prefer, I hear there's a run going on."

Tristan's smile stretched all the wider, and he sank deeper into the couch, crossing his legs and making himself more comfortable. "Oh, I'm here for Cassie, right Cass? She needs somebody who's seen it to make fun of it with later."

I moved to stand right in front of him. "Out of my seat, pup."

Tristan's face fell into a scowl. "Really, man, you're going to pull rank?"

"Yep."

With a grumble, Tristan scooted down to the other end of the couch, leaving Cassie a spot right between us. *Good boy, now sit.* I chuckled to myself.

Wordlessly, Cassie opened the DVD case with a sickening crack and pulled out the precious disc inside. I watched in horror as she manhandled it into the player. My sunshine needed a spanking for treating my stuff that way.

A spanking. Yes, I'd lay her across my legs and rip down the cozy black leggings she wore, exposing the creamy skin of her very fine ass, and give it a little swat. Just the thought of touching her brought back every moment of our encounter in the woods, and I quickly sat back down, clenching my fists when she perched on the couch edge beside me and cleared her throat.

Shit. This was a bad idea. We were sitting too close, and it was all too familiar. The curve of her neck was tantalizing. I wanted to nuzzle into it, to taste, to lick, to nip in the way that had made her squeal on the breeding table. Instead, I adjusted my pants, trying desperately to hide my half-hard cock.

The movie started, and I sighed in relief. There was nothing sexy about a tormented vampire fighting for his very soul, and now I had the pleasure of sharing it with Cassie. The film opened in black and white with a beautiful operatic solo. The coffin stood front and center, still, while the music played.

"That's his coffin," I whispered excitedly to Cassie, my heart swelling when her eyes met mine and she smiled back.

The Heart of the Vampire was one of the worst movies I'd ever watched. It was too weird, with the main character speaking rhymes more often than not, and more monologues than anything. Fuck, it was boring, but Dame…He was so excited it was hard not to feel his passion.

I had to elbow Tristan pretty much every couple of minutes for whispering jokes to me. I really hoped Dame couldn't hear him because he was none too kind. Although, seeing as how Dame outranked him within their squad, my guess is he was trying hard to make sure Dame didn't hear him.

So beautiful. Dame's eyes were alight, his body completely still as he was enraptured by the screen. This really wasn't my thing, but I had a strange thought that I wouldn't mind reading while he watched films like these. Him enjoying his passion; me enjoying mine, smiling at each other every so often. My heart ached. It just wasn't the same with Tristan here snickering in my ear.

What was wrong with me?

I live not for the food in my belly, but for the air in my lungs.

Tristan laughed out loud at the line, and Dame shot him a death glare, startling me out of my daydream. Right, the mission.

Casually, I leaned my head on Dame's shoulder, my heart clenching with how right it felt. He stiffened beneath me. But honestly, he'd been in this weird state of tension the whole time the movie was on, and I didn't know if he was acting any differently. Carefully not to draw attention to what I was doing, I closed my eyes and sniffed.

Yes, his scent was discernible with the air freshener out of the picture. There was the smell of the strong aftershave all the guys wore and under that? Something piney and primal that tickled my nose and went straight to my pussy. I bit my lip on a moan, sitting up straight and giving Dame an apologetic look.

Damn, he'd smelled amazing, but not familiar. No, not familiar at all. Was it because he hadn't been one of my breeding males, or was I just not remembering right? All my senses had jumbled together, making it harder to sort through them now.

With a sigh, I leaned back into the couch. Maybe this was stupid, but I still had Tristan left and he was practically pulling me into his lap, trying to share the joke of a film Dame had picked.

So, I let him, leaning back into his chest and letting his breath tickle my ear.

"Oh no, I'm a vampire now, boo hoo. Think I'll go walk in the rain."

I couldn't help a small chuckle as the rumbling vibrated through his chest and reached me. Fuck, I hoped Dame didn't notice. It really was a bad film, sorry Dame.

Closing my eyes and sniffing, I worked through the identical aftershave to the scent beneath, vanilla and freshly cut grass. Nope, not fucking familiar either.

With a huff, I sat up, tension riddling my frame.

What. The. Fuck. Why couldn't I just remember their scents? You'd think they would be burned into my memory, but no. I had no idea if my assessment of Dame and Tristan was accurate and the agitation left me antsy for the rest of the film. Sitting between them, I waited with clenched fists for the film to finish. Tristan, perhaps sensing my mood, had ceased cracking jokes in my ear and reclined on the opposite armrest, giving the occasional low chuckle. Dame continued his wide-eyed stare at the screen. I'd never pictured him as someone with such deep-seated interests, but here he was, infatuated with a strange film about a sad vampire. It made me want to cuddle into his chest and be a part of the experience, and knowing I could never do that bothered the hell out of me.

My teeth ground together so tightly my jaw hurt. The second the credits rolled, I sprang up, turning to face Dame and Tristan.

"Have either of you ever fucked me?" Well, shit, it was out now. No coming back from this one. My cards were on the table, and while Tristan had the courtesy to look embarrassed and avert his eyes, Dame leveled an icy stare at me.

"You know it's forbidden to ask that question." His tone was cold and a muscle in his jaw twitched, but he didn't look away until I averted my eyes to stare at the spot on the couch I had previously occupied.

"Yeah, well, it's forbidden, but you get to know? I don't even know who fucked me, but you do? That's not fair."

Dame stood up, getting into my face with a snarl. "Not fair? Nothing about this is fair." His eyes burned into mine, a well of sadness bearing down on me one moment and gone the next.

Oh. So close. He was practically vibrating with emotion and close enough to touch. My hand reached out of its own volition, trying to make contact, to soothe the upset I'd put there.

"Dame…" I trailed off, wishing he would kiss me, wishing he would touch me, prove my last attempt to kiss him wrong, that he wanted me, and I hadn't been mistaken in advancing on him.

But he didn't.

With an angry huff, he stormed off back to his room, and I startled at the sound of his door slamming a moment later.

"Don't take it personally." Until he'd spoken, I'd almost forgotten Tristan was there. "There's a lot going on with our guard squad right now, and Dame takes that kind of thing seriously."

I nodded, feeling the disappointment of his statement. Dame's anger had nothing to do with him and I but a completely separate issue.

"For my part, I'm sorry you're not allowed to know who your breeding males are, really I am, but we really are not allowed to tell you. Doing so would get us banned from the breeding program, and well, this might seem like a vacation but most of us just want the option to father a child."

I looked up to see Tristan's eyes growing misty.

I hadn't realized how they might feel. My feelings about motherhood had driven me forward. It seemed like such an easy ride for the guys.

Bang a few girls.

Eat premium food.

Sleep in amazing beds.

But this was also their only chance at parenthood, and what a raw deal it was to not even know if you'd successfully produced a child, to maybe have fathered a child or two or three, but never get to meet them.

"I didn't know. I'm sorry."

Tristan swallowed hard and stood up to give me a sad smile and extend his arms outward in welcome. Relieved, I slipped into his warm embrace, pillowing myself on his chest, and snuggling into his latest monster movie t-shirt.

"Don't worry about it, Cass. Just remember, we're all here for our own reasons, and what we want doesn't really matter. Pack above all, remember?"

I nodded into his shirt, wetting it with my tears.

What was wrong with me, snapping at Cassie like that? I'd stormed out like an angry child. And now I sat on my duvet, fists so tightly clenched I didn't know if I could ever unclench them. Just seeing her standing in front of us outraged had made me furious. As if I was any less of a prisoner in this situation. Like I hadn't wanted to scream who I was to her this whole time and take her to my bed where I would kiss away every last one of her salty tears.

But I could never do it, and my fists felt impossibly tight, the nails digging painfully into my palms. My teeth ground into oblivion as I snarled at nothing. I was so goddamned pissed at myself for not being able to keep it together, for losing control on her like a crazed animal. Her wide eyes had shone with tears as I'd turned from her, locking myself in my bedroom, unable to face her pain.

What a coward I was.

Cassie. Was Tristan comforting her right now after my outburst? Probably, and I felt nothing but gratitude towards him for being there for Cassie when I couldn't be. Cassie deserved better than this, than me. I was the guy always standing on the sidelines, trying to stay close enough to her light to warm my icy soul by even a fraction. But to pull her into my cold depths? No, I could never do that. Even if by some miracle she wanted it—wanted me—to allow any feeling to grow between us was to deny her the dream of being a mother.

"Damn it!" I slammed my fist into my thigh hard enough to leave a bruise.

A mother. Cassie wanted that role, to have children of her own, and I would rather die than take it from her. The way her expression had softened and her eyes had glazed over when she'd described reading stories to her children, well it was the most beautiful thing I'd ever seen. To deny someone so pure of such a vision was unthinkable. So, I would have my tantrum. I would pound my leg bloody if that's what it took, and when I saw her again, I would be the calm, indifferent bastard I should've been to her all along.

 Chapter 16

Two days and Dame still hadn't hung back from the daily run to game with me. I'd tried knocking on his door, but he'd gone out with the rest of them to run and fuck. Bitterness lodged in my heart at the thought of him choosing to get physical with some other woman instead of playing video games with me.

For all his apparent anger, he still set out all my favourite snacks on the table, but his half was disconcertingly empty, adding to the loneliness of the vacant apartment. He wasn't in the common room for meals, and I didn't see him in the hallway either. The only conclusion I could draw was that he was now avoiding me.

It had been stupid of me to ask him and Tristan if they were one of my breeding males. Stupid, and it had set me way back with Dame. Tristan, on the other hand, was ever present, my personal shadow. He'd explained he was required by Jace, his squad alpha, to attend the runs and he'd had to run laps around the building as punishment for skipping out on it the other day. I didn't fault him, but I was angry with Jace for making it so Tristan couldn't stay back with me.

On the third day, I walked into the common room expecting to get back to my solo campaign and instead found Dame sitting casually in his long abandoned spot, with a controller in his hands like he hadn't just disappeared from my life for two days.

Without a word, I sat down beside him, letting our legs brush. He stiffened and shuffled away, his windbreaker shifting loudly as he did. I craved contact with him—anything but he didn't say a word, just stared at the screen.

The start menu.

He had the start menu open and his cursor was paused on continue. Getting the message, I picked up my controller from its cradle and joined the game.

We played in silence for almost the entire time the others were gone. My body was a mess of tension, not wanting to be the one to speak first after our fight. The thought of saying something that would frighten him off again kept my lips tightly pressed the whole game.

"You can't climb that ridge. There are mines at the top." His voice startled me, and I almost dropped my controller.

"Pardon me?"

He frowned and gave a huff, as if irritated at having to repeat himself. "The ridge you're climbing has explosives at the top. You have to go around."

Those were the first words he said to me after stalking off and staying hidden away for days? The idea was laughable, and I chuckled to myself.

Dame's frown deepened. "What's so funny? I don't want you to get blown up. I'm going to need you to cover me when we approach the tower."

I laughed out loud, giving him a light shove that barely moved his stiff body.

"Okay, no problem, there's some tree cover over there I can use." Feeling better now that we were settling back into our usual dynamic, I grabbed a handful of cheese puffs to stuff my face with and slouched back into my comfy spot, wiggling myself into place.

I'd promised Administrator Samson I would shift and go for runs regularly to help with the nerves, but the thought of running into the black wolf kept me indoors. My body trembled just thinking about how he'd chased me down, and we'd fucked loudly in the heart of the woods. I simultaneously wanted to go out and discover him there again, and never leave the dorm again.

The sex had been hot, but the rejection of him leaving and shifting without letting me see his face still haunted me. He didn't want me to know who he was, and I wanted to avoid any more spontaneous encounters with him until I could force him to reveal himself.

My heat was growing nearer. Already I had signs of it starting—extra arousal, hot flashes, difficulty sleeping, more dreams of The Ram. I'd been shown the way the masks were attached and didn't think I'd be able to get The Ram's mask off to see his face, but if I could somehow mark him, I'd be able to check each of the men of Pack Breeders 103C and discover his identity.

Fortunately, I had an idea. When I'd been washing out the air freshener liquid, some had gotten on my hands and stayed for days. Even showering, the concentrated odour simply wouldn't be removed until a dozen showers. If I could put a drop of the liquid on The Ram, somewhere he wouldn't notice, I'd be able to check that spot on the guys. I had one in my room I could reach if I stood on my bed.

"Hello, my old friend." I grimaced at the overpowering scent and carefully poured some of it into a cup. I'd need to sneak it into my breeding party and hope I had the presence of mind to keep it hidden, and then apply it to The Ram when he came into the room.

I blushed, staring down at the liquid and remembering how good The Ram had made me feel last time. Would he take his time with me and make sure all my needs were met again? My breathing quickened, and I sat down on the bed.

The next day, someone knocked and slid a paper under my door. Quickly snatching it up, I quickly took in the crisp text. My breeding party date, to be shared with three others, was set for only two days after I'd secured my stash of air freshener, leaving me scrambling to think how I was going to pull this off. I snagged a little plastic bag from the kitchen and put a bit of liquid inside the sealed baggie. I'd hold the baggie in my mouth while they set me up and hide it behind my back until The Ram showed up. Then all I had to do was dip my fingers in and run my hand along. But where?

I settled on the lower part of his chest, I was sure it wouldn't be out of character to feel his chest, and it wasn't a place he was likely to sniff himself. Plus, when I went to find the marked man, all I would need to do would be to offer some free hugs, and I'd have an excuse to snuggle into a few chests. How very not suspicious for the shy girl who hides out in her room most of the time, but I didn't see another option.

Plan in motion, I settled in and enjoyed the last couple of days relaxing with Dame and reading quietly in my room, trying to forget how wound up my body was.

The day of my breeding party came, and while I hadn't slept the night before or had much to eat, I was eager to mark The Ram and discover his identity. A bright blonde woman with laugh lines framing her eyes and wearing a white lab coat came to take me to my breeding room with a warm smile and a comforting hand on my shoulder. I guess my nerves were apparent. As we walked toward the hallway of breeding rooms, she launched into the same spiel I'd heard last time about what to expect, ensuring I'd had some food and water before starting as a heat could go on for over twenty-four hours.

"Of course, we have breeding males in reserve if it seems you will exhaust your current set."

I gulped, hoping I wouldn't, that I would end with The Ram as it had my previous heat. Would they be in the same order? I couldn't ask, it would show too much interest, but I so wanted to know.

The blonde smiled and pulled open a white door to reveal the familiar cozy breeding room with its hospital bed and leg straps. Waters lined the wall, reminding me of how this whole process would go, and my part in it.

"Okay, Cassie, you take your clothes off, and we'll get you set up."

Was she going to watch me? The woman stared at me expectantly, and I had a moment of fear realizing she was going to discover the little bag I had hidden in my pocket, but as the silence stretched between us, the woman seemed to take the hint and held up a hand.

"How about I go check on your neighbour while you ready yourself? I understand this can be a...stressful process."

Yeah, like there was a way for being induced into a state of lust-filled madness and getting railed by a collection of unknown men to be a relaxing event.

As soon as the door clicked shut, I stripped, carefully palming the plastic bag and pressing along the fastened edges to make sure it was still sealed before fitting it into my mouth. I pushed it as far into my cheek as I could get it, in case I needed to speak while the blonde set me up.

Naked and aroused just being in this space again, I knocked on the door. The blonde reappeared a moment later, clearly waiting just outside and not checking on my neighbour as she'd claimed. That had been kind of her, and I smiled in greeting when she shuffled inside.

"Okay, I'll get you strapped in now and then we'll induce you. Hop up on the bed, please."

I did as I was told, leaning back onto the waterproof mattress while she attached the straps to my ankles.

"You groomed?" Her words caught me off guard, and I balked.

"Groomed?" I tried hard to make my voice sound normal around the plastic bag in my mouth and was pleased when it sounded only slightly huskier than normal.

"Yes, your pubic hair."

Shit, I'd forgotten we were supposed to do that. "No, I'm sorry."

"Nothing to worry about, Cassie. Lots of girls forget, but it's a good idea for hygiene, what with all the fluids going back and forth." She gave a laugh that made me wonder if she'd ever been a breeder. "I always keep some supplies handy. Just a sec." The blonde disappeared out the door again, and when she returned a few minutes later, she had a bowl of water, soap, and a razor. "Okay, spread 'em. I'll be quick, I promise, and you won't have any irritation with this cream I'm going to use. You have to be made ready, Cassie."

I'd done all this myself the first time, fumbling with the razor and nicking myself more than a few times, but the woman was clearly an expert, and I wondered how many pussies she shaved on a daily basis. The thought made me snort, and I gave her an apologetic look when she peered up at me, wanting to be let in on the joke.

"There, that's much better." She moved to the little blue basket in the corner and brought over a familiar vial. "Ready?"

She had kind eyes. I could do this.

"Ready."

The flower's effects were instant, but this time I was ready for them. Gone was the trembling girl hiding her freckles. Unlike my first time, I now knew I was desirable, and as the burning began in my core and spread across my skin, I waited eagerly for the door to open and admit the first man.

Reaching out a steady hand, I grabbed for the controller and pressed the button exactly two times.

Only no one came. Moaning, I twisted, crossing my legs to try and hold off the building arousal. This was sexual torture, and I ran my hands up and down my feverish flesh, dipping into my slick knowing I would only truly find relief when I was filled and pounded into the bed.

It wasn't until I was so painfully aroused that all I could manage were a few pitiful moans that the door opened, and a familiar masked face appeared.

The Hawk. He was the first last time; I was sure of it. I remembered his mask and the birdlike way he had cocked his head. If he was first again, that meant the order might be the same.

He stepped up to the bed, and I felt his tip at my entrance. My eyes rolled back, and I pushed myself down towards him, desperately seeking more. He sank to the hilt, moving easily through my saturated pussy with a *shlick* sound. I cried out as the feeling of fullness consumed me, and every frazzled nerve screamed out in relief.

The rhythm he found was erratic, but I was so wound up that his friction and warmth were enough to push me over the edge. I screamed my release, and he picked up the pace, pulling me toward and away from him—*shlick, shlick, shlick*—until he came with a grunt and a few final gentle thrusts that sent last minute tendrils of pleasure pulsing through my core.

He pulled away, turned from me, and helped himself to some tissues and a water bottle. While he did so, I tried to think if he was familiar. He had to have been housed with me—all my breeding males were, but nothing about the way he moved triggered a memory.

Heat tore through me again, burning deep within my core, stronger, and I gripped the bedrails as I lay back down, arching my back. The Hawk was spent, and I wanted him gone, wanted him to get the hell out so the next man could come and fill me. The emptiness in my core would not be denied, and my pussy clenched around nothing. My heat had started slowly last time, and it was the same again. The Hawk was a warmup.

Plague Doctor was next, and I recognized his enormous belly and meaty hands. I thought he might be one of the two guys who were always dominating the TV, more interested in it and each other than anything else going on around them. I decided I didn't care, wiggling myself down to the edge of the bed, and offered my pussy up on some kind of demented platter. The need was degrading, but it wouldn't be denied, and I knew the heights it could take me.

I gasped when he grabbed my hips and slammed home with one thrust. He was more vocal than last time, snarling and grunting as he fucked me. I couldn't help but think about how the two guys on the TV were always yelling and jumping around on the couch together. It didn't bother me, not now. What I might have found unappealing in my normal state only turned me the hell on in my heat state. I came long before he did, consumed with the fast, hard pace he set and the animalistic sounds of pleasure he made as he slammed his cock in and out of my dripping pussy, still saturated with cum from The Hawk.

He pushed on my abdomen, thrusting in and out madly, and I felt myself building again. With a helpless cry, my body spiraled out of control and still, he pounded into me, until the pulsing at my core grew ever stronger, sending me higher and higher.

He came with a guttural cry, tilting his head up to the ceiling. Fuck, that was hot. If he was one of the guys who dominated the TV, I forgave him right then and there. He grabbed a water and a few tissues, exiting the room without looking back once.

I moaned into the bed, knowing all the sex I'd had was only sending me farther and farther into the depths of my heat. Everything was becoming hazy, indistinct. I was a bundle of pleasure and need as the next man came in to fill me with his cum.

All I could do was mewl and wriggle when I was empty, cry out in throes of pleasure when the next cock came to fill me. I didn't see masks or faces for an unknown amount of time, and I didn't even notice when The Ram came in.

He was already inside me, caressing my thighs before the haze lifted enough I was able to realize it was him.

Fuck, his body was just as beautiful as I remembered it, his bruising grip holding me firmly while his thumbs caressed the smooth skin of my inner thighs. He began slow tortuous thrusts designed to drive me nuts. But I knew he would lose control soon, and I wanted badly for him to fuck me as hard as he had at my last breeding party.

As hard as he had in the woods, away from the regimented pack breeding program. Out there, I hadn't been high on hormones, but I'd been desperate for him just the same…A small orgasm shook my frame, leaving me trembling, and he paused. Gasping, I reached down to feel his cock, protocol be damned. He was rock hard and soaked with my fluids and those of the ones who had come before him. He slid through my hand as smooth as silk as he sank into me and pulled away. I wasn't supposed to touch him, and I expected him to protest, but he stayed silent. I should stop, lay back down so he could pound his seed into me as all the others had, but I couldn't resist. Not with him, and I raked my nails along his hard abs in appreciation. Fuck, he was so cut. I wanted to lick the ridges crisscrossing his abdomen. His head fell back, and he shuddered.

What I'd done to him—it'd felt good. Maybe he wasn't saying anything about touching him because he liked my touch. As much as I liked his. Doubtful, especially with need burning bright in my core, making every sensation a battle between torture and divinity. But that bit of control over him was intoxicating, and I gripped his cock again, trying to encourage him to pick up the pace. I was done with this slow bullshit. I wanted it rough and hard the way he'd taken me in the woods.

Growling, he pushed in hard enough to slap his balls against my skin, and I moaned my approval, laying back and arching into him. Something crinkled beneath me. Right, the bag I'd brought with me. This was it. I had to mark him, had to find out who he was. I snaked a hand behind my back, trying to ignore his increasing pace, how the way he took me felt so fucking good.

With one hand behind my back, I cracked the seal and dipped two fingers into the liquid within. It stung, but I barely felt it. The Ram had climbed onto the bed now with me, on his knees and planted firmly between my legs as he jackhammered himself into my needy pussy. It was all I could do to lay back and take it, pleasure tearing through me. I'd come for him in the forest a few times, but now that I was in my heat, I didn't think I would ever stop.

Tears leaked down my face, and he folded himself over me, the latex mask brushing my nipples. Now, I reached down and swiped my wet hand across his chest, moaning loudly in the hopes of distracting him.

He didn't notice. Job done, I let myself enjoy him and the way he took me without restraint, barreling into my body with a wild abandon that left me riding wave upon wave of pussy clenching pleasure. It was almost too much, and I forgot to care about the breeding program, that this was all to get me pregnant. None of it mattered but the explosion of pleasure barreling through me and leaving me a blissed out mess beneath The Ram.

He came, his guttural groan pulling me to greater heights. I moaned my pleasure right along with him, needing an outlet for the endless clenching of my pleasure-stricken body. The Ram remained above me, his sweat-soaked chest against mine, and a wave of tenderness stole over me. Tentatively, I reached my arms up to embrace him, but he was pulling away, standing up to retrieve his tissues and water like all the rest.

I watched him, his body, the way he moved. Did I know who he was? I hadn't met the guys last time, but now I had. Was he familiar? I didn't know but I'd marked him, and I couldn't wait to hug every man in the apartment until he was revealed to me. I'd marked him right on his lower left pec, a perfectly easy spot to snuggle into for a friendly hug.

He paused at the door with his hand on the knob, and that pause told me everything I needed to know. The way he took me, the way he owned me, he knew there was something between us.

And soon I'd be able to confront him about it in person.

As before, my heat ended with The Ram—whether it was my body's natural stopping point or I just subconsciously knew sex with anyone else after him was meaningless—the relentless need faded along with the searing heat tormenting my core, leaving me weak and shaky. I found the cord and pushed the red button to indicate I was done.

The blonde lab coordinator returned and looked me over.

"How'd you do, Cassie? Mind if I take a look?"

I shook my head, laying back dutifully as she prodded at my leaking pussy and made the occasional satisfied sound.

"Good, I see a lot of opportunity for pregnancy this cycle. You, my dear, are stuffed. Now let me just get you three bottles of water, and I want you to drink them all down, but go slow. We'll have you lay down for an extra half an hour while you recover and those swimmers get to work. Oh, Cassie, you are going to have *such* beautiful babies. I just know it." Her smile was akin to that of a proud mother, but my return smile was uncertain.

Babies, right. I was here to make babies, but that meant my time with Pack Breeders 103C was limited. If I got pregnant this cycle, it'd mean I'd have the next four weeks before moving back into the family compound to raise my children. A hand flitted across my abdomen, the words *stuffed* and *a good chance* sticking in my mind. I wanted this, wanted them badly, but there was more to my wants than there had been when I'd joined the breeding program.

All that was left was for me to reveal The Ram and confront him.

Chapter 17

The shaking in my limbs was bad enough that I needed to stay in the recovery room for a couple of hours. My blonde coordinator, whose name turned out to be Nancy, brought me beef jerky and some candy to help me get my energy back up. The process took entirely too long, and I was eager to get back to the apartment so I could plan out my next move.

At least my forced confinement gave me time to think through how I would explain away my upcoming hugging frenzy. When the idea came to me, I knew it would work. It was so simple.

Everyone knew what a lightweight I was with alcohol, and while I wasn't normally big on hugging strangers, everybody had been my best friend that night. Well, they had before I'd puked my guts out and blacked out.

By the time I was given leave to go, I had it all figured out. Tristan had mentioned there would be a celebration in honour of the heat's end, and it was the last time potential mothers would be allowed to drink until their pregnancy status was determined. The celebration presented me with the perfect opportunity to be silly-overly-friendly-drunk-en-Cassie again. But I wouldn't drink, not really. I'd have a sip, and then dump the rest of my beer out on a planned bathroom break. No one would be the wiser, and I could hug whoever I wanted without suspicion. The last thing I wanted was to get drunk again and lose my wits before I could sniff out The Ram.

The door opened with a bang and did not reveal the cheery blonde I'd been expecting. Instead, a grouchy older man, with a shaved head and frown wrinkles so deep I wondered if he even could smile anymore, appeared in the doorway.

"I have orders to escort you back to Pack Breeders 103C."

When I didn't move right away, he took a step forward into the room, his big black combat boots heavy on the floor. "We need this room for the next group. Now let's get going."

I climbed off the bed and rose unsteadily to my feet. With a snarl, the man stepped forward and gripped me roughly under the elbow. Whether to provide support or force me along, I wasn't sure.

He walked me back that way, clearly disgusted with having to assist me to walk, but committed to getting me back as soon as possible. He seemed pissed, like he had other duties he'd rather attend to, and he left me clinging to the door of the apartment without even a farewell.

I opened the door to see several pairs of eyes watching me.

"Hey guys, how's it going?" I tried to sound like my normal chipper self, but I was just so fucking tired. I took a step into the room, full of a confidence I didn't feel and tripped forward. I was caught just as I fell, my hands clutching on the sleeve of a familiar shiny black windbreaker. I looked up into Dame's worried face.

"You okay?"

Dame worried? It was hard to picture, but I loved to think he might be worried about me. I mustered up my best reassuring smile.

"I'm okay, just a bit shaky after the heat. Do you think you could help me to bed?"

His eyes softened, and he gently pulled me up to my feet, gripping under my armpits. Once I was steady, he took my elbow the way the military man had, but with a tenderness I found endearing. I wished it hadn't been my elbow though, but that he'd wrapped a comforting arm around my shoulders to help support me back to my room.

That just wasn't Dame. As much as I wished he'd have returned my kiss or offered me a drop of affection, he wasn't interested, and I breathed through the reminder of his indifference.

We reached my door, and I leaned into the knob as I opened it. He stood awkwardly behind me, waiting.

"Thanks, but I can take it from here."

"You sure you're not going to fall again? Why don't I take you inside?"

I frowned to myself, turning halfway towards him. "No, really, it's okay."

"Yeah well, I'm not going to have you fall on my watch, so give me your arm, Sunshine, or I'll take it." He growled the last, and I saw a challenge swirling in the depths of his dark eyes that I was too tired to fight. With a slow nod, I held out my arm. He gripped it with a lightness at odds with his attitude, offering me support as I hobbled inside.

So far, nobody had been in my room, and I'd come to think of it as my safe haven. I'd left my forbidden books out on the nightstand, and I watched nervously as he eyed the titles.

"You shouldn't have these."

"No."

"Is this why you didn't want me to come inside?"

"Maybe I don't know if you can keep a secret."

He smiled at that, giving a low, moody chuckle as if laughing at a private joke.

"I can and I will. Goodnight, Cassie."

I sank into the comfortable mattress and watched his retreating form.

"Goodnight, Dame."

I knew there was something wrong the moment Cassie opened the door to the apartment. Her colour was off, her freckles standing out against her unusually pale skin. Even her smile had suffered, appearing as a ghost of her usually vibrant self. When she'd started to fall, it could've been my heart tumbling to the ground. Luckily, I'd gotten there just in time to catch her and keep her from hitting the floor and injuring herself.

The intense guilt over not staying with her and making sure she was okay after our breeding session weighed heavily in my mind. I should've been there helping her out of her heat, making sure she was all right. Not fucking her and leaving like some kind of uncaring asshole who was only fucking her as part of my duty to the pack, and nothing more.

Too bad that's all I was to her, as much as my idiot heart wanted to pretend otherwise.

Then there were those books of hers. All romance, all forbidden. Human mating rituals and courtships were said to pollute the youth with visions of mates and families instead of the pack.

She'd been right to try and stumble her way into the room solo. If someone found she had those books, there would be a harsh punishment. Maybe even a period of isolation from society, and a re-education session to ensure she would be a good pack member. Hell, they might even take away her status as a breeder and future pack mother if they thought she would corrupt the kids.

The kids. She'd told me she was telling the children of 7C her own made-up stories, and I certainly hoped they were about the love of one's pack and not the love of a single person to the exclusion of all others. Maybe that worked for humans, but the alpha had found a different way, a better way.

Only, after having Cassie, I didn't know how I was supposed to just return to my guard squad and pretend like I'd never met her. Never spent time with her. Never found heaven in her body.

She'd touched me. Even though I knew it wasn't allowed. Even though that kind of connection in the breeding room was a punishable offense. She'd touched me and it had felt so fucking good I hadn't been able to do anything, but let myself slip into the pleasure of her grip on my hard cock. Consumed with lust, she'd wanted me, and I had to remind myself that she'd wanted me in the woods too.

Me, The Ram. Not me Dame, and I prayed I could get through this next month without her knowing who I really was. Cassie would be pregnant this time. I knew she would be. I could feel it. She'd be pregnant, and we could both go home. Back to our lives.

Pack above all.

Fuck.

CASSIE

I'd never been more grateful to my mystery benefactor as I was the next two days when I mostly just slept and ate the delicious food delivered to my door. He always seemed to know exactly what I wanted, and I looked out curiously each time to find delightfully greasy foods that made my stomach rumble. He'd been upping the fats and sugars, which made me feel he'd seen the way I'd collapsed upon coming home.

Home. In a way, this had become my home, or rather, I'd found a home here. Routines, friends, independence from my mother and 7C where I'd spent my life before now. Unlike 7C, the apartment of Pack Breeders 103C was all mine—a place where I had blossomed and grown from a shy girl to a woman. Now the countdown to find out if I was pregnant and going back, my dream of being a pack mother realized, began.

The party was tonight. Tristan had stopped by to let me know, and while I still just wanted to sleep and eat, I knew I couldn't miss this opportunity. Not with the mark I'd put on The Ram already two days old. So, I put on a pretty coral dress with spaghetti straps and a v-neck, giving a slight twirl to appreciate the nearly floor-length flowy material swishing around my ankles.

I headed out immediately, no hesitation in my step.

"Hey, Cassie."

Jace.

I stiffened. "Hey."

"How are you feeling? We've all been worried about you after you basically walked in and fell down." Jace chuckled like my nearly fainting was hilarious.

Yeah, fucking hilarious. *What a dick.*

"Much better, thanks. Is that the beer over there?" I nodded to a big cooler full of ice with bottles peeking out from the top. I mean, it was obviously the beer, but I didn't know what else to say to get out of the conversation.

"Yeah, want me to—"

"No, I can get my own, thanks." I brushed past him, hurrying over to grab a bottle. There was a metal bottle opener on the table beside the cooler, and I tried to fit it on top like I'd seen the other breeders do. It took me far too long, and I looked around nervously while fiddling it, imagining someone watching and laughing at my efforts. At last, the bottle gave a satisfying pop, and the lid came loose.

The yeasty smell of beer tickled my nose, and I took a careful sip. I'd need to take at least a few, so people thought I was drinking. My back against the cooler, I scanned the crowd. There, Tristan was over by the speakers, talking animatedly to the same long-haired brunette I'd seen him with a couple of times. Her teeth flashed in a wide smile and she giggled, hiding it behind a hand. She was clearly enjoying herself, and I felt a stab of jealousy at the sight, but I'd never really felt that way about Tristan. He was the definition of sweet and funny. He was smoking hot, no mistake, but he didn't do it for me.

I kept looking, not knowing who I was looking for, but it became obvious to me when I came up empty.

Dame. I was looking for Dame, and of fucking course, he wasn't here. I shouldn't have been surprised, not really. The man had made no mystery of how little he enjoyed socializing. Except with me, of course. I'd even say he enjoyed my company. I lifted the beer to hide my smile and the heat of my cheeks.

After a few more sips in plain sight, I went to the bathroom and dumped out the rest of my beer, reentering the room with my head thrown back and the bottle between my lips as if I'd just downed the rest. I joined one of the chattering circles and waited, but nobody seemed to have noticed.

Showtime. I began giggling a little extra and gesturing more with my hands, stumbling around the party just enough as to make my supposedly drunken state obvious. In truth, the small amount I had drunk, nearly the neck of the beer, had made me feel lightheaded and less nervous, making it simple to play my part and play it well.

After demonstrating my intoxication for a little while longer, I started with the hugs.

"I love you," I told some random guy whose name I didn't remember, hugging him, and cuddling into the left side of his chest to give a stealthy sniff. Nope, not that dude. I hugged everyone in sight, even the girls, to dampen suspicion, but no one had The Ram's mark.

Tristan's group was last, and I did my fake stumble over to where he stood, my heart pounding in my veins. What would I do if he was The Ram? I'd just decided I didn't have romantic feelings for him. *Fuck.*

"Hey Cass, you doing all right?" Tristan eyed my sloppy gait with trepidation, and I gave him a dopey grin in reply.

"S-s-sure, Buddy. I'm just loving on l-life." Another grin.

There were two other guys he was talking to, but with the idea of him being The Ram tangled up my thoughts, and I launched myself into his chest nearly knocking him over.

Pressing my nose into the left side of his chest, I took a long sniff for any trace of my mark, but there wasn't any. With a relieved laugh, I pulled away to stare up into Tristan's startled face.

"Whoa, Cass, I think it'd be a good idea for you to stop drinking tonight, yeah?"

I crinkled my nose at him in reply, glad he could remain my Tristan my friend, without the complication of his being the man who owned my body.

Neither of the other two guys had my mark either, but there were still a few people missing from the party.

And I had yet to hug Jace. Every time I thought of approaching him and throwing myself into his slimy embrace, I cringed. Once I'd hugged everyone else at the party and had failed to find my mark, I knew I had no choice but to get it over with and rule him out.

With a deep breath, I approached him. He was chatting up a fancy brunette with big hoop earrings and a slinky, low-cut black dress. As if she needed to attract more attention to her breasts when they were already on display.

"Jace, hey, can I talk to you for a second?"

Surprised, he looked up from his intended and eyed me. "Sure, I guess, yeah." Hesitant at first, a vomit-inducing grin soon appeared on his face.

"I just wanted to talk, you know? We never talk anymore. Like, really talk." God, I hoped I sounded drunk enough.

"Yeah, baby, sure, we can talk about whatever you want."

"It's just, I'm going to be a mother soon, and well, you could be the father of my children for all we know. I really think we should go back to being friends. Like, really good friends." I gestured big with my hands when I said it as though big friends meant actual size. Maybe it was dumb, but he seemed to buy it.

"Just friends, huh?" Shit, he looked genuinely sad.

"Yeah, just friends, but like, really big ones." I gestured with my hands again, and he laughed.

Now. I threw myself at him, but he hugged me back so quickly I didn't get my head into the right spot to check for the mark. I struggled a bit, and when his grip loosened, I was able to turn my head and get a good whiff.

Not Jace. *Thank. Fucking. God.* I pulled away to smile at him.

"See you later, buddy!" I held up my hand to give him a fist bump, and he returned it with an explosion sound and a playful laugh.

Honestly, it felt better to have made some form of peace with Jace. Dame was adamant he never would have harmed me, and while he hadn't, the way he'd been so pushy still gave me shivers. But what I'd said was true. I could be pregnant right now, and he could be the father.

The Ram undiscovered, I moped around the common room, squeezing on the couch next to the video game guys. I wasn't nervous around them anymore, so what if we liked totally different games? They were still my people.

Somehow, the mark must've washed off. That was the only explanation. I'd checked everyone at the party and even hugged a few twice to make extra sure. Dame was the only one not present, and I'd long since ruled him out as lacking the fiery passion so central to The Ram.

Yes, it must've washed off, but when I'd gotten it on my hands it had taken a few days and lots of handwashing to remove the smell, and what I'd rubbed into The Ram's chest was no small amount. I'd distinctly seen a long wet smear from my fingers, enough that it should've lasted for a week, even with regular showers.

Chapter 18

My melancholy mood lasted into the next day, and even the sight of Dame waiting on the couch, snacks already set out and a curious pitcher of fizzy green pop, didn't lift my spirits.

I flopped down next to him.

"Hey."

"Hey." Yeah, classic Dame, the man of few words.

I sighed heavily, resting my head on his shoulder. Tears welled up in my eyes, and I angrily swiped them away. Aside from Tristan, Dame was my only friend here, and I needed a friend's comfort.

The muscles of his arm tensed beneath me as he played some solo target practice. Fucker was always one step ahead of me, always honing his skills.

"What's wrong?"

His question caught me off guard, and I looked up to see a touch of warmth in his dark eyes. It was too much, and the tears came harder.

"Hey, hey, Cassie, it's all right." He turned fully towards me, and I fell into his arms, sobs wracking my body. Dame awkwardly patted me on the back.

My eyes snapped open.

No. I sniffed to clear the tears and settled more firmly into his chest. I thought, but I could be wrong.

"Don't you ever take this windbreaker off? What have you got on under there? Are you even wearing a shirt?"

"Yeah, I have a shirt on." A smile pulled at his lips.

Without asking his permission, I reached up to grab the zipper at his neck and upon yanking it down, I was hit full in the face with a blast of my air freshener mark.

Dame. Was. The. Ram.

The realization hit me in a few different ways. My mind struggled to reconcile Dame's cold and distant behaviour, his quiet moodiness, with the passion of The Ram while my heart knew it was right. I'd always had a thing for Dame. Right from the beginning, I'd craved his company. Hell, I'd even tried to kiss him, but he'd rejected me. Why? If he was The Ram, then he definitely wanted me, so why reject me in the apartment? He'd made it clear how badly he'd wanted me outside of the breeding party when he'd chased me down in the forest and fucked me into the ground.

I groaned, sitting back into the couch and letting my head fall back. The forest, the breeding party, all this time, it had been Dame.

I peeked at him from the corner of my eye and found him watching me with those intense, dark eyes of his. Beautiful eyes, so deep and so dark that they'd pulled me in right away.

Dame was The Ram. The man who owned my body. We'd spent so many days together, just the two of us gaming, and he'd never revealed himself. Hurt, I broke his gaze, looking back up at the ceiling and fighting off a fresh wave of tears.

"Are you okay?"

The concern in his voice was genuine, and I looked over to see worry etched into his sculpted face.

"It's you."

He frowned. "What's me?"

His denial pissed me off, and I sat up on my knees in front of him. But knowing what he was capable of, need pulsed through me. The way he'd touched me. Those nimble fingers.

"You fucking know what." My voice came out in a husky whisper, my body wound up, and my pussy already dripping knowing who he was.

He held my gaze for only a moment before turning his attention back to his game.

"I don't know what you're talking about, Cassie, but you're acting crazy."

I laughed, knowing full well that the shrill sound only served to prove him right. I was definitely acting crazy, but I was also right.

"You're The Ram."

He dropped his controller into his lap and turned to me, his mouth open in surprise. I grinned in satisfaction, sitting back on my heels. I'd ruffled the infallible Dame's composure.

"I'm—I don't know what you mean."

Bullshit. I would never have done it to Dame before, but knowing he was The Ram and how badly he secretly wanted me was empowering. I grabbed the controller out of his lap. Tossing it on the couch beside us, I straddled his lap and folded my arms across my chest as I stared him down.

"Yes, you do." There, I was right, I saw it in the moment before he looked away.

He was breathing fast, panting, and I reveled in my newfound power, wrapping my arms around his neck, and running my nose along his scratchy stubble to nibble along his jawline and ending at his ear. I took the lobe in my mouth and sucked before moving down his neck.

Dame moaned beneath me, and I felt him starting to get hard. I laughed at the joy of seeing his face. Of finding him out here in the real world, where we could do this, and not be in the breeding room. No turning away, no running off. Just Dame and I, our bodies entwined as one.

"Cassie, stop."

I trailed my tongue back up to his ear. "No."

He shuddered, and I felt how much he was trying to hold himself back. Maybe this was why he hadn't kissed me back. Fuck, losing control looked good on him. His hand gripped my arm in an effort to stop me, but my tongue had free reign.

"I'll never stop, not now that I know who you are. Fuck, it's so good to see your face." I choked up a bit. I'd never thought Dame could be The Ram, but it'd been him all along. My friend, my confidant, my gaming buddy, and my secret lover. I dragged my tongue along his neck, savouring his taste.

His taste, seeing his face for the first time—everything about him drove me crazy, and getting to experience all of him made it so much better than our previous encounters. I rubbed my needy pussy into the bulge of his jeans, and he sucked in a sharp breath.

"Cassie, listen. You don't want to start something with me. Even in this place, I'm an outsider. I'm a moody asshole, and I know it. You should be with someone who can be right there with you talking and laughing at parties—not me."

I chuckled into his neck, reveling in his shiver of need when I did so. "What, someone like Tristan?"

That got him riled up, as I knew it would, and he grabbed my shoulders to pull me back and scowl.

"No, definitely not Tristan, but somebody else. I'll only bring you down."

As if he hadn't been the one holding me up all this time. I turned serious, fiddling with the zipper of his windbreaker.

"Dame, you don't realize how perfect you are. You may be a moody asshole sometimes, but you're *my* moody asshole, and I like it. I like you. Everything about you." It was true. I liked how I was one of the few people he felt comfortable talking with. I liked when he gave me one-word answers so I could poke and prod him into expressing himself. His weird love of artsy horror films, and the way he called me Sunshine.

My eyes were misty when I looked up at him. There was still hesitation in his eyes. I wanted to kiss it away, but when I leaned forward, he held up a hand between us.

"Cassie, please, you know even if I wanted to, I know you're not someone who wants multiple partners, and sleeping together exclusively is outlawed. We could get in serious trouble here."

A smile rose unbidden to my lips. *Serious trouble, eh?* That was as good a confession he wanted me as I was likely to get. The most Dameish confession. Only he could make *serious trouble* into a romantic declaration.

For all his protesting, his body was screaming yes, his hips rolling slowly against mine. I wondered if he even noticed.

"Dame, come on, isn't this what we're supposed to be doing? Fucking every chance we get outside of the breeding parties. It's why they housed us all together in the first place."

His hand rested lightly on my arm.

"Yeah, with *multiple* partners, not this thing between us."

Yes, another admission. But as much as he might protest, there was no stopping the chemistry we shared. I smirked, moving back to nuzzle into his neck and rub against his straining bulge. I couldn't wait to get his clothes off and find the body I knew he was hiding under his baggy windbreaker and loose fit jeans. Those abs.

"We'll just have to keep this secret then because no is not an option. Not for me, and not for you." I pulled back to find his eyes just as lust-crazed as mine must be. Our breath mingled, and I nipped at his lip. "Is it?"

His hand fisted in my hair and he kissed me hard on the lips while his other hand snaked around my back to pull me closer. The seam of his lips parted, and our tongues slid against each other all molten heat. His need matched my own, and I lost myself to it, to him in what would be our first ever kiss.

Our first, but far from our last. Kissing Dame was everything. His hands gripped my butt and lifted me effortlessly, driving his face into my neck. He panted against my skin, and I cried out at how the sensation rippled across my skin. His mouth, this connection, it had all been missing before. Then he was sucking and kissing, tugging at my shirt. I whipped it off, flinging it who knows where, and he moved down, yanking my bra aside to expose my nipples. He paused.

"So beautiful. You have no idea how badly I've wanted my mouth on you."

I didn't have time to think before he pulled one of my hardened nipples into his mouth and sucked, dragging his teeth along the bottom edge and winding my body tighter. It was all I could do to clutch his head to my chest and throw my head back as I worked through the influx of pleasure.

"Oh, Dame, I need—"

"I know, Sunshine."

Fuck, I loved it when he called me that. I'd thought it was good before but now, in his husky bedroom voice? It was perfection. He undid his jeans and pulled them down. I took the hint, sliding to the side and pulling off my leggings as fast as I could. Then I was back in his arms, kissing him, nipping his lips, wanting to do every possible thing with this man. I cried out as he lined himself up at my entrance. The skin-to-skin contact felt divine, but I still wanted his shirt off, wanted him just as naked as I was. I struggled to push his windbreaker off.

"Take your clothes off."

"Soon."

Soon? What the fuck did that mean? Without another word, he gripped my hips and eased me down on his cock. We both groaned as he sank in deep. I leaned my forehead into his neck, needing a moment to adjust to the increased sensation. But he gripped my thighs, spreading me. With startling ease, he lifted me and slammed me back down. I cried out at the friction, clawing at his black cotton t-shirt—filled with a need to see him, to press my flesh against his, and know that this was happening, that it was real.

His pace picked up, and I felt myself coming undone—spiraling closer to the edge of release. Burying his face in my neck, he panted against my skin as he impaled me. I was an animal, grabbing at his shoulders as my world exploded. Slamming me into the wall, he fucked me like a man possessed, and I loved every minute. Dame. Careful Dame. Quiet

Dame. But he'd never truly been that way. Under it all, he'd had a fiery current, and I longed to find just how deep it went.

Now I burned, crying out when he nipped my neck. His hands pinning my hips as he hammered into me like nothing else mattered. I was barreling helplessly towards an orgasm when I heard laughter and someone turning the knob.

"Dame," I shouted.

He peered over his shoulder. Assessing the situation, he took hold of my ass and carried me with us still connected. A quick dash down the hallway, and we were at a room I assumed was his. He yanked the door open. Easily holding me with one hand, he slammed it behind us and turned to press me against the wood. With his forehead pressed to mine, and his dark eyes trained on me, I could practically feel the lust dripping off him. He was practically feral with need, and I was quickly finding the power I had over him was almost as intoxicating as his touch.

Our hearts pounded in sync. I was drunk on him.

"Where were we?" he asked, his pupils dilated, kiss-swollen lips parted.

"Let me show you," I whispered, not sure I could speak above a whisper ever again. Tenderly, I kissed his bottom lip, still red from where I'd bitten it. I laced my fingers behind his neck. But there was a quiet spell cast over the both of us after being interrupted, and he returned the kiss just as tenderly as it had been given.

The passion was there, I couldn't imagine it ever disappearing, but it was under the surface, a bubbling mass ready to consume us once the thin crust of earth we stood on disintegrated.

"Is this your room?"

"Mmhmm." His kisses, just as soft, trailed along my jaw, to the spot at my neck he seemed to favour. Sucking on the delicate skin, I shivered from the tantalizing roughness of the scrape of his teeth. My body came alive, and I squirmed against his still hard cock. His hand moved to my breast. When the toughened fingertips played with my soft nipples, I couldn't keep from squealing.

But he didn't move where I needed him to, and though we remained connected, all my eager squirming against him could not provide the friction I craved.

"Dame. Please." My breathy words were thick with desperation. Dame paused at my neck, pulling back to look me over with those dark eyes of his, and I realized he was remembering how I'd begged him the first time we'd met. Even without the heat, I was just as desperate for him as I'd been then. Cupping his cheek, I ran a thumb across the light stubble. "Please."

Watching my face, he lifted me a few inches and pulled me back down. My head thumped back against the wooden door, and I bucked my hips in a silent plea for more. He groaned in response, the sound more animal than man. Grabbing me, he turned towards the bed, laying me down gently. I whimpered at the loss of contact, but then he pushed my legs apart and knelt between them. I remembered this position; him being on the bed with me in our breeding room, and I sat up enough to palm his cheek.

He caught my hand and held it there, turning to kiss me on the wrist. His eyes spoke a thousand words. He'd chosen this position on purpose, knowing it was the one where we'd last left off, when he hadn't been able to make himself known to me.

"Kiss me," I begged, wanting the slick of his tongue, something else we'd been denied for too long.

He obliged, leaning forward to press his hot mouth against mine, the seam of my lips parted eagerly for him. Tasting him was everything. Every moment of worry, and wonder at my mystery ram, every time I'd touched myself to the memory of him in the breeding room, dreamt of ripping the mask from his face had all been building to this.

He positioned his tip at my entrance and moved in slowly, inch by inch, until I was full of him. Shit, he made me feel like I was in heat again; the burning consuming me from head-to-toe. Every sensation heightened, my pussy dripping with an appetite I knew he could sate.

Massaging my thighs in slow circles felt so good, but it wasn't what I needed, and I whimpered. His thumb found my clit, and I threw my head back, wriggling against him as a burning need ripped through me. I jerked my hips against him, fighting for enough space to create the friction I needed.

I could see the moment he lost control, and the punishing pace he set made me miss the bed rails from my breeding room. My fingers scrambled to find purchase on Dame's coverlet. The friction was almost too much, and his damned thumb just kept pressing mercilessly into my swollen bud. The tension inside of me exploded, and I cried out, but I found Dame's fingers in my mouth, a warning in his eyes. Message received, I bit down as gently as I could manage while I clenched around him, and my body shook with the spasms of my orgasm.

But he wasn't done yet. Leaning over me, his palms flat on either side of my head, he caged me in. The expression of lust in his dark eyes was unbelievably sexy, and I could feel he was building towards his own release. The tension in his body grew more intense, his pace quickening. The sight of him hovering above me, losing himself in my body, forced a response I didn't realize I was capable of outside of my heat, and against all reason, I began building again.

He came with a groan I remembered well from our previous encounters, a sound like he'd achieved heaven and I was the cause. A sound that drove me over the edge once more, and left me twitching as I worked through the explosive pressure of my second release.

This was the moment he'd left every other time, and I tensed beneath him, watching him with vulnerable eyes. I could remember well each time he'd ruined me for anyone else and walked away, but this time was different. I was sure he'd only run because he was keeping his identity a secret.

Panic settled heavily on my heart when I realized his dark eyes had gone hazy and absent like he'd checked out, like now I knew his identity and he'd still leave. I'd have lost The Ram and Dame in one fell swoop.

"Dame?" The moment I called his name in a high-pitched squeak, he snapped out of it, his hand moving to stroke my cheek, his brow furrowed.

"What's wrong?" He kissed my lips and then my cheeks, and it was only then I realized I'd been crying. Tears dripped traitorously down my face, betraying my fear and anxiety.

"Nothing." But he wasn't convinced, and I hated his deepening frown and the way he was looking me over critically. Dark eyes traveled the length of my body, searching out any nicks or scratches as if he'd done something wrong. I had no choice but to explain.

"I'm fine, really. It's just that, well, every other time we've slept together, you've left."

The words hung between us, spoken on a whispery breath, all my idiot fears laid on the table before us. His face transformed, into a wide grin, and he chuckled. Fully chuckled. It was as close to a laugh as I'd ever heard from Dame, and I knew how rare it was.

"That's it? You're worried I'm going to leave *you*?" Then he did laugh, a barking sound that made him sound very out of practice. I lay there blinking at him, not understanding.

"Come here." He pulled me into his arms, kissing my face, and chuckling. "Cassie in no world would I be the one to leave you. You've always been too good for me, Sunshine, and while I had to leave before, I didn't want to. I wanted this. Of course, I wanted this, and maybe that was part of the problem." He sighed, growing pensive. "Make no mistake, Cassie, in two weeks time, we'll find out if you're pregnant, and if you are, they'll take you back home, and it will break my heart all the more for this stolen time with you. This forbidden time." He reached out and cupped my cheek. "But that just makes me want to cherish every last moment we have together before you have to go." Now he was the one who looked self-conscious and vulnerable, averting his eyes the way he had when I'd first sat down beside him on the couch. "Of course—if this isn't what you wanted, if you've changed your mind—you can leave, I won't hold it against you. I know that I'm not the easiest to be around."

It was my turn to laugh, and I gripped his chin pulling it towards me until he was forced to meet my eyes. "Stop this nonsense about my choosing to leave. I won't. I don't. In fact, I refuse to leave, so get used to it, D."

He rolled his eyes at my teasing tone. He should never have told me he hated to be called D. It was too easy to pull out when I wanted to get under his skin.

"Because this is my room now." I grinned, stretching out on his bed, and looking around for the first time. This was the same room I'd woken up in after my drunken escapade. The realization didn't surprise me. Just knowing he'd taken care of me that night warmed my heart. I looked up to find confusion on his beautiful face.

I was pretty sure I could kiss that away. I winked at him and settled back into the covers dreamily. Dame's coverlet was rougher than my blanket, and I wasn't a fan. I'd have to bring my own bedding, and my pillow, too. I'd grown used to the thing. Now, if there was some way to hook up a game system in here, and get Tristan to make deliveries, we would never leave again. I was serious when I said this was my room now.

My room

My bed.

My man.

Cassie snored, and I fucking loved it. Who would've thought sweet, delicate Cassie made little piggy noises in her sleep? I watched as bubbles formed between her lips. Her face was free of all tension, perfectly at peace. She'd slept in my bed once before after her encounter with Jace, but she'd been restless, her blonde hair tangling as she tossed and turned, near constantly.

This time was different. Now she slept as if this was the same bed she'd been sleeping in her whole life. But she'd said it was her bed now, and I wanted it to be. I'd give her both pillows and all the blankets if it meant keeping her in my private den.

The thought of Cassie always being here in my bed, and the memory of how I'd watched her last time unable to touch was almost enough for me to wake her up. How I longed to press my hard cock into her mouth the way I'd imagined all those nights ago. But I didn't want to be demanding, and disturbing such a restful sleep felt like a crime. I watched her again, struggling to comprehend the way she'd reacted when she had discovered my identity.

After she'd fallen asleep, I'd laid awake trying to figure out how she'd done it. Then I remembered the way she'd pulled open my windbreaker and sniffed at my chest. A quick assessment proved just how clever my girl was. I'd thought the air freshener smell was stronger these past few days, but I'd assumed they'd changed them out for new ones or something. Never did I think Cassie had marked me with the stuff in an effort to uncover my identity.

I hadn't been able to deny it, or her, not with the way she looked at me. My denials felt weak even to my ears, and then she'd touched me and I'd been lost. Intoxicated by her taste, her sounds, and the feel of her smooth, eager skin beneath my hands. She'd still wanted me. Begged for my touch, even knowing I was Dame, the loser boy who hadn't been able to say more than two words to her for the first few weeks. Now, I spoke to her more than I'd ever spoken to anybody. She prodded, never accepting my answers unless I explained myself, and I fucking loved it.

Because she cared, just like she cared for everyone I'd never thought, never dreamed she could care about me and want this thing between us. But now? She was forcing me to believe it, and I smirked to myself in the dark where a beautiful angel slept next to me not knowing I was a thing of darkness. Even so, I was determined to stay near her for a taste of the warmth and light she provided.

Could it be true? Could she really want me, want us? I tried to steady my breathing, gently wrapping an arm around her and cuddling into her shoulder to give the bare skin a whisper of a kiss I hoped wouldn't be enough to wake her.

My angel, my sunshine, my everything. I only had two weeks with her before we'd find out if her breeding program had been a success. If it was, she'd be going home. How was I ever going to let her go?

CASSIE

Light streamed through Dame's window stinging my sensitive eyes and pulling me from a deep sleep. He'd forgotten to close the blinds, and I squinted into the beam hitting me directly in the eye. Dame slept beside me, an arm draped across my middle, his head bent and his hot breath on my shoulder. Fuck, he was hot, and I took my time looking him over in the bright light, suddenly thankful he'd forgotten the blinds.

The covers bunched at his waist, giving me an excellent view of his broad shoulders and chest muscles. Even his arms were ripped, and I nearly panted with excitement remembering how effortlessly he'd carried me to his room. What other things could we do with that strength of his?

I didn't want him sleeping anymore, and I turned towards him, carefully extracting my arm. Wiggling lower on the bed so we were eye level, I brushed my lips against his, heat rushing to my core. He stirred, blinking sleepily at me, his dark eyes still hazy with sleep and appearing soft brown in the light of day. Damn, he felt good to wake up to.

"Morning."

"Good morning." He reached up to stroke my face, and I brought my hand up to cup his cheek. I peppered his mouth and his stubbly face with butterfly kisses. Dame gave a grumpy groan that reeked with secret contentment at my ministrations.

With a yawn and a stretch, he turned over and was blinded by the same sunbeam. He threw an arm over his face and turned back toward me.

"Ugh, sorry. I guess I forgot to close the blinds." But he didn't say anything or make a move beyond that, and I realized he was still playing shy, even after the way he'd dominated my body the night before. He was a sensitive soul, but I wasn't above corrupting him.

"I don't mind. It's nice and bright. Perfect for seeing certain things," I purred, nestling into his neck and running my hands across the muscled expanse of his chest and down his chiseled abs. Those I traced with my fingers, finally having the time to do so. He tensed beneath my touch, the muscles going taut.

"Cassie." My name was a plea, and I dipped my hand lower to find him hard as a rock. Fuck, already? I must be better than I thought, unless he'd been dreaming of this very thing happening.

Running my hand over the length of him, I traced the veins and divots the way I'd traced his abs. Mine. This was mine. He was mine.

Dame shivered, and I kissed his lips, dragging my tongue along the seam of his mouth until he took the hint and opened to admit me.

Mmm, morning breath, but on Dame, it tasted good. My arms snaked around his neck, and his hand took hold of my hip, holding me in place like he was trying to control himself.

I wouldn't let him. I didn't want him holding back from me ever again, and I pulled back the blanket. Wiggling free, I gently nudged his shoulder until he lay flat on his back, and I had full access to his body. He put his hands behind his head and watched me guardedly, as if there wasn't so much to admire I was practically speechless.

Every inch of him was lean and toned, and I trailed a hand down his chest and over the ridges of his cut abs to grasp his hard cock. It was a thing of beauty, and so ready for me I could see a drop of precum at his slit. With a contented coo, I licked it up, shuddering at the salty-sweet taste of his sex.

Dame's sharp intake of breath emboldened me. I may have no idea what I was doing, but he liked it, and I circled the head of his cock with my tongue, my fingers wrapping around his thick base. When I sucked the tip, his ab muscles tensed, and I smiled to myself, doing it again, empowered at how easily the man beneath me was coming undone.

His head pressed back into the pillow, his eyes closed. The distrust I'd seen earlier was replaced with carnal need as I took him deeper into my mouth. Tentatively, I stroked up and down his length while I sucked on the head, licking excitedly at the tip when another drop of precum appeared.

"Cassie," Dame said my name in a grunt, and then he was sitting up, moving us towards the edge of the bed. I pulled my mouth away, worried I'd done something wrong. "No, just, shit, Cassie, don't stop."

With what I hoped was a sultry smile, I slipped off the bed and let him sit up proper. With his legs on either side of me, I had a perfect view of him. I circled his cock gently and ran my hand up and down the length with the lightest pressure. His need-filled moan went straight to my core, emboldening me to increase the pressure of my strokes. Only when he was shaking did I lower my head and take him into my mouth.

Thrusting into my mouth, Dame was lost, his hands clenching the coverlet. I did my best to take him, but I gagged when he went deep enough to hit the back of my throat. I refused to pull away. I was too mesmerized by my new vantage point, watching Dame—The Ram come undone by my hands and my mouth.

His abs contracted, and then he came, his cock pulsing beautifully as he emptied himself. The taste of him was unlike anything I could have imagined, and I took every last drop, sucking even as he came, already hungry for more.

He stared at me, wide-eyed, his lips partedmouth open as he watched me reluctantly let him loose and stand up. I giggled at the shock on his face, pushing him back on the bed and kissing his lips, his cheeks, until he kissed me back, his arms coming up to hold me.

Getting Dame off had sent my body reeling, and I rubbed my wetness against his hard stomach. The taste of his cum and his mouth sent me spiraling into a state of such profound need I couldn't deny.

"Cassie."

I kissed him to shut him up, jamming my tongue into his mouth, but he gently pushed my shoulders. I reluctantly released him, still caging his head between my arms.

"Your turn, Sunshine."

His voice was husky, sex mixed with sleep, and I nipped at his lip. I'd always liked his voice, and now I wondered if it was possible to orgasm just from someone talking to you. Maybe I could get Dame to read from one of my books later. There was a sex scene involving both main characters fucking while riding a horse, and I was practically coming just thinking about him reading it to me in that low husky tone.

"Lay back."

Oh. Eagerly, I flipped onto my back, and it was his turn to straddle me. The look of tenderness in his eyes tugged at my heart. I wanted to pull it from my chest and give it to him raw and bleeding. He kissed me then moved down to nuzzle into my neck. The sound of his sharp inhale at a spot just behind my ear sent a shiver of pleasure straight to my core. There was something deeply animalistic in the way he breathed me in, and I wanted more—wanted him to bite me, mark me as his, possess me, and fill me with his seed until there was no more him or me, but only us.

"You smell so good, Cass."

Oh shit, he'd shortened my name, and I fucking loved the familiarity of it, like he'd found a new way for us to be closer. I arched my neck to give him a better angle, mewling, and wiggling beneath him. He was half hard already. I wanted him to take me, but he moved down my body, hovering an inch above me, braced on his forearms, nipping and kissing at the skin of my neck, my breasts, my ribcage, until he was positioned between my legs. I grunted my displeasure at the loss of contact, but he only smirked, his dark eyes mischievous.

"There's plenty of time for that later. Right now, I want to have a taste." The hunger in his tone and the way his eyes flashed down to my quivering pussy made me think he'd been dreaming of this moment.

Shit, I was in trouble. I laid back, propping my head up on my hands the way he had so I could watch.

He wasted no time, his tongue gliding through my slick, licking me from pussy to the swollen nub of my clit. Slowly, he traced my sex with his tongue, as if memorizing every part until I was wild with need. I gripped his dark spiky hair and pulled him towards my needy clit.

Thank god he took the hint. Two fingers dipped into my pussy as his tongue fucked my clit, sucking and nipping at the bud, hammering it with his tongue in perfect time to the thrusts of his fingers. The tension inside of me, already wound so tight, and I clung to his hand, digging my nails in deep as the dam inside of me burst and exploded, the orgasm shaking through me. He didn't slow, seeking out every last bit of pleasure until I was a trembling boneless mess on the bed, looking up at him in awe. *Those nimble fingers.*

With a satisfied look, he wiped his wet mouth on his forearm. I swear I could come again just watching him lick his lips. He pulled on tight black briefs, and I turned around on the bed, my head propped on folded elbows. Next his jeans, a plain black shirt, and his usual windbreaker, which he zipped up to his neck. Fuck, it was such a pity to cover his beautiful body, and I couldn't help but pout.

"What's the matter?"

Busted. I couldn't very well tell him I wanted to stare at his abs all day. That his body was a work of art I wanted to put on display in the middle of the room so I could walk around him and examine him from every angle, so I settled on a more obvious question.

"Where are you going?"

He smiled down at me. "*I* am going to get you some breakfast. What do you want?"

My stomach grumbled at the mention of food, and I laughed. I guess maybe I was a little hungry, but I didn't want him gone for long, nor did I want to put him through any trouble.

"Just some toast, please."

He snorted, sitting on the bed next to me, and bending over to kiss my head, taking in an extra breath of air as he did.

"You don't even like toast. How about I make you that cheese and red pepper omelette with grated parmesan? You'll just have to tell me whether you like it with chives or arugula on top. You always eat both, so I've never known which one you prefer." His lips were still buried in my hair, and I looked up to find him watching me expectantly. He wore an expression of impatience, like he was asking me what my favourite colour was, and couldn't understand what was taking me so long to respond.

"That was you? You've been the one bringing me food?" Mouth hanging open, I stared at him in surprise. Dame was my mysterious benefactor, *and* Dame was The Ram? He'd been the one taking care of me all this time, never taking credit, always dropping the food and slinking away. He was too good to be true, the absolute fucking perfect man.

"Of course." He frowned down at me as if my reaction confused him, and the four course meals he'd been serving me for the past month and a half were the most natural thing in the world. Then he gave me an indulgent smile, bending to kiss my still open mouth, and dropping another kiss on the tip of my nose. "I love to cook for you."

My jaw dropped another inch, and I wished I could go with him and watch him cook for me. I remembered how he'd made his own eggs in front of me once, all practiced ease with the frying pan. I should've known. He looked away and smiled shyly to himself before dropping another kiss on my head and standing up. He was at the door by the time I found my voice.

"I like them both. The arugula and the chives. I'd always wondered how they'd taste all together."

He looked back at me, his hand on the knob, eyes shining, the curve of his lip just as sultry as ever.

"As you wish."

CHAPTER 20

I couldn't remember ever being this happy. There must've been a time when I was a kid or out running in the woods, but no. None of those fleeting moments compared to this. It was hard not to rush through cooking Cassie's omelette so I could get back to her, but this would be the first time I got to see her eating any of my cooking, and I refused to serve her anything burnt.

The omelette was a perfect golden-brown colour, and I was just plating it when Tristan walked into the common room wearing a rumpled shirt with some stupid new green monster on it. He rubbed his short hair sleepily and yawned.

"Tristan," I called cheerily from across the room, earning me a few looks from the group sitting groggily at the dining table opposite the bar. "Tristan, old buddy, old pal." I grinned when he quickly walked over as if the unusually affectionate way I was acting embarrassed him. Worked for me. "Hey, good morning. Did you sleep well?" I couldn't stop smiling today, didn't know if I'd ever stop smiling, a strange contortion of my muscles that felt unnatural on my face.

With a wary look, Tristan sat on the stool across from where I was preparing Cassie's plate. I'd made her a four egg omelette today and a glass of fresh pressed orange juice. I needed my girl to keep her strength up if she was going to withstand the very many fantasies I'd pushed down and out of sight since I'd first laid eyes on her in the breeding room.

"Yes, fine." His eyes roved my face, and his posture was tense—distrustful. "What is it you want?" Now that I had Cassie all to myself, hiding out in my room, saturating my sheets with her glorious scent, there was only one thing missing. I grinned.

"I have a favour to ask."

Tristan's answering groan only made me smile all the more.

"Oh my gawsh, thish ish amazing."

I don't normally speak with my mouth full, but the first bite of Dame's omelette was so damned good, and I couldn't resist telling him right away. This was the first time I'd had the chef in front of me to thank, and I grinned at him around the food stuffed in my cheeks. True to his word, he hadn't taken long, and I'd gotten changed back into one of the black shirts in his closet. It fit me like a nightshirt and was as covered as I wished to be with Dame returning any minute. What would it be like to walk in and see me wrapped up in his scent, trying to make myself as his in whatever way I could? His clothes had been the only bit of Dame about the room.

Everything was impossibly clean, like no one lived here, with a single desk against the wall and a rolling office chair Dame sat down in upon his return. A peek into his closet had revealed multiple sets of his usual wardrobe: black shirt, jeans, black windbreaker with a red stripe, hand weights, and a pair of resistance bands, but that was it. Where was all his stuff? He'd been living here at least as long as me, but his room felt like he'd just moved in. I decided I would help him personalize the room, especially if we were here for a few more heat cycles. At least a few more, I promised myself, banishing all thoughts of us parting. Another forkful of the omelette and I was completely distracted.

The dish was salty with a bit of sweetness from the red peppers, and I swear he'd cooked it in fresh butter. My tastebuds thanked him for that, tingling at the perfect amount of salt and umami.

After our first night together, I'd been starving, and I greedily dove into the beautifully plated food he'd spent time setting up. Feeling somewhat guilty when I disturbed the adorable curlicue of arugula and delicate shaved parmesan on top.

I was nearly halfway done before I looked up to see what Dame was eating. He'd brought a bowl of cereal for himself, and when I saw what was inside, I burst out laughing, bits of egg flying everywhere.

"No way." Laughter worked its way deep through my belly, and I tipped over on the bed giggling. Dame frowned down at his bowl.

"What?"

"You eat the bran flakes." I'd suspected he was the only one in the apartment eating them, but to have it confirmed? It was too much, and I struggled to control myself as giggles erupted from my throat and tears leaked from my eyes.

"Well, yeah, they're the perfect amount of fiber in the morning. I do my proteins with lunch and keep it light at dinner."

Fighting to regain control of myself, I sat cross-legged on the bed.

"Of course you do." It was so Dame of him to plan out every bit of his meals. I bet he factored the pretzels and chips from our snacks into his diet as well. But then again, I was reaping the rewards of all his efforts in the form of his ripped body, so I couldn't exactly complain. Those abs killed me, and I wished he was topless right now so I could admire them.

"What is it?" He frowned back down at the cereal bowl and met my eyes with a question.

"Nothing, Dame, it's perfect. You're perfect." With a toothy grin, I pushed the half-eaten omelette plate to the side and went up on my knees to throw my arms around his neck and kiss him. Dame's arms came up to hold me back, and when I broke the kiss, he still looked slightly confused but with a new curl to his lips that gave me butterflies.

"Well, all right, I guess."

I cleared my throat, self-consciously looking back at the bits of egg I'd spewed on his always-clean coverlet.

"Sorry, I'll clean this up." He went to stop me, but I held up a hand, not to be deterred. Grabbing the white cloth napkin he'd included with my meal, I gathered up the egg bits. I felt bad. He clearly went to great lengths to keep his room pristinely clean, and I'd spilled food on his bed of all places.

Finished with the task, I sat on the bed, giving it a testing bounce. It was the same mattress as I had in my room and grinned at him excitedly.

"So, what do you want to do?" God, I hoped that sounded sexy. With my index finger, I traced slow circles around his wide forearm.

"Well, Tristan will be here soon with your surprise."

My mouth hung open. What did Tristan have to do with anything? "A surprise?"

Dame cleared his throat, dropping his metal spoon with a clang into his now empty bowl.

"Yeah, I can't wait to see your face." The shy smile he gave me was so damned cute. His dark eyes shining with vulnerability. I leaned forward to press my lips against the sexy curve of his mouth, sighing when he opened up for me to taste him. Bran flakes, *fuck*. He kissed me back, moving the bowl aside, and joining me on the bed.

He caged me against the bed, hovering above me on his forearms, his cock hard against my stomach and his face nuzzling into my neck. The little moans he made as he kissed and sucked at the skin behind my ear hinted at the passion he kept just under the surface. A passion that had burned me more than a few times and left me craving more, but then I remembered what he'd said.

"Dame, didn't you say Tristan was coming?"

He paused his ministrations, reluctantly pulling back to look me full in the face. "Yeah, but nobody said we had to answer right away."

I snickered, wrapping my arms around his neck and pulling him back down against me, wanting his warmth next to mine. More than that, I was sick of seeing him in clothes and my hand slid across the slick fabric of his windbreaker, searching for the zipper.

"You want this off?" He seemed surprised, and I didn't get it.

"Of course, I want to see you." I plucked the fabric of his windbreaker. "I don't want this between us. I don't want anything between us." The vulnerability in his handsome face was heartbreaking, and he looked away as if it was too much. "What's the matter?"

"I'm just—I'm not used to this. I'm not good at being seen." There was a hidden pain there, like he'd been seen by someone else and it hadn't gone well.

The thought was physically painful, and I wanted to ask him about it but the last thing I wanted was for him to dwell in the dark place of a bad memory.

Instead, I placed my hands on either side of his face and turned his head until he was forced to look at me. "Well, I see you, I see you so clearly, Dame, and I–I" I bit my lip against what I wanted to say. We were tiptoeing around an exclusive relationship. It wasn't allowed, wasn't possible, but it had happened all the same. "I love you."

The moment the words left my lips, Dame's eyes snapped to mine, his dark eyes burning.

"You can't mean that, and you shouldn't say that word. Pack above all, Cassie. You know the rules." There was a hard edge to his tone, and I tried to gentle it by cupping his cheeks tenderly.

"But it's true, and I don't care if I'm not supposed to say it."

He growled, dropping his head to my chest.

"You could be sent to the fields for saying that Cassie, or worse, exiled."

They hadn't exiled anyone in over fifty years, but he was right. They could. But what I heard most clearly—more than his warning, more than his angry tone—was his lack of reciprocation, and the echoing silence around us only added to my misery.

I hadn't meant to say it, but the way he always underestimated himself made me want to say every possible thing to him that would help him realize how perfect he was. The words had slipped out.

My eyes welled with tears, and I looked away.

"Cassie." My name on his lips was a plea. "I'm sorry. I didn't mean to be angry with you—I just. Let's just enjoy the time we have together, for however long it is."

I looked up into the dark depths of his stunning eyes and was lost.

"Yes, Dame." Even if he didn't love me, even if we were destined to be parted the moment a pregnancy was achieved, my heart didn't care.

He kissed me tenderly, his thumb brushing away a tear. He kissed my cheek where the tear had been, and I felt my heart warm. My arms trailed up to snake around his neck, hands clasping. He hadn't said it back, but we still had time. I lost myself in the addictive feel of his hard body against my soft one, the taste of him, his sounds, until time ceased to exist and there was only this. Only us.

I barely heard the knocking at the door until Dame pulled reluctantly away. I sat up, straightening Dame's shirt and putting my leggings back on. Dame looked back at me, his hand on the knob, and only opened the door when I smoothed my hair back to contain the frizz and gave a nod.

Dame opened the door to admit a smiling Tristan, wheeling a big black cart behind him. Balanced on top was the TV from Tristan's room. On a shelf underneath was a fucking game system. My mouth must've been hanging open because Dame grinned. Fuck, Dame grinning was a rarity, but there it was. I squealed, standing up and jumping up and down on the bed with excitement.

"No way!"

Tristan wheeled the cart to the center of the room and started plugging things in.

"You like it?" Dame watched me like it was his favourite thing in the world.

"Yes, I fucking like it! Holy shit, how did you get a game system?"

He smirked. "It wasn't so hard. There are actually a few spares that glitch out sometimes, but this is one I'd been secretly repairing. Yep, nobody's going to come looking for it, which means..."

I gave him a toothy grin.

"Game on, sunshine."

"Yes!" In more ways than one. I had my man, and now we had games. Everything was perfect, and I bounced myself into a sitting position, looking eagerly at Dame as he pulled my neon green controller from behind his back.

CHAPTER 21

Playing video games with a half-naked Cassie was my new favourite thing. Seeing her wrapped up in my shirt did all kinds of things to me. It felt so right having her in my room, wearing my things, filling my dark corner with so much sunlight I could barely breathe.

The unnatural smile still clung to my face. No matter how much I wanted to play it cool and keep it casual, the damned betraying curve of my lips spoiled everything.

"Dame, Dame, get that guy over there. He's flanking you. He's flanking you!"

I chuckled to myself as Cassie bounced around excitedly beside me, heedless of the way the mattress shook, jostling me so I needed to keep a firm grip on my controller. Her hair was a frizzy mess, surrounding her freckled face like a halo, and I loved that she didn't feel the need to smooth it back down for me. I wanted to run my hand through the errant strands and do it for her, but something made me hesitate.

As much as Cassie had been all over me since she'd discovered my identity, it was still hard for me to initiate things, to expect her disgusted reaction when I did something she didn't like. And I would. I'd do something incredibly stupid that would make her want to take back the damnable words she'd spoken earlier.

I love you. As if she meant them. As if we were allowed to feel. How badly I'd wanted to weep into the soft crook of her delicate neck and confess the depths of my heart to her. To tell her the truth, that it was all for her, every single beat. But to do so would be to condemn her. If I allowed this thing between us to be real, if I spoke the words, they'd find out. I wouldn't be able to keep Cassie safe. They'd revoke her status as a potential pack mother and send her to the fields. Cassie's dream of motherhood would be lost, and it would be my fault.

"Dame. *Shit.* Dame, wake the fuck up!"

I grunted at the punch to my right bicep, refocusing on the game to find my character under heavy fire.

Fuck. I put on the shield I'd been saving and moved back, knowing the AIs of the game would pursue me all the harder if I tried to advance on their base. My best chance was to go back the way I'd come, find some cover, and regroup.

When I'd put some distance between us, I found some foliage and healed, looking up when I noticed Cassie had stiffened beside me. She was watching me, incredulous.

"Shit, Dame, I've never seen you mess up that badly." Her expression softened, and she put a gentle hand on my arm. "You okay?"

Only Cassie would know my making a perfectly normal gaming mistake meant something was not okay. *Fuck, I loved her.* I nodded, looking away and refusing to meet her eyes. This would be so much simpler if it were just sex.

"Well, I think maybe you need a distraction."

Why would I need a distraction? I was already distracted—by her, by us, by the thought of returning to my guard squad and somehow carrying on with my life once all this was over.

"A distraction?"

With a toothy grin, Cassie crawled onto my lap and wiggled down onto my helplessly stiffening cock.

"Yeah, baby, you're too serious all the time. You need to lighten up, you need..."

Fuck, she rubbed herself against the rapidly growing bulge in my pants, and I gasped at the friction. She only wore panties under her stolen shirt, and the thought made me rabid. I reached out with a tentative hand around her waist, and she made a low sound of encouragement deep in her throat. I pulled the offending shirt out of the way, and she leaned back into me, giving me a perfect view of her taut naval and the sweet little white cotton panties she wore. Just a little layer of cotton between her bare pussy and my eager fingers.

I wanted to rip them off, tear them off her until they were unwearable shreds. The sight of them pissed me off, and I growled, hooking a finger under the edge and tugging.

"Better," she murmured in a breathy whisper, taking my other hand, and bringing it up to her breast. It fits perfectly into my hand, and I palmed it eagerly. Her answering moan was everything, and I adjusted myself to sit more upright. I breathed lightly on the spot behind her ear she seemed so tantalizingly responsive to.

"I thought you wanted to play the game."

"Can't we do both?"

Shit. This was beyond hot. I reached over to retrieve her controller and handed it to her. She took it with a sexy little hum that made me think I wouldn't be playing my best round. Undoing my jeans, I tugged them down letting my cock spring free between us. Cassie stood to remove her panties and sat back down on my lap, just in front of my straining hard-on. I retrieved my controller, wrapped my arms around Cassie, and held it in the front.

Well, this was about to be a real lesson in control. Her pussy was drenched, and she slid forward to rub her slick against me. I groaned, mashing the buttons on the controller and accidentally starting our round. Cassie sat forward eagerly, and I had to peer over her shoulder just to see.

"Don't forget to pick up the ammo." Her voice was husky, and she rubbed herself against me even as she said it. I wanted to pick her up and impale her on my cock, but that wasn't the game we were playing. So, I stumbled my character around, trying to keep an eye out and not get sniped while gritting my teeth hard enough to hurt. I'd had a hard on while gaming with Cassie before—it was nearly impossible not to with her always right beside me, so heartbreakingly beautiful—but never with her softness on my lap, her pussy wet and begging to be fucked.

We crested the hill, and Cassie started getting more into the game, bouncing up and down on my lap until I was hard as stone, my balls tight.

"Dame, cover me. I'll get to the tower." Cassie's character moved to go across the open field ahead of the tower, and I gave her a spray of cover fire. Fucking clumsy, and I was never clumsy when I was gaming, but it did the job well enough that she was able to slip in and claim the tower for us.

"Yes!" She sat back against me, laughing, and I put the controller down, immediately reaching forward and playing with her clit.

"Mmm, you did good, baby. You want your reward?"

I had no idea what the reward was, but yes, I wanted it.

"Yes."

Cassie went on her knees, positioning my tip at her soaking entrance. She looked back at me with a smirk before arching her neck and sitting back into me. She slid down easily, and I was relieved to feel the evidence she'd been just as turned on during our round. So tight and wet, my aching hard on disappeared into her sweet cunt, and I reverently smoothed my hands along her ass and hips.

Fucking Heaven.

She started bouncing, heaving herself up and down on my cock like it was her job. She paused only to take my hand and bring it around to rub her clit, which I was only too eager to do. After so much teasing, I was already close to coming. I held myself back from the edge, rubbing her clit furiously as her pace increased, her back arching the way it did when she was close to coming, blonde tendrils of hair hitting me in the face as she leaned back into me, chasing her orgasm, chasing heaven with me right along beside her.

Her walls clenched, and I let go of my control with a growl, grabbing her hips and slamming her down to hold her in place as I pulsed my release deep inside her beautiful body. Panting hard, my rough hands turned gentle as I massaged her hips, rocking her gently against me as we came down.

Cassie turned around to face me, not paying attention to my softening flesh or the mess between us. She kissed me, and her eyes were so green, so filled with love and a promise I could never accept that there were no words between us. All I could do was bring my arms up to rub her back, kissing her rosebud lips with just as much tenderness as she'd shown me. I cupped her cheek, brushing my thumb along the freckles.

Her smile returned, and I felt an answering one settle on my features. She always did this, always pulled the joy out of me like she was coaxing a living, breathing, shy thing out of hiding. Like it was worth the effort, like I was worth the effort.

"Want to go get us some snacks for our next round?"

My heart swelled until it was almost too much. Fuck, I loved this woman.

CASSIE

After a midnight raid on my room with both of our duffels being used to transport my stuff, I was pretty well moved into Dame's room, and I fucking loved seeing him all the time. The next week was shared between gaming, fucking, and Dame watching his ridiculous horror dramas while I happily read beside him—just as I'd once imagined. We talked, but not enough. I couldn't figure out why Dame still seemed closed off with me about some things.

He never spoke of his family or his squad, and it was getting old, but I kept reminding myself that while our time together was limited, there still was plenty of time remaining. I'd crack him like an egg soon enough. Already he seemed more comfortable touching me, the questioning look in his eyes fading.

We still gamed in the main room while the others went out for their daily runs. The gaming setup there had a bigger screen, a newer console, and easy access to snacks. There was a new game our group had just traded with another breeding unit, and Dame was eager to show it to me. The graphics were supposed to be incredible, and I waited impatiently on the couch in my lounge shorts, my legs pulled up to my chest, chin on my knee.

Dame was preparing our snacks, and it was giving me a bit too much time to think without his very distracting presence. I liked to think we had time together, but if I should somehow get pregnant this cycle, our time together would amount to one more week. Already, I felt the separation from him, even knowing he was in the kitchen at my back and would return soon.

A chip bag was tossed over my shoulder and onto the coffee table, landing with a crinkly thud. Weird, Dame usually served our chips in bowls. Curious, I unfolded my legs and sat forward to take a better look at the bag.

"What do you think about that, Sunshine?"

Eyes wide, I took in the label. "No fucking way."

"Yes, way." Dame's grinning face came into view, and I jumped up into his arms with a squeal of excitement.

"How did you get these? I only ever tried them when I was a kid. Didn't the factory shut down?" Ketchup chips had always been my absolute favourite snack. I'd been broken-hearted when a new alpha took over the region and shut down the factory. He'd deemed them unimportant—as if the delightfully thin red powdered crisps could be anything but important.

"Alpha Cane reopened the factory. Apparently, these little buggers make for some excellent trade."

"Fuck, yeah they do." I laughed. "We used to get them all the time in 7C."

Dame smirked. "Yeah well, 7C got the worst pop so I guess it balanced out."

I pulled back, hands still clasped behind Dame's neck. He'd pronounced 7C like Sevensy, a way of saying my house name that I'd only ever heard used by those who lived there. Everyone else pronounced the "c".

"Dame, did you—were you in 7C?"

Dame looked anywhere but at my face, his thumbs rubbing nervously at my back.

"Yeah, I was." He didn't sound like he wanted to explain further, but then he never did. It was always up to me to push him, and I knew from a painful amount of experience that it would do him good in the end.

"Whereabouts? Did we go to school together?" A million questions threatened to burst from my lips, but I stuck with two. 7C was huge with a school of children for each corner. Maybe he'd been on the complete opposite side, but the way he kept avoiding my eyes made me think there was more to it, and I gave him a little shake.

"Dame, come on, tell me."

He looked hesitantly up to meet my steady gaze. "I was down on Mulberry Street."

The sharpness of my indrawn breath was almost painful. He'd grown up right around the corner from me, and what's worse—

"Oh, Dame, I'm so sorry. Did... did something happen to your mom?"

Mulberry Street was for orphaned kids, a few older women tending to a gaggle of ragtag kids outside of communal hours.

"No actually. Well, I guess you could say she happened to herself." He gave a defeated sigh and sat down on the nearest patch of couch. With his hands on his knees, and his broad shoulders eased back into his seat with a frown pinching his brow, he looked masculine and vulnerable at the same time. I wanted to hug the pain away, but I settled for slipping my tiny hand into his big one and giving it a squeeze.

"My mom, well." He released a shaky breath. "She liked having kids, but she wasn't exactly great at taking care of them. I was the fourth of seven children in five years." Wow, that was a lot of fucking kids in a short period of time. I rubbed his palm soothingly and waited for him to continue. "Every time she'd have a single or a pair of twins, she'd wait just long enough for her breeding cycle to begin again and head back into the program. I don't know why really, except I guess I do now. Maybe there was a thrill to being here, to being part of a breeding unit. Anyway, I guess her genealogy was valuable enough to the pack that they let her keep coming back, until they finally cut her off, told her she was done with the program. Not that she ever came back to take care of her children." Dame's voice turned bitter, and he squeezed my hand painfully tight, his dark eyes burning as he looked into empty space. I bit my lip to keep from crying out. If squeezing my hand helped banish any of the darkness swirling in his eyes, I could stand it. "She came back and set herself up in a different corner from all of us. I guess taking care of other people's kids was easier than taking care of her own."

The silence between us was heavy with emotion, and I struggled to find a way through it, to reach him in his pain.

"Did you have a twin?" I was a single myself, but twins were the norm. At least if he'd had a twin, he'd have had someone right there growing up alongside him. But the slight shake of his head broke my heart all over again. "What about your other siblings?"

He sighed, sitting back and easing up on my hand, drained of the anger I'd felt from him a moment ago.

"We were spread out to a few different side streets. At seven kids, we were a pretty large family unit of siblings, and you know they try to discourage close familial bonds."

I looked down at my hand still nestled into his. "Yeah."

"It's just the way it is. No family but pack family. Pack above all, Cassie."

"Yeah, I mean, I guess so." Fuck, that sounded miserable.

"But hey, don't feel bad about it. I had Jace. I didn't tell you this before, but Jace is actually my half-brother." He frowned. "A fact I only became aware of when we joined the same guard squad and started talking about our past over a few beers one day. The aunties who ran the side street were always kind."

Ah, he had Jace, Jace who I hated, and he was more important to Dame than I'd ever realized. His brother. Fuck. I'd have to work on resolving the grudge I held towards him, but it made sense now why he was always defending Jace, always following him.

"So, if you were in the same corner as me, we would've gone to school together. We're the same year. Right?" He looked at me, and I hated the sadness I saw there.

"Right."

Fucking one-word answer bullshit.

"I don't remember you, but did we ever talk or anything?"

Dame licked his lips, his mouth settling into an uneasy line. "We were in the same class, Cassie."

"What?" I stared at him in shock. Dame had been in my class? He didn't look familiar to me at all, and what's worse, he'd never looked familiar. I groaned, pressing a fist angrily to my forehead, hoping to mush my stupid brain into making some kind of sense. How the fuck could I forget someone like Dame?

"It's okay, Sunshine. It would surprise me more if you remembered me." He gave a sad little laugh at himself. "I barely spoke to anyone and always stayed away from the other kids at break. You were always surrounded by friends, so happy." Miserable, I stroked his palm, wishing I hadn't been such an oblivious asshole of a kid. "But,"—he moved closer to me, wrapping an arm around my waist and pulling me into his chest—"you asked me to play dodgeball a few times. More than a few, actually." He nuzzled his nose into my cheek. "You were the only one who ever asked."

That did it. I was blubbering like a baby; the tears streaming down my cheek at the thought of poor lonely Dame with no friends and no family. Dame rubbed comforting circles on my back, making shushing sounds, consoling me when he was the one who had just shared his troubled childhood and given me my first real insight into why he was so quiet and closed off all the time. I wept for the lonely little boy Dame had been while the man he'd become held me.

"You were my sunshine, Cassie, then and forever. No matter what happens between us, I want you to know that." His words only made me cry harder, the sobs shaking my body hard enough to hurt.

Chapter 22

"I said to hide behind the barrier. What the fuck are you doing standing on top of a car like a prime fucking target?"

I glared at Dame, and he glared right back. Fuck him, he was doing a shit job of listening.

"Yeah, and if I'd stayed behind the barrier, I wouldn't have been able to save your ass when that guy popped up in the window across the street." Neither of us was looking at the screen now, and I could feel the anger rolling off of Dame in waves. I threw up my hands, got to my feet, and paced while talking.

"Yeah well, if you had kept a med pack on you like I'd *asked* you to do then I could take a hit." My teeth clenched tightly, making my words come out as a hiss. What the fuck was I even so angry about? I stopped walking and looked at Dame, who stared down at his controller, grumbling something about stats and achievements.

"Are stats and achievements the only thing that matters to you? What about the mission?" The deer-in-the-headlights look he gave me was infuriating, and I balled my hands into fists, ready to storm out when I realized how stupid this whole thing was.

Storm out? On *Dame*? I literally waited by the door when he went out to make our meals or use the washroom. The thought of being parted from him was stupidly painful, and here I was thinking about leaving because we weren't working very well together as a team in our game? I sat down hard on the bed beside him.

"What is wrong with me?" I never got this worked up, this irrationally angry, ex-cept…With a swallow, I realized it'd been over three weeks since my last shift. I'd avoided it after my encounter with Dame in the woods, and then Dame and I had gotten together properly, and I'd never wanted to leave his bed again. He was tense too, and I looked at the stiffness in his neck with interest.

"When's the last time you shifted?" I studied his face trying to gauge his reaction.

Dame looked sharply at me, the tension in his neck snapping like a cable. He paused before speaking. He paused.

"Not, not since you and I met in the woods."

I'd thought not. In my mind, at the time, The Ram was out there every night stalking around waiting for me, and I'd steadfastly avoided going out to meet him. Afraid of the pain his rejection would bring when he'd leave me covered in his seed and naked on the dirty ground.

But, in reality, he'd been avoiding me just as much as I'd been avoiding him.

"Dame, me too. I haven't shifted since that night either." He nodded, his jaw standing out against his skin. "It's making us crazy."

Dame frowned, looking up at me in confusion.

"Okay, before that night in the woods, you shifted regularly, right?"

"Yeah."

"Well, I'm saying all this random anger, this pent-up frustration is from not shifting. The administrator told me that's why they have the daily runs scheduled in the breeder units, to give all the breeders a chance to shift."

He nodded slowly. "Right, that would make sense. I've never really gone a length of time without shifting and roaming the woods. We spend about half of our time as wolves when we're guarding."

"Okay, so this means we'd better get out there tonight after everyone falls asleep, unless you want to join today's run."

Dame's frown deepened, creating a deep divot in his forehead. "No way, I love having the common room to ourselves."

"Okay then, tonight." I was salivating, thinking of how fucking incredible his black wolf had been. The thought of being hunted by him again, of knowing he would stay afterwards, that we'd walk back to our room hand-in-hand was liberating. I could feel it already easing all the hurt his leaving last time had caused.

We had to wait until everyone went to sleep, and Dame was the one to check if the coast was clear since we didn't want anyone to realize I stayed pretty much full-time in his room. He was already the one who scoped out the bathroom for me and made sure I wasn't caught coming out of his room.

It was a full moon, and my skin pebbled when we stepped outside into the clearing before the forest. The air was cold and it prickled across my skin, but the excitement pounding in my head kept me warm enough to strip off my clothes.

Excitement. I was excited to shift for pretty much the first time. The chore of it forgotten now that I knew the black wolf waited for me.

Dame stripped, pulling each bit of clothing off with quick, firm movements, and I watched in wide-eyed admiration as his body was slowly encased in moonlight. The silvery light glinted off every one of his deadly muscles, disappearing in the ridges and valleys, making everything more pronounced and giving the impression he was a sculpture carved from grey stone.

Mine. The thought came to me with such force I knew if I saw another woman flirting with him, I would rip her throat out. Sweet, nonviolent, little Cassie would take on anyone, anywhere, to keep the man before me. I licked my lips, realizing Dame was naked and watching me with a smirk on his face. He knew exactly what he did to me, and it was brutally unfair.

"Ready?"

His words pulled me out of my latest fantasy where I'd been riding on the black wolf's back, feeling its muscles bunch and release as we raced through the woods.

"Yep." My voice came out in an embarrassing high-pitched squeak that was miles away from the casual "yep" it had been in my head. Oh well, my nipples were already tight, and I'm pretty sure Dame could smell the arousal on me from where he stood. Not like he didn't already know I was hot for him. I chuckled to myself, giving Dame the side eye and catching him smiling back.

He was getting better at smiling and it showed, the expression coming to him easier and more frequently.

This was the part I hated, but I let out a breath and released my human form. Spiraling into nothingness, lost until I caught the wolf part of myself and held it in mind. Then my body dropped to the ground, and I stretched, shaking out the tingles in my muscles as I settled into my new shape. I looked over to find a massive black wolf at my side.

He was just like I remembered him, his fur thick and silvery in the moonlight. I could still feel his fangs on my scruff and his words in my ear demanding I shift. Dame turned to meet my eyes, and I could see the night reflected back at me. His eyes scanned my wolf, taking me in, like he was remembering every detail, just like I had.

This was going to be fun. With a playful pounce in his direction, I took off into the woods, my tail high in the air.

Chapter 23

Of course, she'd run right from the start. I'd barely had a chance to take her in and process how her scent had changed in her wolf form when she pounced like a young pup and made a break for the trees. Her wolf was smaller than mine, and I knew I could catch her. The thought of following her intoxicating scent–Cassie's but more intense and with a wildness that made my blood sing–through the woods knowing what was waiting for me when I finally caught her was almost too much. It made me want to go slow, to give her all the time she thought she needed to put some distance between us.

Distance I would easily cover, knowing what awaited me when I finally wrestled the lithe brown wolf to the ground. Only this time, there'd be no holding her so she couldn't see my face. No running off into the woods, terrified she'd figure out who I was.

Walking at a languid pace, I followed her trail, snorting when I realized she was zigzagging through the trees to slow me down.

Fat chance. Tracking people through the woods was what I did, and I settled into a light jog, keeping my course straight, her trail wafting her scent over to me from either side.

She'd gone deep into the woods, and I was guessing she must be tired. I was disturbingly winded, a consequence of days spent lounging around the apartment instead of doing perimeter checks. Sure, I still did my hand weights and pushups in the morning while Cassie slept in, but my cardio had gone to shit.

Pushing through a tangle of bushes, I saw her.

Shit. I should've known. She was at the same stream where I'd first been drawn to her howl. This time she didn't drink, just stood stock-still. The heart on her chest shined in the moonlight, her russet fur lightened by the silver glow. Beautiful.

I padded forward, awestruck. The moon hadn't been out last time, and I'd been too enraptured to look, but now I couldn't look away.

Cassie widened her stance, dropping her head in submission. But there was a challenge in her eyes that sparked a fire in me, and when she took off into the dark of the trees, I sprinted after her like a man possessed. The need to catch her. To pin her down and take her driving me forward at a speed I hadn't known I was capable of.

I was rabid, filled with feral need as her slender form darted just ahead of me through the trees, forcing me down a more complicated path my bulk couldn't handle. She burst into a clearing and I rejoiced. With no trees, my superior speed was no match for hers, and I was on her in a few bounds. Knocking her to the ground, I winced at the sound of air being knocked out of her.

Shit. Lost in the chase, in the joy of catching and possessing that I hadn't been able to control my enthusiasm. She lay still beneath me, pressed into the ground. Icy fear gripped my heart in a vise. Shifting, I ran my hands soothingly over her fur, turning her over gently to assess the damage. Her eyes met mine with a playful spark, and I was relieved when she shifted back into her human form beneath me. Brown fur was replaced by smooth skin, and her human face appeared before me. A sultry smile curved her lips.

"Why'd you stop?"

What? I gaped at her, my heart still pounding with dread. She must've realized it because she reached up to run her hands across my chest.

"Don't you remember what we did last time? How rough you were with me?" Her voice came out in a throaty purr dripping with lust, but all I could do was blink back at her.

Oh. She wasn't hurt. She'd been waiting for me to take her by the scruff like the first night I'd caught her. That night, I hadn't thought of anything but claiming, of fulfilling the animalistic need to mate. If she wanted that again, I was only too happy to give it to her. Wrapping a handful of her dirty blonde hair around my fist, I pulled her head back to expose her creamy white throat.

"You liked it when I let myself go out here with you?" I breathed along the side of her neck, letting my breath touch some of her favourite areas. "You like to be hunted."

Her throat pulsed with a swallow, and she shuddered beneath me. *Fuck, this was hot.*

"Should I press your face into the ground again, make you taste the dirt while I fuck you?"

Her answering moan was all the permission my aching cock needed, and I climbed off her to push her onto her stomach, my hand in her hair controlling her every move.

Yes, just like this, my beautiful Cassie squirming for me beneath the moonlight. The animal within me was pleased, and I massaged her ass, parting the cheek with one hand to catch a glimpse of her glistening pussy. Of course, she was soaked. There was something about the chase that did this to both of us, and I dipped two fingers violently into her pussy without warning, rubbing at her inner walls and imagining it was my cock and not my hand fucking her.

She cried out, and I pressed her face further into the ground, using my thumb to circle her clit while my fingers fucked her pussy. Shit, she was already close and the sight of her left me impossibly hard. I pulled out my fingers, and she made a noise of protest, but then I slammed my cock home, and she squirmed, trying to adjust her position.

I didn't let her, setting a punishing pace and demanding she keep up. The air filled with my snarls and growls, my thumb rubbing her clit mercilessly. Her walls clenched around me, and still, I pounded into her. The sound of her screams and my growls mixed with the wet slap of skin in the echoing forest. I moved onto my knees, pulling her along with me and slamming into her again. Impaling her on my cock, I took her as deeply as I could go. And it still wasn't enough. It was never deep enough, and I pressed down on the small of her back as I chased my release. I used my weight to go deeper–the lust-filled squeals she was making were music to my ears.

"Come on, Sunshine."

She was building up again, and this time I meant to meet her. Everything snapped inside of me. Groaning, I emptied myself into her, giving her everything I had. Like a man possessed, I pulled and pushed at her hips hard enough to mark her delicate skin. She trembled with her release, and I threw my head back as her pussy clenched around me tight enough to milk me for every last drop of cum. The way our bodies responded to each other, how in sync we were, was perfection.

I massaged her ass gently, pulling her back and forth on my softening flesh as her body trembled through the last of her orgasm. I released her hair, and she spun around to face me as though scared she wouldn't find me there. Even after all the time we'd spent together, every shared kiss and joke, she was still afraid I'd leave her out here. She studied me, and I hated the worry in her emerald eyes. Reaching up, I stroked her cheek, brushing a stray tear away with my thumb.

"Oh, Cassie. I'm not going anywhere, Sunshine. I—I'm not leaving."

I had been about to say something else, the very thing I'd promised myself never to say to her, but I'd caught myself at the last moment.

She fell into my arms, nuzzling into my neck. And under the light of the moon, I held her, wishing I could tell her how I felt about her. How I would never leave. How she would turn to find me beside her always, but I couldn't. I never could. All I could do was hold her and stroke her beautiful hair, letting my body tell her all the things I could never say.

CHAPTER 24

CASSIE

"You want to make us some of those fries with the orange sauce?"

Dame sighed beside me, giving me a long-suffering expression that looked sexier without his shirt on. It'd been an easy sell when I'd promised to come out to the empty common room in only my underwear. No clothes for me, no top for him.

"You mean, my parmesan crusted frites with sriracha aioli?"

I snorted with laughter at the pained look on his face. It was so fun to get under his skin.

"Yeah, the fries with orange sauce."

His mouth fell open for a moment and then he grinned, reaching out to tickle my middle with both hands.

"Well, maybe I just won't make it for you then."

I gasped, trying to catch my breath. He followed me, blowing into the skin of my neck, his fingers tickling my rib cage. I laughed until I was a puddle of mirth, exhausted. Only then did he stop, his lips at my ear.

"Now, what would you like me to make us, Sunshine?"

I grinned, wrapping my arms around his neck.

"I would like some of your *amazing* parmesan crusted frites with sriracha aioli."

He grunted, and his fingers started skating up to my exposed armpits.

"Please."

He nuzzled my neck, dropping a quick kiss behind my ear, and stood up. "You got it."

With a dreamy sigh, I turned around to peer over the back of the couch and watch him cook. We had at least another hour before the others got back, and while I wasn't that hungry, the sight of Dame cooking always did it for me. That and my man seemed to enjoy making my favourite treats, a passion of his I was only too happy to indulge in.

Two more days until my period was due, two more days until I could relieve the budding fear that I might have gotten pregnant this cycle and have to leave my little bit of heaven wrapped up in spiky black hair, with dark arresting eyes.

I sighed, stretching out on the couch, my head going into the groove of Dame's still warm spot. The pleather felt luxurious against my bare skin.

"Dame?"

"Hm?"

"What's it like in the guard squad?"

He was quiet for a moment.

"Cold, mostly. We spend a lot of time surveying the perimeter for trespassers, and while we do have a shared cottage, anyone out on patrol usually just meets at the camp near the border to warm up."

That didn't sound like the best life. While I would return to the comfort of 7C to be supported through parenting my child or children, he'd be going back to that. My nails scraped at the pleather armrest above my head.

"So, this is like a vacation for you?"

He grunted. "Yeah, a lot of the guys think of it that way, and I think that might be the goal. To give the guard squads something to look forward to, as well as believing they might have a pup or two. They really make this place pretty awesome."

I mulled it over, chewing my lip. "Plus all the sex."

"Yes." He didn't elaborate, and I felt a ball of jealousy lodged in my chest.

"How long were you in the program before I arrived?"

He sighed, and I heard the sound of him dropping our fries into the deep fryer with a sizzle.

"Two months."

Holy shit. I bolted upright, looking at him over the back of the couch and trying to catch his eye.

"Two months?"

"Yeah."

Shit, he'd been here for two months before I'd arrived, and by the way he was avoiding my eyes, I'd guess he hadn't been quite so shy with the other girls. I lay back down, questions streaming through my head, one after the other. Had he been exclusive with anyone else? How many girls had he slept with? Had he been in love with any of them? For all I knew, Dame had been in a secret romance with someone whose breeding cycle had come before mine and *shit*. He could have a child.

Dame came around the corner to place a little bowl of orange-coloured creamy dip on the table.

"But you don't need to worry about that, and no, I'm sure I don't have any children." He drew a deep breath, and I watched him carefully as he took a seat beside me, his bare back brushing up against my side—flesh on flesh. "I was only assigned to one other breeder before you, and she was removed from the program when she was unable to conceive. I've never slept with anyone who's conceived, which is kind of why I'm still here."

I frowned at that. "What do you mean?"

"Well, they want us to be here for a successful breeding cycle. Right now, I know for a fact I don't have any children. I wouldn't be able to say that if someone I'd slept with had conceived. It helps foster loyalty."

Nodding thoughtfully, I reached out to take his hand, smoothing out the fist he'd been jamming into his thigh.

There was one more question I'd been meaning to ask him, one that I'd kept close and been unable to vocalize until now. I rubbed his knuckles with my thumb.

"And now, are you only assigned to me, or do you have more than one breeder this cycle?"

His head snapped up, but I didn't meet his eyes. "No. Cassie, look at me."

Cautiously, I brought my eyes up to meet his. There was a passion and a tenderness in the dark depths that was almost frightening.

"There is only you." His grip tightened almost painfully on my hand, and I smiled shyly. Even if he didn't say the words, Dame always made me feel special.

The acrid scent of smoke tickled my nose, and Dame jumped up.

"Oh shit, my frites!"

The fact he had called them frites even in a moment of panic made me laugh, and I lay back on the couch dreaming of all the days we still had together—of romping in the woods as wolves, cuddling up to play games, not to mention the multitude of delectable meals he made for me.

I just needed my damned period to start, so the twisted-up knot in my stomach could unwind.

Cassie was quiet, and I didn't like it. Quiet Cassie was like a dog that didn't bark or a cat that didn't meow—it was fundamentally wrong and against nature. Her testing day was coming up, and I knew it was bothering her, but there was nothing I could say or do to help. We could only both wait it out, hoping her period came early so we could both breathe again.

What the fuck was I supposed to do if she was pregnant? The possibility hung over our heads, always there in every interaction. But it was just my fear, and I tried to tell myself that these things often took time with most girls being in the program for three to four cycles to conceive. This was only Cassie's second cycle—surely we had more time.

But when her period didn't come and an older blonde woman with a warm smile came in to bring the breeding women tests, I felt the icy grip of dread at the back of my neck. What's worse, in the common room with everyone around us, Cassie and I couldn't be seen getting close. We shared a glance just before she headed to the bathroom, a pink stick of plastic clutched in her white-knuckled hands. The fear in her eyes had me on edge, and I wanted badly to go hug her and tell her it was all going to be okay, but how could it?

Everyone seemed to be in the common room at the same time while the three breeders from Cassie's heat cycle went to test. We were a mess of knotted muscles and nervous conversation. Ten minutes felt like hours, and when the first girl emerged with a sad shake of her head and tears in her honey-brown eyes, I breathed a sigh of relief.

See, I told myself, *not everyone ends up pregnant.* The second girl emerged, a cute blonde with her hair pinned up wearing a sequined heart on her t-shirt. She did an overdramatic spin before flashing the test at us.

"Negative." She sang the word, and a few of the guys in the back gave a whoop. I guess nobody minded if she stuck around. She'd arrived around the same time as Cassie. I didn't know her name, hadn't bothered to pay much attention to any of the girls since Cassie had come onto the scene, but she hadn't been shy like Cassie.

Beautiful, sweet, joyful, Cassie. My everything, my sunshine.

Time passed and still no Cassie. Everyone was waiting now, the tension thick in the room full of potential fathers. At last, Cassie appeared around the corner, and her tear-stained face nearly cleaved my heart in two. She looked only at me, and I knew before she said a word—before she showed the test.

She was pregnant, and she was going home in two days. The world crumbled around me, and I could barely process all the excitement in the room. Cheering and clapping fell on my deadened ears as Cassie stood there red-faced, playing with the damning test in her hand. The test that would take her away from me. The one that would destroy us. In a haze, I stood, intending—I don't know what. To go to her, to take the test and fling it across the room, maybe stomp on it, and just pretend she wasn't pregnant, that it was negative and we still had time.

Someone swept her away with an arm around her shoulder, and she looked back, searching for me. I caught her eye, seeing my panic reflected in them. Then she was pulled away and toward a celebration at the kitchen counter, fresh fizzy pop for the new mother. Just another pack mother joining the ranks, entrusted with the pack's future.

Nausea churned in my stomach and the world spun, the dark hardwood threatening to come up and meet me. I realized I was going to be sick only a few moments before it happened. I just managed the dash down the hallway into the bathroom, before heaving my guts out into the white porcelain bowl. The whole while I wondered if this was the toilet Cassie had used, if this was where she'd done the test that had ruined our life together.

A smile stayed glued to my face as I was passed around to be hugged and fawned over by the others, but inside I was numb. My limbs were lifeless, breathing was something I had to remember to do, and my heart? My heart was a useless brick in my chest, weighing me down.

All I could think of was the look in Dame's eyes when I'd walked out into the common room. He'd known right away, and the devastation I saw in his eyes matched my own so completely that it had broken the last bit of strength I had. I wanted to run to him, to scream, to pretend the test had been negative, but they'd watched me take it. Everyone had gushed when the plus sign came into being.

Their happiness baffled me, and I'd stayed in the bathroom stall letting the tears stream down my face for a long time before coming out to join them. I'd told them I was emotional and hormonal, and they'd clucked, petting my head like we'd been best friends since coming here. *Of course, Cassie, whatever you need, Cassie.* But I didn't need them or all this attention. The one thing I needed was Dame, and he'd left the common room the second he'd seen my face and it had made my announcement for me.

Dame. Was he okay? I had no idea where he'd gone, but the look in his dark eyes had me worried. Worried for him and for us as I was patted on the back and congratulated by a slew of potential fathers. I saw the chubby videogame guy give a high five to his friend and knew my suspicions were confirmed. He'd been one of my breeding males, which meant he was a potential father. My hand drifted down to press into the flowing fabric of my loose white cotton shirt.

My children. I could still see them in my mind, a boy and a girl—a double, of course—and such a precious gift to me. To my mother, to the pack itself. Raising them in the family compound and having them sit front and center at story time, my dream was right there in front of me. Every bit of it. But I was miserable. The life I was facing wouldn't include Dame.

Two days, that was all I had to say goodbye to everyone here and pack my things to go back home. As if home could ever be anywhere Dame wasn't. I forced a painful breath in, fighting back the tears threatening to spring from my eyes. I needed to see him, but I couldn't, not with a whole crowd of people bent on congratulating me and each other on my successful breeding cycle.

Tomorrow they'd have a party for me to celebrate the pregnancy, and then I'd pack my bag and head back to 7C and a Dame-less existence. My life there stretched out in front of me, a life not without joy, but lacking the very essence of what I needed to be happy. My love, my *mate*, the very thing we were never supposed to have.

A few tears squeezed their way out throughout the evening, but I was able to explain them away as tears of happiness. In part because they were. Having children was so important to me, but they couldn't be true tears of happiness, not knowing what I would be giving up.

This is why mates weren't allowed. If I hadn't pursued Dame so doggedly, tried to find out who the man wearing the ram mask was, my heart would be singing right now. Instead, I've had a taste of what it was like to find the other half of myself, and now I would be ripped away to raise children that may or may not be his.

The realization hit me like a new blow when I was already on the ground bleeding. *Dame might not be the father.* That was the point, after all, and while I had slept with Dame in the breeding room and dozens of times since, there had been others. The chubby video gamer could be the father, or the guy standing at the back sipping a beer with a proud smile tilting his lips.

Every part of this situation made me sick, and when I finally managed to excuse myself, I went straight to my room to collapse on the bed, shaking and crying.

How could I face him knowing I was going home in two days, that he would go back to his squad and I would go back to 7C to raise my children? What would I even say? All the words had been spoken between us in that one glance—it was over. The dream of us was done.

Only after crying until my eyes burned and my stomach muscles ached, I decided it wasn't. Sitting up with hair still clinging to my tear-soaked face, I put a hand on my belly.

"It's all right, Little Ones." I wanted more for them than this, and I would make sure they had it, and I had an idea how to make it work.

CHAPTER 25

When Cassie finally came to my room, I barely processed it. Alone in the dark, and still fully clothed, I'd pictured her walking in many times over, and not once was I able to find the right words to say. So, when she ran to me, tucking herself into my chest, and squeezing me tight as she nuzzled in, my heart bled anew. Tears I didn't know I had left flowed from my eyes, falling on her head and staining her blonde hair, darkening it as I could only darken her life with my miserable presence.

"Dame, it's okay. I've figured it out."

Surprised, I pushed her to arm's length and looked into her overly bright green eyes. There was something unhinged about the way she grinned back at me.

"We can still be together. We'll just, well, we'll leave." She gave a nervous laugh, but all I could do was stare at her in shock.

Leave? Of course, to her, it was the perfect solution. We would leave and be proper mates together, problem solved. Only she'd been raised in the interior of our pack boundaries, she'd never patrolled the perimeter. Sweet Cassie had no idea the security the pack provided us or what the guards had to do to maintain it.

The hollowed out hungry eyes of starving human scavengers, desperately trying to break through our ranks to steal the pack's provisions. The occasional lone wolf, not looking any better off. All of them, hungry, dirty, miserable. What life was that for her, for the children growing in her belly? Whether they were mine or not, I didn't care. They were Cassie's, and if they had even a fraction of her light, I would love them with my whole being. But I wouldn't be able to protect them, or her, from starvation, from the lack of shelter in a cruel world run by packs, where if you didn't belong, you were an outsider who had nothing but the fight to survive.

All these thoughts passed through my mind in a moment and when I came back to reality, Cassie was still watching me, an oversized grin stretched across her face as she waited for me to acknowledge the dream she had in her head.

A dream of us. Of her children. Together and happy. It was so beautiful, and I wanted to live in that dream forever with her. But she didn't know what she was asking, and I couldn't do it to her, not to Cassie. Swallowing hard, I prepared to lie–to break her heart and save her life.

"I can't. I don't even know if that baby is mine."

Her face crumbled, the light in her green eyes dimming behind a wall of tears. I didn't care. I wanted to scream it at her, and it was torture watching her face fall, the fragile hope in her eyes dying. "And I won't leave the pack, Cassie. This is my home."

You're my home. The words were there under my false ones, but I forced out the next damning sentence, an image of a gaunt Cassie holding a crying baby firmly in my mind.

"Pack above all."

I saw the second the words hit home, and the tears spilled over, pouring down her cheeks. She leaned toward me, reeling as if she might fall, and I held up my hands to steady her, but she spun away, leaving my room in a whirlwind of blonde hair.

She left me in the darkness. My sunshine was gone. There was no light where I dwelled now. I had just killed it.

CASSIE

The thought of leaving the room and attending my party made me sick, but I was the only breeder who had conceived this heat cycle, and the celebration was entirely for me. So, I pulled myself out of my tangled blankets and put on some jeans and a turtleneck, tying my hair in a ponytail. I didn't bother to do much with my face beyond pressing my cool hands into my hot cheeks in hopes of disguising how much I'd been crying.

I was certain there was evidence of it, that the others would take one look at my face and know the truth: I didn't want this. Not anymore. But no one said anything to that effect when I emerged from my room and greeted the crowd with a shy wave of my still-trembling hand. They cheered like I was some kind of fucking celebrity, and a woman I didn't know slung her arm heavily across my shoulder like we were old friends.

"Hey, Cassie. To Cassie, the newest pack mother!"

A chorus of *hear, hear* went up through the crowd, and I winced, almost failing to take the fizzy drink being pressed into my hand. It wasn't alcohol but pop. Just another reminder that I was pregnant now and going back to 7C the next day.

My haunted eyes sought out Dame in the crowd, hungry for the sight of him, but when I saw him standing next to a leggy brunette at the bar, I reached out to steady myself against my new best friend. The world rocked, spinning on its axis and pulling me with it. He was talking to a woman, engaging, his smile like a dagger into my already dying heart.

The burst of pain at the sight of him interacting with someone when I knew he hated it, when I'd only ever seen him hang back at parties, cut deep. But I couldn't look away. Everything about him drew me in. His smiles, the way his windbreaker hung off his incredible body. I found myself moving towards him, not caring about the woman he was talking to or the way the girl at my side protested and nearly fell when I slipped out from under her arm.

"Dame?" My voice came out in a croak, but it was loud enough for him to hear. His dark eyes met mine. The emptiness in them was fleeting, a false cheeriness taking hold.

"Oh, hey Cassie. Have you met Amanda? This is her second time through the breeding program. She arrived yesterday and will be induced sometime next week."

That stung. Was he staying? He'd told me they sent breeding males home once they'd been here for a successful cycle. I mumbled something by way of greeting in reply, my eyes never leaving Dame's face, not caring about some random girl named Amanda.

"Can we talk?"

His gaze bored into mine, grief mixed with anger. He looked away, a line of tension standing out in his jaw.

"No."

One word. That was all he would give me, but it said so much. He didn't mean *no talking*. He just meant *no*. No to me, no to us, no to the possibility of my finding comfort in his steady arms. No to the home I had found in his body.

I nodded, tears blurring my vision.

"I'm going home tomorrow."

Dame's jaw twitched when I said home, and the sight gave me hope. I reached out to touch his arm, but he rolled his shoulders and shrugged my hand off.

"Yes, back to raise your children, as a pack mother should."

Should. My world was filled with shoulds and I was only realizing it now. I should be a good pack mother, I should go back to 7C and fulfill my duty to the pack, and I absolutely shouldn't be in love with Dame. But I was, and this wedge he jammed between us was more damaging and painful than anything I'd ever experienced. It was ripping me apart inside, and I reached out to him again. Not touching this time, but just hovering my hand helplessly in the air. So close, but so far away from the other half of my soul.

Dame cleared his throat and turned more towards Amanda, shutting me out. Then he whispered something in her ear, and her blue eyes went wide with excitement. He grabbed her hand and left toward the rooms without a glance back at me.

Tristan came up to me in a rush, pulling me into his arms, and I nuzzled into the soft cotton of his graphic tee.

"It's okay, Cassie. I've got you."

Fuck.

If hell was an actual place, I was bound for it after what I'd done to Cassie. But as much as it had killed me to do it, I'd effectively dismantled my relationship with Cassie, freeing her to go back to 7C, not knowing how miserable I was to be parted from her. I couldn't imagine ever being okay again, and when Amanda stripped down to bare a gorgeously tanned body with large bouncing breasts. I felt nothing.

By the flirty smile she gave me, it was clear she expected more but with my heart in so many pieces, I didn't think it could ever be put back together again. I had nothing to give. Nodding appreciatively at her, she gave a girlish giggle and spun in a circle, her chin-length brown hair twirling around her.

She was pretty. Some part of my brain processed it, and how unfair I was being by inviting her back to my room with no intention of following through. But it had been important that Cassie see me doing so. The pain I caused her might cost me my soul, but it was the only way I could give her the life she deserved.

Safe and cared for within the confines of the pack, telling her stories to the children, and tucking her own fat cherubs into bed. That was the image I held onto when the heartbreak in her eyes had been painfully apparent.

I was doing this for her. I would do anything for her.

"Um, Dame, don't you want to touch me?" Amanda was right in front of me now, her tits jiggling in time with her giggles. Any man would be feral with need at the sight of such beauty.

Any man but me.

"Why don't you dance for me?"

I was stalling and I knew it, but it worked. She went to it bending and gyrating seductively like she was dancing for a living, breathing man and not the corpse I was without Cassie by my side.

She fell into my chest with a breathy gasp, nuzzling into my neck, her hands going down to find my very limp dick. When she discovered exactly how uninterested I was, she gave an angry huff.

"What the fuck, Dame?"

I didn't have words, nor did I care as she began yanking her clothes on, glaring at me every chance she got.

"I thought you said I should come back to your room, that you wanted me?"

Was that what I'd said? I had no idea. With Cassie at my back, I'd only thought of inviting Amanda back to my room, the final nail in mine and Cassie's coffin.

She had to push me aside to get me to the door.

"Limp Dick Dame," she muttered on her way out.

Well, that was a fun new nickname.

CHAPTER 26

Everything I'd brought fit neatly into the nondescript black duffel as I looked around the room, checking through my drawers and under my bed lest I'd forgotten something. I hadn't. I'd already checked three times, it was just another excuse to linger, but the reality was my suitcase was packed—the clothes folded neatly and my forbidden books buried midway down, in case someone took my bag and felt the edges poking out of the bottom.

Those books were all I had of love and romance now that Dame had left me completely and utterly alone. Fictional characters who were devoted to a fault, and love so strong it could overcome any obstacle.

But the real world wasn't like that, and part of me had wanted to rip up the pages, tear apart the lies, and defile the covers. Only I hadn't. Instead, I'd tucked them carefully into my bag. As much as things had ended badly with Dame, I'd still experienced love with him. The books just left out how badly it hurt when love was ripped away.

With a sigh, I zipped the bag up and slung it over my shoulder, looking back at the freshly made bed. Sometime when I'd been sleeping, Dame had come and dropped off all my stuff just inside the door. Waking up to see he hadn't even had the gall to look me in the eye when he did it had been hard, and even now—even knowing he'd taken another lover and thrown me out of his room, of his life—I wanted so badly to see him one last time before I left.

Maybe that's why I was dawdling. Stupid.

With a huff, I pulled my ponytail tight enough to hurt, securing the strap across my shoulder, and walked out into the hallway.

The common room was surprisingly empty. Everyone had gathered to be my well-wishers at the party last night, but no one cared to send me off, and I felt the sting of it. Even knowing their friendship had been false to begin with, it had been nice to think they cared.

Tristan was there though, and I smiled into his warm brown eyes, heading over to where he stood at the counter. I found strength in his friendship. He wasn't alone, and I sized up the cute brunette at his side, her pixie-high cheekbones emphasized by straight bangs. I'd seen him with her before. A few times.

"Hi, Cassie." At least she seemed cheerful enough, but I didn't have the stomach for much conversation. She seemed to take the hint, turning to Tristan.

"Meet up with you later, okay?"

Tristan lit up and gave the girl an eager nod. I watched her walk away, not surprised at all when she peeked over her shoulder and gave Tristan a little parting wave.

"How are you feeling today?" Tristan's concerned voice was enough to make tears prick my eyes again. He alone had been there for me when Dame had left, and I'd crumpled into his arms. What the others thought happened, I had no idea, but he'd understood when no one else did, and I was grateful.

"Better, thanks."

He nodded, leaning back into the counter, and cracking his neck. "That's good." Licking his lips, he leaned forward, his height still outmatched mine even with the way he was slouched against the counter. "Listen, Cassie, about Dame."

I held up a hand. "I don't want to talk about Dame." Even saying his name was torture. I'd just been starting to crawl my way out of the despair pit he'd dropped me in, and it was disappointing to feel how easily I was sliding back down at the mere mention of him.

"No, I know. I just. I wanted to say, well, he's a fucking idiot."

My eyes shot up to meet his. Dame was someone he admired, a leader of his guard squad.

"Thank you."

He smiled, his eyes soft. "You're welcome."

A knock on the door made me jump, and I found myself right back against Tristan's chest, his comfort calling to me in my moment of distress.

"Sorry," I muttered, extracting myself.

The door opened to reveal my lab coordinator from this past breeding cycle. Her grinning face was exactly what I needed, and when she rushed into the room with arms open wide, I happily sank into her embrace. She didn't let go, just squeezed, and held me until I settled against her, the tension draining from my limbs.

"How are you, Cassie? How are you feeling? I hear big congratulations are in order," she said the last with a laugh, pulling apart, at last, to hold me at arm's length, and peer down at my flat abdomen. Her hands traveled down to clasp mine. "Are you ready to be a mother?" By the sparkle in her eyes, she expected me to be jumping up and down with excitement, but I couldn't manage it. Not knowing I was leaving with her, and that I would never see Dame again.

I managed a watery smile, and she squeezed my hands.

"Oh honey, let's get you home." Her grin was so joy-filled and genuine that I lost myself in it, trying to hold the image of my twins in mind. Only they both kept turning into little carbon copies of Dame, his same dark eyes and hair. What would it be like to look at little versions of Dame every day, but never see him again?

My breathing turned ragged, and I excused myself to the bathroom. Splashing some cold water on my face helped bring me back to reality. Lifting my head, I stared at the girl in the mirror, aghast. I looked like a wreck, frizzy blonde hair sticking out of an unkempt ponytail, tight in some spots and loose in others. My pale face covered in ugly red splotches from an endless river of tears.

What sort of a pack mother was I?

With a shaky hand, I smoothed my hair down and left the bathroom, but I couldn't help pausing at Dame's door, my hand poised to knock.

Would he even answer? The thought of him choosing not to come to the door, of that being our last interaction, was too much and my hand fell to my side.

Goodbye, Dame. I mouthed the words but didn't give them voice. I couldn't. It was too final, but I could kiss my knuckle and pretend it was a goodbye kiss.

It was time to go back. I would have my children and be a mother. My time with Dame was over, and now I needed to be the woman I'd been before him. And to be her, I had to banish Dame from my mind and my body.

By the time I emerged back into the common room, the smile on my face felt a little truer, and the relief in Tristan's eyes was palpable.

Today was the day. Cassie would be going back to the family compound, and while I was sure I'd ruin everything if I saw her. That I'd take her into my arms and never let her go, that the jig would be up, and she'd know I'd been pretending. But I couldn't help myself from staying pressed against my door. Straining for the sound of her voice and hoping I would be able to hear it through the thick wood, just one. Last. Time.

I didn't, but I swear there was a moment when I could sense her nearby. My greedy soul had made one last desperate plea for me to go to her. The effort of holding myself back left me shaky, the metal doorknob I'd gripped bent out of shape from all of my tension. Maybe they would make me replace it, have me do some kind of extra labour to compensate for the cost of the golden knob I'd ruined.

Ruined, yes, the knob was a wreck of mangled metal. I smiled down in satisfaction at the sight.

At least I'd left my mark on this place. Looking around, it was like I'd never lived here, never laughed with Cassie, and made love to her on what she called our bed. The room was wiped clean of everything she had brought, and I'd thrown my meager belongings into the standard-issue black duffel.

The space was barren. The white walls stripped of any life and awaiting the touch of their new owner. I hoped they did better than I had. With a sigh, I slung the duffel over my shoulder and checked my watch. An hour had passed since she was supposed to leave, and I didn't hear her when I popped my head out the door.

She was gone, and it was my turn next.

It was surreal being back at the squad house. Everything was exactly as we'd left it, bedrooms branching off a large common space with a fireplace and foosball table. My open concept kitchen was a mess, and I tsked at the buildup around the gas burners. *Damned pups.* I couldn't wait to sit back and have a beer while they scrubbed the shit out of the stainless steel.

I found my way to my room, tossing the duffel on the bed. Nobody had been here for the past three months. Dust covered my bedside lamp and along the back of my maple headboard. But as much as I demanded perfection of my space and my body, I couldn't help but imagine what Cassie would do to my room if she was here. I could practically see her clothes scattered around and her precious book collection on the nightstand.

No way should I be imagining that here, where Cassie had never been and would never be, but I was. My bones ached with how much I missed her, and I sank back into the familiarity of my lumpy mattress, letting it lull me into a dreamless sleep.

Life at the squad house was painfully repetitive, and I awoke to the smell of sausages being fried up. It must be the night shift switch. But I didn't expect to see Jace at the helm, tossing brown sausages in the pan with a crackle.

"Hey, sleepyhead."

What the hell?

"What are you doing here?"

Jace frowned over at me, pausing to sling a kitchen towel over his shoulder.

"What does it look like? I'm cooking dinner. Well, dinner for some, breakfast for others." He gave me an eyebrow waggle that was no doubt a dig at the fact I'd crashed the moment I'd walked in the door. With a grunt, I sat on a stool opposite him.

A cold rage settled into my heart, and I stood up in one fluid motion.

"Cassie. You were one of her breeders." We'd never talked about it, and I'd been too scared to ask. But if he was here, it meant one of his breeding females had achieved a successful pregnancy. With Cassie being the only one to have conceived this past cycle, it had to be true.

"Yeah, so what? I did my duty. She did her duty. Now she's back where she belongs and we've got work to do, D. These pups have done okay keeping our station afloat, but there have been reports of scavengers on our borders. Now is not the time to get distracted."

Defeated, I sat back down. He was right. Even if he hadn't wanted her, sleeping with Cassie had been his duty to the pack. What did it matter anyway? So, what if Jace could be the father of her children?

Cassie had been my distraction, but now she was my purpose, and if all I could do for her was to keep her and her children safe, I would.

With a curt nod, I stood and met Jace head-on.

"Where do you need me?"

He grinned in response, gesturing towards me with a spatula. "See? There's my boy! I want you out on the east end of our perimeter and take one of the pups with you as a shadow. Let them see how it's done." I moved to leave, but Jace called my name. "Take a sausage for the road. Gotta keep your energy up."

I didn't know what a poorly cooked bit of gristle like the one he offered would do for me, but I went to grab a fork and spear it from the offered pan.

"Good to have you back, buddy."

Scavengers tested our borders, and I spent the next two weeks helping to shore up our defenses and ward away the starving rag-covered humans when they came near. That is until one old guy with a sharpened stick got a good jab into my shoulder, and I was forced to return to the squad house to get patched up.

I'd thought Jace would be out running along the border and supporting Tristan and the others, but I found him seated at the counter, a paper in his hands. I might've been curious, but I was too tired and my shoulder hurt. Grunting my greeting, I made a beeline for my room and passed out cold, still wearing my blood-soaked clothes.

When I woke up, my wound was mostly healed, and I gave a tentative stretch of the arm, pleased with the progress. At this rate, I'd be able to get back out by nightfall at the latest. Upon exiting my room, I was surprised to find Tristan sitting on the couch, staring at nothing in particular. He looked rough with mud caked into his hair and smeared across his face on one side. He didn't look up at my approach, just stared straight ahead without acknowledging me.

"We lost Will. A group of humans attacked quad 103 trying to get through to the food stores. We followed his howl, but he was dead by the time we got there."

I hissed in a breath. This wave of attacks had been brutal. With winter coming, the local human scavengers had been growing more desperate.

"The alpha will honour him." He would, guards dying defending the pack always received a hero's funeral with the alpha himself presiding. Tristan choked up, and while I wasn't a hugger or very good at comforting people, I did sit down beside him on the couch, offering up my stony presence. "Sorry, man."

"Yeah. Thanks." We'd all lost someone in defense of the pack, but I could see this one was hitting Tristan differently.

"You okay?"

He turned towards me, and his eyes were half mad.

"Do you ever wish we could just go back to the breeding compound? That life was better there? Maybe they'd take me on as a permanent breeder. What do you think?"

My mouth hung open, and I struggled for the words.

"Tristan, man, that place, that whole damn place, was an illusion. And it's an illusion we protect for those in the interior." I thought of Cassie. Sweet, sheltered Cassie, living far away from death and grief, from starvation and cold.

He gave a sad nod.

"But it wasn't, not really. You and Cassie—"

Cutting him off with a snarl, I sat upright, poised to leave. "Don't you dare say her name."

He balked.

"Me? What the fuck, Dame, you were the one who broke her heart."

How fucking dare he? Rage consumed me, and I was on Tristan in an instant, my hand gripping his throat tightly enough to make his eyes bug out. He yielded to my display, the perfect subordinate, struggling to keep his hands down and put up no resistance.

"Bah." I released him, sitting back on the couch to stare up at the ceiling, as if I would find the answers somewhere in the exposed beams. "She never belonged with me, Tristan. She belongs with them, in the family compound, away from all this. Breaking her heart was," I paused, my lips twisting with disgust, "necessary."

"Yeah, but why does it have to be this way? I get why you did it. You're still an asshole, but I get it."

With a bitter laugh, I turned to face him. "Pack above all, brother."

He paled. "Fuck the pack, and fuck this." Tristan stood in a huff, storming out of the common area and slamming his door.

For my part, I just sat there laughing alone in the common area, laughing like a madman. My shoulder ached from an injury sustained keeping the pack and its food stores safe from outsiders. Laughing because I just couldn't cry anymore.

If one more fucking person hugged me, I swear I was going to scream in their face. My personal Cassie alarm was going to go off, and it wouldn't stop until they were all at least six feet away.

Ever since I'd returned to 7C pregnant, nobody could keep their hands off me. Touching my belly, hugging me, kissing my cheeks. Everything seemed to be fair game, and I was sick of it. The more I settled into my new old life, the more I found it filled with emptiness, and the more I cursed the pregnancy that had cut short my time with Dame.

My mother was surprisingly quiet, offering me a whispered congratulations and a brief warm hug upon my return. There were plans to be made, cradles to be brought into our space until the babes were old enough that I was granted my own place to raise them.

How scary to think I'd soon be a mother, soon to be raising children, and teaching them about the pack. About unfaltering loyalty to an alpha who clearly didn't give much of a shit about his subjects. A man who would outlaw the precious gift of love.

"Cassie, have you thought of any names yet, dear? Never too early." My latest visitor was an auntie in her fifties with deep smile lines and short brown hair that only made her plump face appear all the rounder. I could see the greed in her face. She wanted to hold my babies, to mother them. They all did.

My mind went blank.

Names. Yes, I'd chosen names once, in the time before I'd gone into the breeding program, but I couldn't think of them now. My future children. What would they look like? Be like? What would I call them? It all used to be important to me, but I hadn't thought of their names in months. Hand caressing my belly, I offered my unborn children an apology as I worked to conjure up the image of them that had once come so easily to my mind.

In my fantasies, they'd both looked like me, with dirty blonde hair with freckled cheeks. There'd been no trace of their father, but now? They were miniature Dames, all spiky black hair and dark flashing eyes. Swallowing my grief, I realized the woman was waiting patiently for an answer.

What would I call them? I tried to think of names, any would do, but nothing came to mind. My lips were dry, and I licked at them, buying some time.

"I don't have the right ones picked out yet. I think maybe they'll come to me when I see their faces."

The woman's eyes twinkled merrily. "Of course, dear." She patted my hands fondly and pulled a brown paper bag out of her satchel. "For you."

She offered the bag to me, and I took it, curiously peering inside to see a collection of rainbow-coloured candies, all homemade, the sugar pulled into a variety of shapes. Sweets like those were the best, each delightfully different from the next, but I couldn't bring myself to feel interested in the treasure within my bag.

Whether it was the babies or my preoccupied mind, I didn't know, but my appetite wasn't there. I smiled warmly at the auntie, giving the bag a shake.

"Thank you so much, Auntie. I'm going to enjoy these." A lie, but a kind one, and her crinkly smile well-worn into the lines of her face was sweet.

No one meant any harm, I knew that. They were all excited for me and for themselves. Soon there would be new pups to hold and care for, to coddle and teach.

My days were purposefully boring. The aunties and my mother forced me to rest and do as little as possible. I was still permitted to tell stories to the children before bed, but otherwise, I played games by myself and had entirely too much time to think.

Dame's rejection haunted me, and I hated playing video games without him. But I hated my books even more with their promises of love and commitment, promises I knew I would never receive, could never receive.

At least my children were growing well. A blood test had revealed my pregnancy to be a double, as I had suspected, and fondling my still flat abdomen had become the only true comfort in my world.

Minutes turned into hours, which turned into days, and then weeks without my going outside or doing much of anything. Even talking felt like too much effort, and I could barely stomach the food I was brought. I needed Dame, his cooking, his hard-won smiles. The need was so deep-rooted I found it hard to get through even the simplest of interactions, knowing they weren't the ones I wanted. I slept a lot, welcoming oblivion, and knowing my body needed the extra rest.

Until one day, my escape was disturbed, and I rolled around in a pain not deep enough to wake me but not enough to sleep through. A sharp stab in my middle left me gasping in pain and bolting upright. Looking down to find my sheets soaked with blood.

"Mom!" She was there in a heartbeat, and I held up my blood-covered hands, seeing the fear and shock I felt mirrored on her face.

"Oh, Cassie, let's get you to the bathroom." She hooked me under the arms, and supported me to stand, gently tugging me along. Bloody footprints trailed down the hall behind me, but it was the pitying looks from each person we passed that shook me to the core.

My children, my precious children, the only good thing I had left in this world, and I'd lost them. The same auntie who had asked after my children's names peered out of her home, one hand lightly holding her door covering aside. A violent cramp tore through me and I cried out in pain, pausing to work through a pain strong enough to shoot down my legs.

"Almost there. Come now, Cassie."

But I didn't want to go there. Didn't want to lose the babies, and I put a hand where the blood flowed as if I could somehow stop what was happening to me. The ultimate betrayal of my body.

There was no stopping it and after an hour spent on the toilet, watching my blood pool against the white porcelain, I was visited by the midwife. She tenderly pressed on my abdomen, and I squealed when the pressure caused a new gush of blood to pour out of me.

Eagerly, I watched her face, hopeful this didn't mean what I thought it meant, that the pitying eyes from the hallway were wrong, but I saw no hope there, just a pale-faced auntie with her thin lips pressed into a tight line.

They were lost. My pregnancy was lost.

My anchor was gone, and I was adrift.

Chapter 27

DAME

Being apart from Cassie was like having an open wound I couldn't treat. An aching phantom limb I could feel, but not touch. The pain of her loss was a living thing, hidden somewhere beneath unblemished skin—untouchable and ever present, torturing my every breath. So, I escaped to the woods, running myself ragged to help secure our borders, hoping to find some solace in pushing myself to physical limits I'd never known before.

Even there, she haunted me. A whisper of a brown tail, a howl carrying on the night air from one of the pups changing into the howl that had drawn me to her when we'd first met as wolves. The woods were filled with ghosts of her, and so was the squad house. There was nowhere I could go where I didn't ache with the need to see her, to touch her, to claim her as a mate and end my suffering.

But I knew she could find her happiness as a mother. She might be sad I had ended things between us, that my lies had been so easily believed, but the babies would solve that.

I had no such good to look forward to, just a miserable life out in the cold, defending the pack borders for her. Not for the alpha, but for Cassie.

More humans encroached on our territory. The need for me to be out there patrolling enough to justify the physical abuse I put myself through. My shoulder still hadn't healed, but I welcomed the pull of pain on each extension of the limb and the burn of my muscles as I pushed them to the extreme. Those sensations kept me grounded and chased the ghosts of Cassie away, if even just for a little bit.

At least the starving humans were a good reminder of why I did this, and while some tried to attack us—to breach our barrier, and steal from our food stores—most were easily cowed, their sunken eyes wide with fear when I growled in warning.

The work was fucking depressing, and while I knew I shouldn't, I found myself catching a few squirrels and leaving them on the well-traveled paths where I knew more humans would be coming. Maybe squirrel meat wasn't the most nutritious, but my offerings were my own and not taken from the pack. A small rebellion against the way things were.

You either had a pack or you were dead.

I only returned to the squad house when I was forced to do so or risk passing out in the chill of night. I existed for the pack, not for myself, and the pack needed me to stay strong. Cassie needed me to stay strong. So, I hauled my exhausted body and heavy limbs through the door to collapse on the couch, sleeping there instead of my bed, heedless of the sounds around me.

Waking up to a boot in the face was unexpected. Sitting up with a snarl, I shoved it away, looking up to find Jace staring down at me, disappointment etched into his features.

"What the fuck is wrong with you, man?"

Disappointed and pissed, neither looked good on Jace, and I struggled into a sitting position.

"I don't know what you mean." My words came out in a snarl as I pushed through the pain of a dozen torn up muscles.

"Well, you're fucking killing yourself out there, and you're even more of a moody asshole than ever."

"Fuck you."

"No, fuck you, Dame. I need you strong. I need you to get your fucking head in the game. Bash said he caught you fucking *feeding* the humans."

With a huff, I twined my hands together, pressing my palms together until it hurt. Fucking Bash.

"I just like to hunt sometimes, and sure, maybe I dropped a kill or two. There's no crime in that. I didn't take anything from the pack."

Crouching over, Jace got in my face.

"Yes, you did. You took your time and your strength away from the pack,to what? Postpone the inevitable? Humans had their time, and we do not have enough to go around. Pack above all."

My lip curled up in scorn.

"Is this about Cassie?"

My eyes shot to his face, and I studied his expression. "No."

"The fuck it isn't. Listen, we had a fun time. A wonderful vacation and now it's time to get back to work. She's a pack mother off having her babies and raising the future of the pack, and you—no, fucking look at me." My eyes had drifted away, thoughts of Cassie consuming my vision, but I reluctantly met Jace's fiery gaze. "Have a job to do. As do we all."

My jaw was tight, but I agreed with Jace no matter how fucked up it was, and I gave a firm nod.

"Good boy. Now, stay the fuck put for a day and heal your injuries. Tristan will take point with the pups."

I nodded again, leaning back into the couch and wishing the soft fabric was a brown pleather. That I was in another time, another place.

As much as I hated Jace, he was right, and even sitting upright, sleep beckoned to me again. My exhausted body begged me to get the rest it needed to heal.

When I awoke, it was to the sound of someone clattering around my kitchen, and I peered over the couch back to find a grim-faced Tristan washing a stack of dirty pans. The fuck.

"Tristan, man, why don't you get one of the pups to do that?"

Weary brown eyes met mine, and Tristan looked confused for a moment, as if he had no idea what I was talking about or what he was doing.

I could relate.

"You okay, man?"

Tristan set a gristle-covered pan aside and sighed. The cotton t-shirt he wore was inside out, whatever monster movie logo obscured. A tag hung down his neck at the front. Inside out and backwards—what a mess.

"Yeah, I just—" He covered his face with a sudsy hand. "How does Jace do it? How does he go into the breeding program and come out the same?"

I didn't have an answer for him, but I was starting to suspect Tristan and I had more in common than I'd thought.

"What's her name?" Tristan gave me a sharp look, his eyes red-rimmed.

"Sam. Well, Samantha, but she hates when people call her that." He gave a small laugh and the ghost of a smile appeared on his face.

I gave a nod, standing up to clap a hand on his back. "Pretty name."

"Yeah, it is." Seeing Tristan so broken-hearted was wrong. He was supposed to be the cheerful one, the smile to my scowl. But now he just heaved a sigh and stared down at the dirty pan in his hand like he could find the answer somewhere in the hardened white fat. "You know, I wasn't even her breeder." Tristan's shoulders shuddered with the force of a small, shaky laugh. "She's pregnant now, and I'm almost certainly not the father but I don't care. I just want to be with her."

Words failed me, and I gave him an awkward pat on the back.

"I get it." A pained hiss was the only response I could manage, but it was enough.

Tristan's eyes were shining when he looked up at me. "Why do they do this to us? We've given them everything." He didn't say it, as though not willing to damn himself by speaking out against the pack, but I understood who and what he meant.

"We have."

"Isn't it natural to have a mate? A family? That used to be the way things were."

I sighed, unable to look into Tristan's grief-stricken face a moment longer.

"Yeah, and it didn't work. That's why the alpha did this, to protect us. Everyone knows the pack wars nearly tore our society apart."

Tristan gripped my arm, forcing my eyes to meet his feverish ones. "Do you really believe that? I've heard things about packs up north where they still have mates and claim their children, and they're doing just fine."

Such talk was a punishable offense. I tried to shake my arm free of Tristan's death grip, but he held on with a tenacity I didn't know the tall man possessed.

"We could go there, with Cassie and Sam."

Fuck. I wanted to, but for all we knew those packs were a myth, and if they did exist? No one let in outsiders, and I'd seen enough rag covered stragglers to know it was true. None of the local packs wanted to take on more people who weren't theirs to begin with.

"We'd be sentencing them to death. I won't do it. You go if you want to, but I'm staying here where I know Cassie and her children will be safe."

Grumbling to myself, I grabbed a bowl of cereal and a few strips of freshly made jerky from the fridge. Tristan stood there for a moment, frozen in the same position. Slowly he began moving again, washing the pan in his hand. and then reaching out to wash another from the seemingly endless pile.

Was he really going to go? Would he leave the safety of the pack, the security for the unknown? With a pregnant woman in tow no doubt. No, not just a pregnant woman, his mate.

The jerky was total shit, poorly made with an unsatisfying hollowed-out crunch and not the meatiness I craved, but I choked it down knowing I needed the calories. As soon as I was fueled up, I could leave back to the woods, back to protecting Cassie.

Fuck Jace. I didn't need a day to rest. I needed to run until I was too tired to feel the wave of emotions threatening to consume me.

When I finally left Tristan was still methodologically scrubbing dishes. The run didn't help as much as I'd hoped. My foolish heart had latched onto Tristan's words and the hope they provided. Maybe it wasn't selfish to take Cassie away from here, to offer myself up as a mate to her. If she'd even have me. The lies I'd told her had been cruel and designed to hurt.

A human girl stumbled in the brush, and I watched her ankle turn on a hidden rock, her frail form starting to tumble towards the rocky creek below. Without thinking, I grabbed for her ratty brown coat, catching it in my teeth and yanking her back to safety. Wide, startled eyes met mine, and I didn't know what to do. I'd just saved her, and it felt entirely inappropriate to snarl and put on a show of protecting the border.

She just stared at me, agape. My best guess at her age would be nineteen, but it was hard to tell with her features so obscured by hunger. I felt a stab of pity, imagining Cassie in this girl's state. Practically a skeleton, her beautiful blonde hair hanging limply across her shoulders. The girl smiled, and I forced myself to sit back on my haunches, to prove I wasn't a threat even though I was supposed to be.

"Thank you." She reached out a trembling hand and petted my head. Grumbling to myself in a series of growls, I allowed it and turned, determined to find her some food.

The two squirrels I was able to catch on short notice didn't have much meat on them, but they were a good size. Her wide grin at the sight of them filled a hole in my chest I didn't know needed plugging.

Continuing my patrol along the perimeter, I looked back and gestured with my head back towards the pack border and gave a shake. She nodded in understanding, and I took off into the trees, following the trail we'd beaten into the ground.

Helping someone felt good, felt right, like protecting what we had didn't have to come at the expense of others. It hadn't taken much to pull her to safety, to catch a few sluggish squirrels so she could eat, and I felt a strength in my limbs I hadn't experienced since Cassie.

It was her goodness, I decided, and the warmth of the girl's smile, her gratitude. All of it reminded me of Cassie, and I knew if she'd been there, then she would have helped, too. Hell, she probably would've found a way to take better care of the girl, finding a spare coat for her that wasn't so threadbare.

That night, I chose to stay outside to sleep under the night sky, by one of our designated campgrounds. After making the fire, I changed back into my sturdy wolf, knowing the thick fur would keep me warmer than my naked human flesh.

The sound of a twig snapping woke me, and I shot up with a growl, seeing only a long dead fire at my feet. But there was a scent in the air, and I sniffed at it incredulously.

No, it had happened before, but not often. Fear gripped my heart in a vice as I chased the scent not knowing what I would find or how many of them there would be. There was no time to call for help if this was a true start of war with the Cintras pack to the east.

I came to a halt around a thick evergreen bush and, keeping low to the ground, I observed the scene. And there they were.

Wolves, but in their human form. A man and a woman, the woman's belly pushing out ahead of her, but covered neatly in an oversized warm-looking black coat. Long brown hair fell across her shoulders, and she looked tired, her eyes pinched at the edges. I sighed in relief, knowing this wasn't an open attack and a new turf war, but some loners mistakenly encroaching on our borders.

The man held the woman's hand, stepping in front of her to guide her over a log she couldn't see around her belly and kissing her knuckles once she was safely across. No, not a man, her mate. They were mates, and the love shining in their eyes stopped me in my tracks.

In a moment, I saw what could be, what should be. The couple was out here, but they were free, and the protective hand the man placed on his mate's back told me everything I needed to know.

Neither were starving, and while the woman looked exhausted, she also looked happy. Her eyes crinkled at the corners when the man paused a moment to look back at her, as if he'd been looking away from her for too long and needed the sight of her constantly burned into his eyes.

I understood that feeling all too well—he needed her the way I needed Cassie.

This could be us. The answer to the agony I'd been living with since leaving the breeding compound was right in front of me.

Cassie and I, out in the world, away from the protection of the pack, but also away from the control of it. Surviving and helping each other. Together, as we should be.

Not able to stand the excited energy a moment longer, I revealed myself to the couple, moving towards them—wanting to be a part of their world, trying to understand them. They froze in fear, the man pushing his mate behind him and flinging an arm out to block my advance. The woman crouched behind him, peering over his arm with wide, frightened eyes.

But I didn't growl, and I had no intention of hurting them. The man relaxed when I made no further move towards them, his stance less filled with tension but with enough remaining that he could lunge at me at a moment's notice.

With a gesture over my head back the way I'd come, I gave him a meaningful look and shook my head no. They'd be all right if they stayed clear of the borders. There was a fairly large expanse of land between pack boundaries they could safely traverse. I saw understanding flit across his features as he peered into the darkness behind me.

"Thank you." His words touched something deep inside me.

No, thank you. I wanted to take my human form and say it directly to his face, but I refused to waste another minute. Racing back to the squad house was easy. My legs felt light. I burst through the door to find a few startled pups in the common room, but my eyes sought only Tristan. When I didn't find him in the common room, I went to his room only to find it locked.

Fuck it. I broke the lock of his door with the satisfying crunch of strained metal to find him sleeping topless in bed.

"Tristan, wake up." I fit the mangled door back into place.

"Dame? What? What's going on?" Sleep still clouded his eyes, but I had enough energy for the both of us.

"Let's go get our mates."

CHAPTER 28

"Best thing for her is to get back into the breeding program as soon as possible." The auntie talked about me like I wasn't even in the room, and in a lot of ways I wasn't. It'd been two months since the miscarriage, and while my body had healed, I still felt like life was just going through the motions.

I ate, I slept, I walked around the building for exercise, but in my mind, I was lost. Roaming a forever darkened landscape with no goal, no target, and no hope. The breeding program tickled my mind, bringing me back to reality just long enough to feel the pain of it.

Breeding males were never reused for the same females. I wouldn't be going back to Pack Breeders 103C to find Dame sitting there on the couch waiting for me, a small smile tilting his lips, my neon green controller freshly charged and waiting in my spot beside him. The breeding program without Dame felt like a fresh hell, and new tears leaked from my eyes.

My mother must have noticed, because she shooed the auntie out, and came to kneel on the carpet in front of where I lay on our couch, covered neck to toe in the blue and purple knit blanket she'd made me for my last birthday.

"Cassie, dear, they won't send you back until you're ready to go."

But what was the point of waiting, anyway? Losing Dame, and then my children, had nearly destroyed me. Maybe this time, I could go there with the very pure intention of becoming a mother. There would be no Dame to tempt me into thinking I could be anything more.

"I'll do it."

"Cassie, you don't have to go back into it."

But I wouldn't be deterred by the worry in my mother's eyes. What was the point in putting it off? At least this way I'd have children to pour my love and energy into.

"Please let the administrator know I am ready to re-enter the program."

My mother's eyes turned watery, and I was sure she didn't believe me. But she gave a subtle nod in defeat.

"Okay, Cassie, if that is truly what you wish, I'll let them know."

What I wished? What I wished didn't matter.

The plan was to break into 7C by cover of night, something I discovered Tristan had been doing on the regular. He'd been seeing Sam this whole damned time when he was supposed to be running patrols, and the beta of our guard squad in me wanted to bust his head for doing so. But that wasn't who I was anymore.

Now I was just a man determined to reunite with his mate and carve a way through this world with her.

The former warehouse of 7C came into sight, and I heaved my backpack full of rations and winter gear more firmly onto my shoulders. I would need to make sure Cassie was protected from the elements and well-fed, especially with the pregnancy. It was a daunting task in a world where humans starved just beyond our borders, but it didn't feel like a burden. I would feed her, keep her warm, and protect her. There was no trying to do it. I would pour every bit of my will into seeing it done.

If she would have me. Our final few conversations replayed in my mind. Then there was Amanda, who I'd led Cassie to believe I'd slept with. Would she still want me? Accept my apology? I had no choice but to try, and even the prospect of seeing her again made my heart feel lighter than it had since I'd walked out of our shared bedroom. At least she would allow me to apologize to her. My Cassie would allow that, and if that was all she wanted, I'd go. But if she still wanted to leave together the way she'd claimed, I wouldn't deny either of us anymore.

"Shit, man, how aren't you more nervous?"

I looked over in surprise to study Tristan. He wore a warm grey down-filled jacket, and his hands were stuffed into his pocket. I assumed for warmth, but the trembling in his arms suggested otherwise. He danced from foot to foot, looking around nervously, as if he expected Jace to pop out and catch us at any moment.

"I am nervous." More nervous about what Cassie would say than powering my way through the gap in the border where I'd told Jace that Tristan and I would patrol for the next four hours, but he didn't need to know that.

Waiting for the sun to go down and lights out to go into effect at 7C was torture, but at last, they shut off. The light in the front window switched off even as the perimeter lights turned on, illuminating the immediate area around 7C with floodlights.

Tristan hadn't grown up in 7C, but I had, and while he eyed the illuminated grounds nervously, I grinned. Everyone in 7C knew there was a dark patch near the back left corner, a few breaks in the light easily skirted, and I led Tristan around to the side, crossing my arms in satisfaction when I saw the darkened metal door to my childhood home.

"Okay, cool. So, I'll grab Sam, you grab Cassie, and we'll meet back at the border section we left open?"

"Yeah." I never understood why people felt the need to say more when a one-word answer would do. Cassie would've talked my ear off about the logistics. She and Tristan were alike in that way, and damned if my ear didn't need some talking off right now.

Crouching, I kept low to the ground while I followed the thin patch of shadow between floodlights. It'd been easier as a kid, the path too narrow for a full-sized man, but easily navigated by a ten-year-old. I made it to the door without being seen. Pulling on the door, I winced at the clanging sound, pausing for a moment to make sure I hadn't woken anyone within.

Tristan followed close behind, close enough he could just about step on my heels. With a parting look, we went our separate ways. It was surreal to be back inside 7C after so many years away. The last time I'd walked these corridors, I'd been a kid, but something deep inside me knew the way to my corner, and I found myself outside Cassie's living quarters, the dandelions painted onto the bottom fringe confirming I was at the right dwelling.

Nerves consumed me as I pulled back the curtain and ventured inside, but I didn't find Cassie within. Only an empty bed, and an unfamiliar snore. A quick peek inside confirmed Cassie was not in bed with her mother. Venturing back outside, my limbs heavy as I dragged my feet, I leaned against the partition of Cassie's home.

Staring at nothing, I couldn't believe this was how it ended, that I wouldn't even get a chance to see her. This was it; this was our shot. We couldn't fake Jace out more than once. Crushed, I tried to think where she might be when I heard a sound come from way down the hall where a dim light shined.

The kitchen. I moved towards the light with a rekindled hope.

My decision to rejoin the breeding program had been the right one, I knew it in my heart. With nothing here in the family compound, getting pregnant again was my only path towards any kind of happiness.

So why couldn't I sleep? Ever since I'd decided to remain a breeder and return to the program, I hadn't been able to rest. A feeling of agitation, of nervous energy, kept me moving at all times.

I'd be going to meet a new group of strangers.

I'd have to face the same or a similar apartment to the one I'd shared with Dame.

Puttering around the kitchen, I prepared snacks for the kids the next day, carefully packing the little plastic containers full of cheese cubes and salty crackers. When I got done with those, I washed some plates and left them to drip dry in the overstuffed plastic drying rack. Out of tasks, I sighed, ready to sit down when a sound at the entrance caught my attention.

"Cassie."

Now I was just imagining things, hearing his voice where he would never be, imagining he would ever even say my name with such tenderness again. Only when I looked up to assure myself that I wasn't going crazy, I found Dame standing in the entrance, his dark eyes burning, fists clenched at his side.

"Hi, Sunshine."

A startled squeal tore from my throat at the sight of him. I didn't remember moving, but somehow, I ended up in his arms. Crashing him with enough force to rattle my teeth, I buried my face into his neck. The emotion pouring out of me, encouraged by the feel of his hand rubbing my back gently, and I cried. I fit into him. God, I'd forgotten how well I fit against him, my body molding to his, every one of my senses alive at his touch, his voice, his scent.

Tears of happiness continued to streak down my face, and he pulled me back just long enough to stroke my face and press his lips to mine. Fuck, he was crying, too–the tears streaming down his face as thick as mine. We cried like little children, clinging to each other as if the world was collapsing around us. I kissed him hard, clutching his face with both hands, until I somehow broke from the kiss. The need to talk to him was greater than the need to be comforted by his body.

"Why are you here?" My words came out in a rush, and I studied his face, listening intently. The infuriating feeling of hope filled my chest until it was near to bursting. I was a fool, but he was here, and that had to count for something.

"Because I'm a selfish asshole."

"I-I don't understand."

"Cassie, I'm so sorry, Sunshine. I lied to you before, about how I felt about you, about the pack. I love you, and God Cassie, I've missed you so bad." His lips connected with mine, moving against my mouth urgently.

But how could that be true after the way he'd acted. I would never be able to forget him taking Amanda back to our room.

I broke the kiss, more confused than ever.

"But, Amanda, you-you took her to bed, to our bed." Tears at his betrayal threatened, but I held completely still, gauging his reaction. I waited as he took a shaky breath—wanting to steal that breath with another kiss—but holding myself back, knowing I needed to hear what he had to say and that the next words out of his mouth would seal our fate.

"I never slept with her. I couldn't. How could I when all I want is you? When I couldn't care less about the pack or about being the father of your children because if they're your children, they're mine, too. Cassie, I'm so sorry."

At the mention of my babies, fresh tears worked their way out of my eyes and streamed down my cheeks. Sobs nearly choked me, but I needed to get the words out.

"I lost the pregnancy." Dame's face fell, and I saw a flash of grief in his eyes.

"Oh, Cassie. I'm so sorry." He pulled me back into him, and I nuzzled into his neck, letting all the emotions over the past few months release until I was a sobbing mess.

"I love you, Cassie, and I don't care what we face out there in the world, because we'll face it together." His words pulled me out of the dark void I'd fallen into, and I looked up to see his earnest expression. "If you still want to leave, I-I want to go with you. To be your mate."

To be my mate? My mind was in pieces. I'd just resolved to reenter the breeding program, never to see Dame again, to find a way to be all right again, and now? The way he looked at me, the promise in the depths of his dark eyes. Could I trust it? Could I trust him?

What was the alternative? Having some stranger's children? Never seeing Dame again? My heart hurt just thinking about it. Being apart from him had been physically painful, but with him here and warm and somehow delightfully mine again, my mind was becoming clearer.

Dame. Mate. He'd always been that to me, but he'd pushed back at every opportunity, rejecting me and casting me aside when I'd become pregnant.

"Why?" I didn't elaborate, but I didn't need to. I saw guilt and shame flicker across his expression, warring with a pain so deep I wanted to take back my question, to hold him and never let him go.

He took my hand, staring down at it, and toying with my knuckles while he spoke in a broken, clipped tone.

"I've always loved you, Cassie. Did you know that? When we were children, I was drawn to you, to your light. But I was always the outsider, always watching, in awe of your easy warmth. Then when you came into the breeding program, and I was assigned to you—my feelings for you only grew. You may have said you loved me first, but I loved you long before you knew I existed." He rubbed his thumb over my knuckle to smooth out the skin, his voice breaking. "And if this meeting is all I get now, all you want, I'll leave. If you say the word, I'll go, and you'll never see me again. I know that I hurt you, and I'm sorry. I only ever wanted to do what was right for you and having a place in this pack assured your safety, no, your survival. I just didn't think I could offer you that." Tears dripped from his eyes and splashed across our joined hands.

Dame. My heart broke for him. All this time, all these *years,* and he'd kept these feelings bottled up inside. Tears slid down my cheek to collect at my chin. All this pain, all this time apart, and for what?

No more. I decided right then and there. Dame had been trying to do what was best for me, but he didn't know what was best for me. Whatever the world outside of the pack borders was like, my happiness lay with him.

He wept, and it was the most heart-wrenching sight. My stoic man finally consumed by emotion that had always been just under the surface. But even if it hadn't, even without his tearful confession of love, my heart still belonged to him. It had ever since I'd seen him in my breeding chamber, and then when I'd met him in the common room. Both sides of Dame had captured me so completely that I'd been helpless in his path. A screaming maiden with a train bearing down on her, its weight and speed assuring her inevitable demise.

"Dame." I placed my hand on either side of his face and tilted it up to look at me. "You are my mate, my other half, and you always have been. I go where you go. From now on. Yes?"

He nodded, the movement scratching stubble across my hands.

Leaning my forehead against his, I drank him in.

"I love you, Sunshine."

A ripple of laughter tore through me. "I love you, too."

Dame laughed against me, his warm breath tickling my cheek, and I worried that something in me had broken, that this wasn't real. My mind hadn't been right since I'd lost the babies, and I wanted to see Dame so badly. Could I have conjured him up, made him say the perfect words? Pulling back in alarm, I stabilized myself against his forearms, noticing for the first time that he wasn't wearing his usual windbreaker, but a brown bomber with a white collar.

"Are you okay?" His voice was dripping with concern, and I brought a hand up to his cheek for comfort.

"Mate me."

"What?" Dame's dark eyes swam with confusion.

"There are rumours about how mates work among our kind, that the bond allows mates to communicate in wolf form. I think that would be useful outside of the pack's boundary, don't you?"

Dame frowned. "Maybe, but now, here?"

I nodded. "Yes, baby. Now. Here."

His expression cleared, and I understood something I hadn't before. He would do whatever I needed if it was in his power, and he could tell I needed this.

"So, how do we do this?"

It was my turn to frown. "I don't know. Just do what feels natural. Claim me. Mark me as yours."

Something feral glinted in his eye, and he growled, pressing himself forward against me. He kissed up and down my neck, following the curve, and I arched into it, savouring the feeling of his lips against my skin.

"You're mine?" he asked, and I recognized his voice from that first night in the woods, the depth of it penetrating straight to my bones. The tone lost somewhere between man and animal.

"Yes."

His teeth pierced my skin where my neck met my shoulder, and I cried out in a gasp of pain soon replaced with a wholeness and sense of him followed by a lightning bolt of lust reminiscent of my heat. I gasped, trying to process all the conflicting sensations, but there was no way to sift through them. All I could do was hold on to Dame for dear life as he lapped at my blood hungrily.

"All of your heats are mine."

I moaned my approval. Wrapping my legs around his waist, I lifted myself more fully into his arms and found the bulge in his jeans, rubbing myself against it.

"All of your children are our children."

With a whimper, I worked myself up and down against him, my nightshirt riding up so there was only a thin layer of cotton panties between me and the roughness of his jeans. A roughness that felt amazing against my needy clit.

"Cassie, I'm sorry, but we don't have time for this. We have to get out of here." His tone was urgent, and the logical part of me knew we risked getting caught. But I was beyond logic, and I refused to be denied ever again. I met his eyes in a challenge. If he loved me, if this was real, he'd give me this. With a sigh, he brushed his thumb across my cheek and nodded.

I reached down to rub his length through the jeans, fighting to release the button keeping them closed. But he pulled me back, setting me on top of the kitchen counter in front of him and stepping between my legs.

"Cass, we can't, not here. Once we're away, we'll—"

I shut him up with a hard kiss, my fingers curling into the thick white collar of his coat.

"We're doing this here, and we're doing this now." My voice came out in a growl so unlike me, it almost made me pause. Well, it would have if need hadn't driven me to pull him forward so that I could taste him, kiss him, lick him, bite him.

Claim him. The thought came to me on a furious wave of need, and I pulled back to look into Dame's lust-filled eyes, his face made all the more beautiful by the way it softened with need. A face I wanted to look at every day of my life.

"You're mine?" My voice came out husky, but I didn't mean just his body. He stared at me in confusion, and it was fucking adorable, as if I'd just asked him if his name was really Dame. As if it wasn't a question at all. My heart sang.

"Yes."

"All your children are my children."

"Yes."

"No one and nothing will part us again."

"No, no one and nothing." His voice grew stronger as he understood what I was doing.

"You are my mate."

"Always."

"Love above all." Startled dark eyes met mine at the way I twisted our pack loyalty vow into something new, something stronger.

"Love above all."

I pulled him to me and sank my teeth into his neck on the opposing side from where he'd marked me, and I felt his body come alive beneath my teeth. His blood didn't taste like the copper I expected but sweet like honey, and I lapped it up, knowing everything he was experiencing as my claim took hold of him, body and soul.

"Cass."

I loved my name the way he said my name, in a deep voice thick with desire, and I pulled away from his neck to claim his lips.

His hands fell to work at his jeans, and I felt him pressing against my entrance with only the slip of my cotton panties between us. Moaning into his mouth I reached down to push my panties aside, but he grasped my hand.

"We have to be quiet." He released my hand when I nodded my agreement, wondering how the hell I was going to stay quiet when just the feel of his body and the scent of him already had me near release.

My drenched panties pushed aside easily, and Dame slid into place with one smooth motion. We both groaned at the sensation, and I grabbed behind his head to lift myself into his arms, kissing his cheek, down his neck, anywhere I could reach.

Dame took a firm grip of my ass and began lifting me slowly up and down his length. I was so wet that he moved in and out easily. His grunts sent me spiraling towards a release I wasn't prepared for, and when he moved to circle my clit, it was more than I could take. Stars flooded my vision, and I burrowed into the thick jacket at his shoulder to stifle my screams. Panting hard, Dame came with a shudder, his head dropping as he fought to stay silent through his release.

Together, our bodies pulsed, his filling me with every last drop of cum and mine spasming through the last of an orgasm that had come on so suddenly and so hard that I felt the tingles straight down to my toes.

Gently, Dame placed me on the counter's edge and fastened his pants. We were both breathing hard, and he reached out to run his thumb along my bottom lip before kissing me.

"I love you. It is done. We are mated. Now let's get the fuck out of here." Smiling in satisfaction, I adjusted my underwear and hopped down from the counter to twine my fingers with his. As one, we turned to leave when my mother appeared in the doorframe, her face ashen.

"Cassie, what are you doing?" The hurt in her eyes was painful to see, and I turned into Dame's shoulder, cuddling into the softness of his coat.

"I'm sorry, Mother, but I'm leaving with my mate." The silence was heavy, and I looked up to find my mother watching me carefully, studying my face. I twined my fingers more tightly with Dame's and stood straighter at his side.

"I can see that." Her shrewd eyes narrowed on Dame. "Young man, I need a quick word with my daughter."

Dame looked back and forth between us, but I knew my mother, and while she might be upset with me, she wouldn't turn me in.

"It's okay. Just wait outside. I'll call out if I need you." With a parting look of anguish as if torn between doing as I asked and leaving my side, Dame stepped out of the room, and my mother stepped into it, sizing up Dame with a quirk of her eyebrow as he sidled past.

She turned to me. Her eyes filled with concern.

"Cassie, there's, well, there's so much to tell you." She stepped forward to take my hands, and I blinked at her in surprise. "I hadn't wanted this kind of heartbreak for you, my dear. I tried to warn you away, but I understand it better than I've let on." She took a deep steadying breath and met my eyes. "I met your father in the breeding program, and he became someone special to me, and, well, I couldn't keep it to sex either, and then I became pregnant with you and my world shifted. Let's just say there's a reason I never wanted to go back. I knew he wouldn't be there." A tear streaked its way across her cheek, but I could only blink in surprise.

My mother was a rule follower, a leader, an auntie, and she'd been holding onto this secret for so long, playing the perfect pack mother while suffering inside. I saw in her the future I almost had—a hollow life fulfilling the pack's needs and never my own.

"If it's your choice to leave with this man—"

"My mate," I corrected her.

She nodded in agreement. "Your mate. I won't stop you, but I will miss you." With a defeated sigh, she gave my arms a squeeze. "Come. We must be quick. I'll help you pack."

CHAPTER 29

It didn't take long for me to throw a bunch of clothes into my trusty black duffel. I paused only once to catch Dame's eye, my hand on the pile of books more precious to me than anything else I owned.

He gave a quick nod, and I smiled gratefully back at him, tucking the books into my bag carefully before zipping it shut. Then I turned to my mother, who had been handing me warmer versions of what I was packing.

There were tears in her eyes, and I threw myself into her embrace. I wished I could hug the tears away and promise to visit. But I couldn't and wouldn't, and we both knew it. All I could do was press my face into her hair and breathe her in one last time.

"Thank you." We parted, and she considered me with shining eyes.

"You just go and be happy. Seeing you these past few months, I know you can't find that here. I love you, Cassie."

I wiped my watery eyes. "I love you, too."

We both turned to Dame, and my mother ushered me into his arms, putting her hands over our clasped ones.

"Be safe." The words were spoken more to Dame than to me, but I heard the part she didn't say. *Keep her safe.*

Quietly, we slipped back down the hallway and exited the building, my hand growing sweaty in Dame's as the nerves crept in. My mother had given me a thick woolen coat, and I was hot as we ran through the woods, sweating buckets beneath the thick insulating fabric.

Dame set a quick pace, and we didn't speak as we traveled through the woods. Not until we reached the border, and I saw a familiar face waiting for us.

"Hey, Cassie."

"Tristan!" It was so good to see him, and I launched myself into his arms for a quick hug. It took me a moment to realize he wasn't alone, that a girl from Pack Breeders 103C stood beside him with a shy smile. She was wrapped in a thick coat, like me, but I could still see the roundness of her pregnant belly. Multiple scarves were wrapped snugly around her neck, and she covered a giggle with one mittened hand.

"Hi, Cassie."

"Um, hi, Sam, was it?"

Sam grinned, showing pearly white teeth. "Yep."

I looked back questioningly at Dame, who shrugged. "Tristan and I had the same idea. I trust you don't mind a little company."

With a laugh, I hugged Tristan again, pulling his new mate in for good measure.

"Not one bit." I hugged them both close, knowing we were a pile of thick coats. It felt like I'd just grown my family by two, and I couldn't be happier.

"All right, well, I hate to break up the party, but we have to get moving." Dame was already looking past us at the darkness beyond our border. He had his game face on, all seriousness, and I longed to kiss it away. But he was right, and I broke from Tristan to skip over to Dame's side, tucking my arm into his.

"We'll have to travel in human form so we can bring our gear." We all gave somber nods. It would be faster and easier to travel as wolves, but that wouldn't do our human forms much good when we ended up naked in the dead of winter with no shelter or provisions. "We've stolen goods from the pack now, which means we're officially loners."

Loners, the word for those who were exiled from the pack, those with no community, no home. My arm tightened around Dame's. He was my home now, and I would be taking it with me.

We were quiet as we made our way across the hilly terrain, Tristan keeping a firm grip on Sam's hand as she struggled to navigate the rocks and logs littering our path. Dame kept a tight hold of my hand, but his attention was all around us, his head on a swivel as he watched and listened for any approaching threat.

Just as we got to the other side of a bubbling creek, Dame paused to sniff the air.

He turned to me in alarm.

"Someone tipped them off. Tristan, Jace is coming." There was an alarming urgency in the way he quickly took the last few steps to the other side of the rocky creek.

The fear in Tristan's eyes was heartbreaking, and he pulled Sam into his chest, as though someone was going to snatch her away at any moment.

We pounded through the underbrush, going as quickly as we dared until we reached a clearing and Dame stopped.

"This is as good a spot as any. Tristan, Sam, drop your gear." They'd come to a halt when Dame did, and I took a moment to appreciate the natural leadership he exuded. Whether or not he liked people, they followed him.

After a shared look, they did as he said, leaving two backpacks at our feet. Dame took off his gear as well, stripping off his coat and unbuttoning his pants. Tristan took hold of Sam's hand.

"Thanks, man."

Dame only grunted in response, pulling his shirt over his head, and Tristan took off into the woods with Sam.

"Dame, what are you planning to do exactly?" He toed off his boots, kicking them back towards the pile of packs, and stared out across the clearing.

"It's just Jace. The idiot's come alone, and he won't stop following us. Can't stop following us, so."

"So what?" He was preparing to shift, and the thought of him fighting and getting hurt was terrifying.

"So, this ends here."

I gripped his bare arm, but he didn't turn. His eyes stayed fixed on the point across the clearing.

"Please be careful."

He turned to look at me, his eyes shining with love. "Trust me. It'll be all right. Just stay behind me." There was a confidence in his expression that set me at ease, and I released his bicep, watching as his muscles rippled. The change took hold in a bending, breaking crunch of bones until the black wolf stood in front of me, widening his stance, his head lowered protectively.

DAME

The enormous brown wolf that was Jace lumbered into the clearing like he owned it, dropping his head and snarling when he saw me across the field.

Fuck. Never in my life had I faced off against Jace, not even in play. When we had wrestled, I'd never tried to fight back. Never wanted to, never had a reason to do anything but follow his lead. Only now I did, and my reason stayed crouched low to the ground behind the protective wall I provided.

Jace's eyes shifted behind me to Cassie, and I growled deep in my throat. If he thought he was taking my mate back, he would find my teeth in his throat. I dropped low, ready to spring if he dared to take a step further. And of course, he fucking dared, running at me with his fangs bared.

I met him in the middle, colliding with him in a flurry of teeth and fangs, but Jace had never fought me and that gave me the advantage.

He didn't know what I was capable of when I stopped holding back.

He knocked me off balance with a swipe of his paw, biting into my flank, but I barely felt it. Adrenaline pounded through my body as I twisted to come back at him stronger than ever. Protecting Cassie drove me forward, viscous and without mercy. Grabbing his neck, I flung him down in front of me, pressing into his throat with my teeth in his jugular and growling. The vein pulsed helplessly against my teeth. I needed only to sink my fangs in a bit deeper and Jace's life's blood would spill out onto the forest floor.

Fucking submit already. But he held on, squirming beneath me and snarling, trying to twist his body into a position where he could get the leverage he needed to flip me. I didn't give it to him, and my growl became a deep rumbling warning.

At last, he went limp beneath me, whimpering in defeat, and I released his neck. He twisted onto his side, glaring at me, but we both knew I'd won. That I'd always been able to beat him, and he didn't resume his attack.

Instead, he shifted.

I stared in surprise at Jace's human face, at the blood staining his neck from where I'd bitten him hard enough to wound when I could have chosen to kill.

"What the fuck are you doing? Stealing? Running? You can't just take a pack mother. She belongs to the pack, to the alpha. Are you crazy?" Jace's green eyes were livid as he hauled himself up to stand, clamping a hand over his neck to dampen the flow of blood.

Fine, he wanted to talk, we'd talk.

I took my human form, wincing as the wound in my side flared up amidst the twisting of reforming flesh.

"She's not a pack mother anymore. She's my mate, and we're leaving."

Jace stared at me, aghast.

"Fuck you, man. You don't just get to claim her and take her. She belongs to us. You know how carefully breeding females are chosen. How their bloodlines are meant to strengthen the pack. Did you really think we'd just let you take her and fucking leave?"

I hadn't thought about it. Not really, and it occurred to me that as alpha of our guard squad, Jace had been granted access to more of the pack's secrets than I had.

I should've taken squad alpha from him years ago, and I bared my very human teeth in a genuine threat. My control was moments away from slipping at the mention of him taking Cassie and repossessing her like she was fucking pack property.

"You're not taking her." The pain of the wound at my side faded into the background and my hands clenched into fists, my body ready for a fight. Jace watched me with a cocky smirk on his face.

"Did you really think I'd come for her alone, brother?" Out of the shadows stepped an entire squad of wolves, all of them snarling and advancing. I'd been too distracted fighting Jace to notice their approach, and by the smug curl of his lip, Jace knew it.

The fucker had planned it.

Heedless of my injuries, I embraced the form of my wolf, only hoping I could fight them off long enough to allow Cassie the time she needed to escape.

CASSIE

Dame looked back at me, and I felt it—our bond. I could communicate with his wolf, but it wasn't so much words as it was a deep understanding, and when his yellow eyes made contact with mine, I felt his intention boil down to one word.

Run. He turned back to face the dozens of wolves emerging into the clearing, the fur on his back rising, and I gathered something else through our mate bond.

He was prepared to fight to the death. For me, to give me a chance to escape. Icy fear gripped my heart and held me in place. The thought of Dame torn apart by these assholes was horrifying. No, not my mate, not like this. I would not lose him like this.

Never again.

A tawny wolf barked out a warning, taking a few steps forward, his teeth gnashing at the air, eager for Dame's blood. They were closing in and I stood frozen, not knowing how to help or what to do. But one word hammered through my mind, one thought, and it would not be silenced.

No. Rage funneled through me, boiling down to that one word

No, I would not allow this to happen.

No, I would not lose Dame again.

Walking forward a few steps, I placed myself in front of Dame.

"You will stop." My voice boomed across the open space, and the approaching wolves halted their progress, staring at me. The snarls dropped from their lips. Had I done that?

Dozens of heads dropped, all eyes on me as they awaited my next command. Startled, I looked back to find Dame's eyes on me. He looked as confused as I felt. But whatever this power was, it was clearly to our advantage.

Facing the wolves again, I let my feelings flow through my voice once more.

"You will *not* give chase. You will return to the pack." One by one, they left until only Jace remained. He watched Dame for a long time, and I could feel the frustration pouring off him.

"Screw this." The twist of his lips was that of a childish man, angry at having been bested, and then he shifted back into his wolf form and left with the others, leaving Dame and I alone in the clearing.

Dame shifted and turned to me, eyes wide.

"Cassie, what? Cassie, did you know about this?"

I could only blink back at him, not knowing how to respond. But then he laughed, pulling me into his bare chest and peppering my startled face with kisses. "Sunshine, do you know what this means?"

"No, I have no idea actually, I was just scared for you, and I felt something flow through me." He grinned.

"Cass, you have alpha blood. Those rumours at 7C about the alpha must've been true. Your eyes were glowing silver when you commanded them. God, Cassie, do you know what this means?"

I shook my head dumbly still trying to process what was happening.

My father was the alpha. Everyone in our corner of 7C had heard the rumours, but I'd always dismissed it as gossip. My mother had known though, and now I knew why she'd never gone back to the breeding program after having me. She said she'd loved my father like she'd known who he was. Like she was certain the man she had fallen for was the one who had fathered me. Surely the alpha himself would have a better plan to father children than attending a breeding party.

Apparently not. Dame's laughter brought me back, and it was a glorious sight. I'd never seen him so happy, and I smiled shyly at him, waiting to be let in on the joke. He scooped me up and spun me around.

"Dame, damn, you're freezing. Put your clothes on" I hissed as his ice-cold skin touched my exposed parts, but he didn't seem to care.

"No pack would turn away such a powerful bloodline, Cassie. We can go wherever we want. Hell, we could even start *our own* pack if we wanted to, Sunshine. Up north, where the lands are unclaimed." His words sank in, and then I was laughing right along with him, marveling at the gift I'd been given to make a better life for us. Clinging to his neck, I let him spin me again, feeling like I was flying.

"I just have one question for you, baby."

He stopped with a breathy laugh, setting me down on my feet. "Yeah?"

I leaned in close, forcing him to dip his head to listen.

"Did you bring the med pack?" I gestured towards the oozing gash on his side where Jace's teeth had grazed him, and we both laughed.

Chapter 30

6 Months Later

DAME

Turns out running a pack is a fuck ton of work, but my pregnant mate made it look easy. Sitting behind a desk, her eyes puffy and her belly way out in front of her, she issued orders with a clear, firm voice that sang with her alpha blood and made everybody listen the fuck up. Damned easy, too easy. Her being the leader of our new pack had come naturally to her, and I'd been only too happy to take over pack defenses, with Tristan as my beta.

Just to be safe, we'd traveled north to an area where taking mates was still common, and the first thing we'd done once we'd found some old run-down structures to occupy was talk about the humans. Lycans had never welcomed them, but Cassie saw their value, and under her leadership, we began incorporating humans into our new pack.

Humans and any loners who came along were welcome, after a fairly rigorous vetting process by me, of course. I wouldn't let anyone dangerous near my beautiful mate and our growing family. From the humans eagerly clamouring to join our ranks, we'd found families of doctors who had passed the skills onto each new generation, their knowledge surviving the destruction of mankind and benefiting us now.

If Cassie had her way, we'd become a powerhouse of a pack within the year. The most difficult part of my job was making sure she took the occasional break to look after her changing body.

"Hey, Sunshine."

Her smile lit up the small wood-paneled office she'd taken for herself, and the sight of it always made something inside of me unclench. She sat behind an oak desk. I'd made sure to replace the standard chair with a well-padded one, at least. A great hulking upholstered brown thing that really belonged in a living room, but if it kept my mate comfortable while she grew our children, it belonged right here.

"You up for a game?" I dangled a bright red controller in front of her. There hadn't been a neon green one yet in all my trades with the local packs, but I'd find one. At least we had power now, and a sweet gaming console.

"Maybe in a bit? I just want to finish up this correspondence." Her brow puckered as she stared down at the letter she was writing for Alpha Kevin who had a good supply of solar panels. How she managed to keep track of everything was beyond me. With a long-suffering eye roll, I went to grab the handheld gaming console I'd secretly stashed in my bag and took up the chair opposite her.

"What are you doing?" She quirked her eyebrows at me, her lips tugging up in an amused little smirk that was both cute and sexy.

I frowned. Nothing was amusing about this. It was just obvious what I had to do.

"Well, you're working so I'll just play games in here until you're done."

She gave a laugh, her green eyes twinkling merrily as she turned back to her letter with a hum. Fuck I loved her, and a smile settled on my face as I lounged in the uncomfortable straight-backed chair and settled in.

Casually, as though it weren't a big deal, I reached down into my bag and pulled out a freshly sealed bag of ketchup chips, tossing them onto the desk in front of her without looking up.

Her excited squeal was music to my ears, and I heard the bag popping and her happily crunching a moment later. With a smile, I started my next round.

Love above all.

THE END

About the Author

Faye writes the kind of narratives that give her strength and courage. You can expect dark themes, high stakes, true love, and fierce heroines who struggle through their broken pasts to find human connection and salvation. Her works are best described as dark fantasy with strong romantic subplots featuring non-human characters with entirely human feelings and weaknesses.

She shares her writing space with a wildly supportive husband who regularly leaves her 'cofferings' (coffee offerings), three tiny humans who provide just the right amount of distraction, and a former Egyptian street cat who warms her lap to the purrfect writing temperature.

When she's not writing, you can find her traversing the outdoors and photographing everyday moments, changing her perspective and finding the hidden beauty in ordinary life.

Faye plans on releasing her dark fantasy, When the Stars Whisper, in June 2024. Read on for a sneak peek of this exciting new piece!

The best place to find out more about Faye's future projects is on her socials.

https://www.tiktok.com/@faye.knightly.writer?is_from_webapp=1&sender_device=pc

https://www.instagram.com/faye_knightly_writer

Or check out her link tree to see everything in one place and join her newsletter for book perks!

https://linktr.ee/faye_knightly_writer

Read on for a sneak peek of When the Stars Whisper, a gritty, lion king inspired dark fantasy by Faye Knightly.
Releasing June 2024

When The Stars Whisper
FAYE KNIGHTLY

The short hairs at the back of my neck prickled and my muscles tensed long before I saw the king approach. He came to us in his beast form, the magnificent animal slowly sauntering towards the dais at a relaxed pace. His massive paws crushed the grass he trod on, leaving flat patches in his wake. His brown mane rippled in the light breeze.

The breath caught in my throat at the sight of him, and I squeezed the hands behind my back as I struggled to push the fear down and control my breathing. I was relieved when his golden eyes didn't meet mine. He passed me on the way to the podium, his wild scent and the warmth of his body nearly causing me to break from my place in line, and run for the safety of the woods. It was only once he had moved away that I began to breath again; great panting breaths that shook my small frame, even as I worked to keep my shoulders straight. I could only hope those assembled mistook my reaction for lust. The lioness beside me sighed dreamily and I bit back the desire to spit in her face. Idiot.

Once the great beast stood at the podium, he reared back and began the night's ceremony with a thunderous roar. The power of his call to order poured over me, and my knees began to quake. I fought against it as my bones became jelly and the lionesses around me bent to their knees and lowered their heads to his awesome power; instantly submissive. I resisted until his roar became a heavy weight, and as much as I clenched my jaw and forced my muscles to obey, at last, I fell to my knees, striking them against the ceramic tile of the dais. I could barely feel the pain as I sat there gasping, my head lowering of its own accord as his terrible power continued to ripple through my trembling body. Tears fell freely from my eyes as I tried, in vain, to raise my head. I had never been this close to his roar before, and the sheer strength of it was stifling- like he held my soul in his hand and could choose to crush it at any moment.

After what felt like hours, the terrible oppressive power of his roar ended and I was able to gain control of my body once more. He stood in front of me as a man, only his naked ass and the long tawny hair that fell to his waist visible. Even the king- powerful as he was- had needed tattoos to help him control his lion's rage, and I could just see the bottom of a massive rune at the base of his skin, barely visible beneath the curtain of his thick hair. He could have asked for a robe or some covering, but I knew he wore his nakedness in front of his worshippers like a badge of honour. He didn't care who saw them. He would kill or fuck whoever he wanted.

The bright one's light glinted off his massive shoulders and thick biceps. The king towered over the priests standing patiently at his side.

"On this night, the stars made a choice. Hunted by humans until only the best of us remained, the night sky brightened and the stars whispered of kings and lions. When the darkness fell again that night, a new constellation appeared; the lion. So that all the beings of this earth would know we were ordained by the stars to rule." His low rumbling voice left me drenched in a cold sweat. "Tonight, we remember what was decreed and send our prayers up to the stars so that they may reward us for accepting the rule of the lion." A mumbled "amen" traveled through the crowd as those gathered began fishing in their pockets for the slips of paper carefully prepared with wishes and dreams that they would send up into the clear night sky.

Reaching into the pocket of my jumpsuit, my hand seized on the slip of paper I had prepared. Hopes and dreams to ask of the stars. Looking over the faces in the crowd, I could guess what some of those hopes and dreams might be. Shy palace servants eyed handsome guards, fiddling with their papers, while mothers looked fondly on their assembled children, holding their own papers with a tender touch. Everyone had a request to be sent up into the cool air. My own was simple and my hand tensed on the precious bit of paper I held tightly in my grasp. Such a fragile thing it was, to hope.

One by one, those assembled approached the dais and placed their slip of paper into the wide metal basin in front of the podium. When it was my turn, I slunk forward, taking care to keep my eyes turned downward as I crept down from the dais to place my slip in the metal bowl at the foot of the king's podium. The king's gaze skittered over my body and I felt my skin break out in gooseflesh. I could feel his eyes on me and the feeling stayed when I returned to my position in line.

A priest wearing a long purple robe studded with shining gems to represent the stars, stepped forward and waved a twisted wooden scepter over the holy basin.

"We have heeded the command sent to us from the stars and now we send to you our hopes and dreams so that you may know our desires and grant them to those you deem worthy." With a few quick waves of his hand, a white smoke began to rise from the depths of the basin, and on the white clouds the first few slips of paper emerged. "We ask for the blessing of the stars and for our wishes to be granted." Another hushed 'amen' rippled through the eager crowd as the smoke began to carry the first of many wishes up to the stars. One by one they drifted off on puffs of white until they formed huge white batches of crisp parchment that hovered in the air like a flock of birds before drifting too high to see.

I watched them, and while I heard shouts of excitement from those assembled, I remained still and thoughtful, thinking of my own note to the stars. The stars had chosen me to join the royal family. To serve the king. Perhaps I should be grateful I'd been gifted this life, but all I wanted was out. I thought of my parchment floating amongst the hundreds others as they drifted lazily up to the sparkling sky.

I'd had just one request of the stars. My hopes and my dreams boiled down to a single word hastily scratched onto a piece of ripped parchment.

Freedom.